Falling *for* Love

MARIE FORCE

ZEBRA BOOKS
KENSINGTON PUBLISHING CORP.
www.kensingtonbooks.com

ZEBRA BOOKS are published by

Kensington Publishing Corp.
119 West 40th Street
New York, NY 10018

All Kensington titles, imprints, and distributed lines are available at special quantity discounts for bulk purchases for sales promotion, premiums, fund-raising, educational, or institutional use.

Special book excerpts or customized printings can also be created to fit specific needs. For details, write or phone the office of the Kensington Sales Manager: Attn.: Sales Department. Kensington Publishing Corp., 119 West 40th Street, New York, NY 10018. Phone: 1-800-221-2647.

Zebra and the Z logo Reg. U.S. Pat. & TM Off.
MARIE FORCE and GANSETT ISLAND are registered trademarks with the U.S. Patent and Trademark Office.

First Zebra Books Mass-Market Paperback Printing: May 2019
ISBN-13: 978-1-4201-4690-5
ISBN-10: 1-4201-4690-4

10 9 8 7 6 5 4 3 2 1

Printed in the United States of America

Falling *for* Love

Books by Marie Force

Author's Note

Welcome back to Gansett Island! You first met Grant McCarthy in *Ready for Love*. I have to admit he was a bit of an enigma to me because he's not like a lot of my guys who know exactly what—and who—they want and go after it (her) with all their considerable charm. Grant is rather conflicted. His heart is telling him one thing while his body is sending him a different message altogether. After *Ready for Love*, a lot of you were evenly divided between Team Abby and Team Stephanie. As the architect of Grant's story, I had to choose the best woman for him, and I hope you'll agree with my decision. In this book, you'll hear from some of our old favorites and meet some new friends.

After the earlier trilogy, I asked you to let me know if you wanted to read more about other members of the McCarthy family. Wow, did I get some reader mail! Your enthusiasm for the McCarthy family and their friends has thrilled me, and I've heard your verdict loud and clear. Next up is *Hoping for Love*, with much more to come.

Writing about this family and their life on an island so much like my beloved Block Island has been the most fun I've ever had as a writer. Thank you for embracing my fictional family and for all the lovely reviews you've posted. I appreciate your e-mails and Facebook posts more than you'll ever know. I always love to hear from readers. You can reach me at marie@marieforce.com. If you're not yet on my mailing list and wish to be added for occasional updates on future books, go to marieforce.com.

While *Falling for Love* is intended to be a stand-alone story, you will enjoy it more if you have read *Maid for Love*, *Fool for Love* and *Ready for Love* first.

Thanks to all the wonderful readers who've made it possible for me to realize a dream come true!

xoxo,
Marie

Chapter One

This whole thing was Janey's fault. If she hadn't gotten married, Grant wouldn't have had to watch *his* woman, wearing a slinky, sexy bridesmaid gown, prance around at the wedding with her new *fiancé* hanging all over her. If it hadn't been for Janey and her stupid wedding, Grant wouldn't have felt the need to make Abby jealous by dancing with Stephanie from the marina.

Too bad it hadn't ended there. No, he'd had to make sure Abby was *truly* jealous by leaving with Stephanie. And now, as the hammer in his head reminded him of how much alcohol it had taken to get through the nuptials, the warm body sleeping next to him was an even bigger reminder of what a disaster last night had been.

Damn Janey and her damned wedding.

Grant was trying frantically to remember just how far things had gone with Stephanie. He was pretty sure there'd been some kissing in the cab on the way to his now-married sister's place. Janey had traded him the use of her house in exchange for pet-sitting duties while she and Joe were on their honeymoon. Since their mother had been driving him crazy with questions about the mess he'd made of his life, it had seemed like a good deal at the time because it would get him out of his parents' house. But now he was mad with his sister for getting married in the first place, and the sweet deal didn't seem so sweet anymore.

He wished he could escape, but he couldn't exactly leave his one-night stand in his sister's bed. What to do?

Then the warm body stirred.

Grant stayed perfectly still, hoping she wouldn't look at him or, God forbid, try to talk to him. He'd been with Abby so long he'd never had the chance to indulge in one-night stands. He had no idea what the etiquette was, and with a thousand hammers at work in his head, he had no desire to figure it out.

Out of the corner of his eye, he watched Stephanie—oh *Jesus*, she was totally naked—slide from the bed and get busy rounding up her clothes. Still pretending to be asleep, he caught glimpses of small breasts and pretty pink nipples that quickly had the attention of a part of him that didn't know enough to fake sleep. As his cock rubbed against the sheet, he realized he was naked, too.

He was desperately trying to remember how he'd ended up naked in bed with Stephanie, but he couldn't recall a single thing after being in the cab. Not that being naked with Stephanie hadn't crossed his mind far too often in the last few weeks . . . He'd even bought condoms, just in case his horny body won the war with his better judgment. But he'd never expected to actually go *through* with it. Maybe he hadn't. Maybe nothing actually happened. That was possible, right? Naked didn't automatically mean sex, did it?

Shit, shit, *shit*! If Abby heard about this, he'd never get her back, not to mention what his father, who'd taken a special interest in Stephanie since she came to work for them, would have to say about it.

Stephanie turned her back to the bed to put on the form-fitting black dress she'd worn to the wedding. Her pale skin was creamy white, and his eyes traveled from her shoulders to the two dimples at the bottom of her spine, above her firmly rounded ass. When he first met her, he'd thought she lacked curves. "Boyish" was the word he'd used to describe her. But now that he'd seen her naked, it was clear that her clothes had hidden small but rather interesting curves.

Not that he was interested in her curves. No, the only curves he craved were Abby's, and somehow he had to figure out a way to get her back. First and foremost, he had to stop drinking. Booze—and Janey's damned wedding—had landed him in bed with the wrong woman, and he couldn't let that happen again. If he had any prayer of winning back Abby, he couldn't get caught with another woman. Making Abby jealous was one thing, but his plan had clearly gone awry in a big way.

Stephanie never so much as glanced at the bed as she hooked her high-heeled sandals around her fingers and tiptoed from the room, closing the door behind her.

Grant let out a sigh of relief that he'd been spared the morning-after awkwardness. But then he remembered he was in charge of the family's marina while his father recovered from a recent head injury and his brother tended to his pregnant wife. With Grant stuck running the docks and Stephanie managing the restaurant, he'd have to face her in a few short hours.

Groaning, he turned facedown on the bed and buried his face in the pillow. Something poked his belly, and he fumbled through the rumpled sheet to see what it was. When his hand landed on a torn condom wrapper, Grant's heart nearly stopped beating.

"Shit, shit, *shit!*"

He'd rocked her world, and Stephanie would bet he didn't even remember it. As she shivered in driving wind and cold rain on her way to McCarthy's Gansett Island Marina, she relived the night with Grant McCarthy. Of course she'd figured out what he'd been up to at the wedding. He'd been using her to make Abby jealous. She'd also known he was drunk when they left and that he probably wouldn't remember much of what happened between them.

Still, that didn't stop her from taking full advantage of the opportunity for one night with the first guy she'd been attracted to in years. She was under no illusions that this was the start of something with him. He was in love with Abby and still hoping to reconcile with her, although Abby and her fiancé, Cal, had looked pretty darned cozy at the wedding.

If Stephanie were one to gamble, she'd bet on Abby being done with Grant, and him being the last one to realize it. But even knowing that, there was no way Stephanie was going to get all stupid over a guy who clearly wanted someone else. So they'd had sex. Big deal. Just because she hadn't been with anyone in ages didn't mean she was going to turn this into something it wasn't and would never be.

A tooting horn caught her attention, and she stopped to find Mr. McCarthy's best friend, Ned Saunders, pulling up to the curb in the beat-up woody station wagon that served as his cab.

"Jump in, gal. I'll give ya a ride."

Since she was soaked to the skin, Stephanie was thrilled to see the older man who hung around the marina every day. "Thanks, Ned," she said as she slid into the front seat. The floor was littered with coffee cups and old newspapers.

"Sorry 'bout the mess," he muttered.

"No problem. I'm happy to get out of the storm."

"'Tis a doozy of a nor'easter. Not seeing the newlyweds makin' it off-island today."

"That's too bad. They'll miss their flight, won't they?"

"Looks that way."

Stephanie appreciated that Ned didn't mention anything about her obvious walk of shame. "How long is the storm supposed to last?"

"Coupla days at least."

"The marina will be slow today," Stephanie said, dreading a quiet day to spend alone with Grant.

Ned took the final turn that led to North Harbor. As they passed the McCarthy home, called the "White House" by locals, Stephanie looked away as memories of the night she'd spent with their son resurfaced. Mr. McCarthy had been so nice to her. She'd hate to do anything to mess that up.

"The boy's confused," Ned said, breaking the silence.

"Excuse me?"

"Smartest kid I ever knew," Ned continued as if she hadn't spoken. "From the time he was first able to talk, he's been asking questions, studying people, filing stuff away to use later in his stories. When it comes to people in his own life, though . . . well, sometimes he ain't the sharpest tool in the shed."

Stephanie's entire body was on fire with mortification

as she continued to stare out the window. *How does he know? And what will he tell his best buddy, Grant's dad?*

"Don't think he gets yet that it's really over with Abby. When he finally catches a clue, I suspect it's gonna hurt."

Her mind raced as she hummed with tension. It was like he could see inside her or something!

"A nice girl like you would wanna watch herself in the midst of all that hurtin'."

Her mouth fell open, but damn if she could find the words. Luckily, their arrival at McCarthy's saved her from having to reply.

"Thanks for the ride," Stephanie muttered, reaching for her wallet.

Ned's hand on her arm stopped her from withdrawing money. "My pleasure, honey."

Stephanie was mortified all over again when tears burned her eyes. She made her escape from the car, but the almost paternal way Ned had treated her stayed with her long after his car disappeared from view. It'd been a long time since anyone had showed her that kind of care or concern, and it had felt good.

A ringing cell phone woke Captain Joe Cantrell the morning after his wedding. He wanted to grab the phone and toss it across the suite where he and Janey had spent their wedding night, but more than that, he wanted his lovely *wife* to sleep awhile longer.

After so many years of loving her from afar, thinking of her as his wife made him smile. He took the phone into the bathroom and closed the door. Seeing the office number on the caller ID further irritated him.

"This had better be good," he grumbled into the phone.

"So sorry to bother you, Cap," said Seamus O'Grady. Joe had hired Seamus to run the Gansett Island Ferry Company when he and Janey moved to Ohio so she could attend vet school. "Especially this morning."

"What do you need?" Joe asked with unusual brusqueness.

"I wasn't sure if you'd surfaced yet to take a look at the weather. Tropical Storm Hailey arrived overnight, and we've got a heck of a blow going on. I'm leaning toward stopping service for the rest of the day, but I know you and the wife are planning to take the ten-thirty boat off the island. Didn't want to screw you up."

As Seamus spoke, Joe went to the window and looked out over South Harbor. The wind and rain had whipped Gansett Sound into a froth of whitecaps, and the rain beat hard against the window. It was the kind of day they referred to as a barf-o-rama in the ferry business because they'd have to hose the vomit from the boats after each trip. "Go ahead and make the call," Joe said.

"You sure about that, Cap?"

"Such is the chance we take making travel plans from an island, right?"

"Right you are. Don't worry about a thing here. I gotcha covered. We'll get you and the wife outta here as soon as we can. By the way, it was a great wedding."

"Thanks, Seamus." Joe ended the call and crept out of the bathroom.

"What's wrong?" Janey asked. Her voice was husky and sleepy—and sexy as hell. She reached out a hand to him.

Joe tossed the phone into his suitcase and went to her.

She gave his hand a tug to draw him back into bed.

Feeling like the luckiest son of a bitch on the face of

the earth to finally be married to the woman he'd loved for more than half his life, Joe snuggled into her warm embrace.

"Now tell me what's wrong," she said.

"There's good news and bad news." He kissed lips that were puffy and swollen from a night of passion. "The bad news is they're shutting the ferries down because of the storm."

Janey gasped. She'd been so looking forward to their honeymoon in Aruba, which they'd chosen because it was outside the hurricane belt. So much for that logic.

"How can there be good news after that?" she asked with her lip curling into the same pout she'd sported as a ten-year-old.

Joe maneuvered her so she was under him and brushed tangled blonde hair off her face. "The very good news is we don't have to leave this bed today."

Janey smiled up at him and ran her hands from his shoulders down his back and curved them over his ass, a move that always drove him crazy, as she well knew. "That's very good news indeed."

"I'll get you there, baby," he said as he dipped his head for a kiss. "Might take a day or two, but I'll get you there."

"Doesn't matter where we are. As long as it's just the two of us, that's what matters."

"Have I told you yet today that I love you love you?" he asked.

"Not yet," she said, smiling at the reminder of how he'd once told her he wanted her to *love him* love him.

"Well, I do."

"I think you need to prove it." Flashing a coy grin, she lifted her hips against his erection, letting him know what she wanted.

"Again?" he asked, quirking an eyebrow in amusement. "No one told me I was marrying an insatiable wench."

Janey laughed and guided him to exactly where she wanted him. "Better get used to it, buddy. You're stuck with me now."

He entered her in one smooth thrust. "Thank God for that."

Driving wind and rain woke Mac McCarthy early on the morning after his sister's wedding. His chest tightened with anxiety when it occurred to him that the storm had probably shut down the ferries for the day.

He glanced over at his wife, Maddie, sleeping on her side the way Dr. Cal had instructed to minimize stress on the baby. The thought of being unable to get her help if she needed it made him crazy. A high-risk pregnancy on an island was a fool's errand, but he'd had no luck convincing her to move their family to the mainland until the baby was born.

Hoping the weather wasn't as bad as it sounded, Mac got up to look out the window. Sure enough, it was every bit as bad as it sounded. In the distance, he could see the ocean whipped into a frenzy. Rain was coming down sideways in the blustery wind. Running a hand over his chest, Mac wondered if he was having a heart attack. The tightness had been ever-present since the accident at the marina that left his father injured.

The accident had briefly put him in the hospital, too, which had stressed out Maddie. After she went into premature labor and was put on bed rest for the remainder of her pregnancy, she'd refused to leave their island home. Mac had no choice but to cede to her wishes.

Mac went to his dresser to retrieve his phone. A text

message from the Gansett Island Ferry Company made it official: service was temporarily suspended. With the wind gusting to what sounded like at least fifty miles per hour, the airport would be closed, too. No way out, Mac thought as the pain in his chest intensified.

Nightmare scenarios such as this had driven him crazy for weeks now. Even when the ferries were running, it was a long hour to the mainland and then more time to get to a hospital. In the meantime, what if something happened that Cal couldn't handle? What if Maddie needed something he couldn't get for her? What if something happened to her—

"Mac?"

He turned away from the window and went to her. "I thought you'd sleep awhile yet," he said, smoothing a hand over her caramel-colored hair. "It's early."

"Why are you up?"

"The wind woke me." His chest began to ache again as he wondered how long they'd be without ferry service. He turned on the bedside light so he could see her in the early morning gloom. "How do you feel?"

"Fat. Horrible." Tears filled her golden eyes. "Hideous."

"Aww, baby." He crawled back into bed and drew her—as best he could—into his arms. They hadn't been able to make love in weeks, which wasn't doing much to help his overwhelming anxiety. "Don't say that. You're gorgeous, glowing and radiant." How would they get through two more months of her being stuck in bed all day, every day?

"You have to say that. You did this to me."

She was so petulant and cute that Mac laughed, even though he knew she wouldn't appreciate it.

Fat tears spilled from her eyes and wet her cheeks. "It's not funny."

"I know," he said, kissing away her tears. She'd been so happy and content yesterday at the wedding, surrounded by family and friends. The thought gave him an idea of how he could lift her spirits a bit before everyone scattered again after the storm let up.

Just as he was about to share his idea with her, the bedside light flickered and died.

Chapter Two

The first memory struck Grant while he was in the shower—the best blow job of his life. As he stood under the hot water, images of Stephanie's lithe body and talented lips working their way from his chest to his stomach to his straining erection overwhelmed him. Thinking about it had him hard and ready to go again in two seconds flat.

"Jesus," he muttered, closing his eyes to relive it even as he was filled with guilt. That never had been Abby's favorite thing to do in bed, so he'd gone without more often than not. On the other hand, Stephanie's enthusiasm had been apparent as she licked and sucked and stroked.

Moaning, Grant took matters into his own hand, still thinking about the way it had felt to be engulfed in the heat of her mouth with her pierced tongue lashing him. The memory sent him into a heart-pounding climax, and afterward, he stood panting in the shower until the hot water began to ebb. Stepping out of the shower on wobbly legs, Grant realized the power had gone out.

"Great," he muttered as he reached for a towel. "This day just gets better and better."

Disgusted with himself for getting so worked up over memories of a night that never should've happened, Grant pulled on jeans and a long-sleeved T-shirt. The truth was, he'd gone too long without. That was the only possible explanation for why he'd responded to Stephanie the way he had. More than a year ago, Abby had told him if he went back to Los Angeles after a visit home for Mac's wedding that things were over between them.

To be honest, Grant hadn't believed her. They'd been together so long that he simply couldn't imagine life without her at the center of it. He'd tried to tell her then how close he was to a new deal to write a movie for a big producer. Of course she'd heard that same story a hundred times before and had laid down her ultimatum.

"You can write anywhere in the whole wide world, Grant," she'd said to him, her big brown eyes pleading with him to stay with her on the island where she'd established a successful business after moving home from LA. "Why can't you write in the one place where I want to be?"

Grant hadn't seen any choice but to go and see things through with the producer. However, like everything else since he won the Academy Award for best original screenplay, the deal had fallen through, and he was left with no job, and now no Abby, either.

In the long year away from her, he'd remained faithful to her and under the mistaken assumption that she'd done the same. Until he heard from his mother that not only was Abby dating again, she was *engaged*! To someone else! Grant had played this one all wrong. No doubt about that. But no swashbuckling cowboy doctor from Texas was going to steal his woman without a fight.

He just wished he had the first clue how to proceed in his campaign to win her back. Clearly, sleeping with Stephanie had been a mistake of epic proportions, he thought, as images of that talented pierced tongue made their way through the fog in his brain to torture him once again.

Groaning, he left the bedroom and went in search of something he could wear to stay dry in this weather. Luckily, Joe had left some foul-weather gear in Janey's closet. Grant put on the jacket and managed to corral Janey's menagerie of special-needs pets into the backyard for a quick visit. The weather scared the heck out of several of them who refused to pee, which meant he could expect a mess when he got back later. He fed them and settled them into the room where they stayed when his sister was out.

The whole time, Riley, the German shepherd, glared at him, as if he knew what a scumbag Grant had been the night before. Things were pretty bad if a dog could make him feel guilty.

On his way out the door, he rolled the yellow foul-weather pants into a ball that he tucked under his arm for the mad dash to his father's truck in the driveway.

With his dad still recovering from a head injury and fractured arm, Grant had commandeered the truck for the time being. Although, with his brothers Evan and Adam in town for the wedding—and now stuck here for who knew how long—Grant made a mental note to hide the keys from his younger siblings the way he had when they were teenagers.

During the short ride to the marina, he encountered downed trees and power lines as well as some flooded side streets. He wondered how Stephanie had gotten back to the marina, where she stayed in a room behind the restaurant, and felt guilty about leaving her to fend for herself in the storm.

The windshield wipers on the truck were no match for the pouring rain, so Grant cracked the window, trying to find some added visibility. They hadn't had a storm like this in decades. He remembered being without power once for ten days, when all five McCarthy siblings were still living at home. That had been a *long* ten days.

Arriving at the marina, the first thing he saw was Stephanie's shapely behind sticking out of the toolshed as she wrestled with something. So much for a nice, easy morning, sitting around drinking coffee and shooting the bull with anyone who braved the storm.

Looked like there was real work to be done, which was about the last thing Grant could handle with a percussion section still at work in his skull. He got out of the truck and jogged over to her. The rain had soaked her thin khaki shorts, which highlighted her dark thong. Grant bit back a curse as his body responded predictably to the view. "Let me help," he said, sounding angrier than he'd intended.

Startled by his sudden appearance, she spun around, wide-eyed. That's when the second memory of the night before decided to show up—the same wide-eyed look she'd given him as he entered her for the first time.

"For Christ's sake," he muttered as he stepped around her to get to the generator she'd been trying to remove from the shed.

"What's your problem?" she asked, wiping the rain from her face with the sleeve of a windbreaker that was far less of a jacket than she needed for this storm.

"No problem." He grunted under the strain of trying to lift the generator.

"Let me help you before you throw your back out." They had to shout to be heard over the roar of the wind.

"You were doing it yourself. Why can't I?"

"I couldn't budge it."

Grant turned and grabbed the back half while she took the front. Somehow, they managed to muscle it to the small deck outside the marina's kitchen.

"I'll get the gas can," she said when it was in place.

"I will. Where is it?"

"I'm perfectly capable of doing it."

Grant closed his eyes and counted to ten, praying for relief from the pounding in his skull and the stubborn woman. "I said I'll get it. Just tell me where it is."

"Figure it out." She turned and walked away from him, giving him yet another view of her soaking-wet ass, which of course his addled brain morphed into the nude version he'd seen earlier. He'd had more boners in the two hours since he woke up with her than he normally had in two days, which was absolutely infuriating.

As he stomped back into the rain to search for the gas can, he wondered why his body reacted so strongly to her when he didn't even *like* her. She was prickly and mouthy and stubborn as hell. Usually, she wasn't much to look at either. Her hair was always spiky and messy-looking. She was skinny and had a pierced tongue—he couldn't imagine letting someone drill a hole in his tongue, although he had liked the feel of the stud on his shaft. *Stop it! Stop thinking about that!*

Despite his overwhelming desire to forget, the memory of her pierced tongue working up and down the side of his cock returned for yet another visit. "*Goddamn it*," he screamed into the roaring wind. "I don't *want* her! *I don't want to think about what happened with her anymore!* I *want* Abby. I *love* Abby."

Feeling somewhat better after the conversation with the wind, he located the astoundingly heavy gas can and dragged it to the doorway of the shed, just as a gust of wind caused the door to slam shut. On his hand. Grant let out an ungodly scream as pain whipped up his arm. "Son of a *bitch*!"

The door swung open. "Bro?" Mac appeared out of

the gloom and rain, his head covered by a navy-blue foul-weather jacket. "Who're you screaming at?"

Clutching his hand, Grant couldn't get a word past the agony.

"What's wrong with you?" Mac asked, drawing him out of the shed and into the light.

"Hand," Grant managed to say. "Door."

"Shit," Mac said. "Let me see."

Grant pulled his other hand away and nearly passed out at the sight of blood pouring from an open wound in his palm.

Mac put an arm around Grant to lead him inside. "Don't faint."

"Oh man," Stephanie said when she saw them coming. "What happened?"

"From what I can gather," Mac said, "the door slammed shut on his hand."

Stephanie took a close, assessing look. "Needs stitches." She unearthed a clean white cloth and wrapped it around Grant's injured hand.

"Go easy, will you?" Grant snapped.

She scowled at him and finished wrapping tape around the cloth.

"Can you take him?" Mac asked her. "I came to get the other generator for the house, but I need to get back to Maddie and Thomas."

"I can take myself," Grant said, standing and then swaying when the room tilted.

"Sit your ass down before you pass out and crack your skull." Mac pushed his brother back into the chair. "Dad's busted skull is enough for one summer."

"I'll take him," Stephanie said. "We need to get the generator going for the fridge and freezer, though."

"I'll take care of that before I split. We can close up here for the day. I checked last night and all the boats are tied down tight for the storm. Won't be anyone coming or going today."

"Okay," Stephanie said.

As they worked out the logistics, Grant held back the growing need to puke.

"I was going to tell you guys that since Joe and Janey are stuck here, they're coming over to open their wedding gifts tonight. We're making a tropical storm party out of it, so come on over."

Grant moaned, reminding them of his injury.

"Stop being such a baby," Stephanie said. "It's a scratch."

Mac laughed and sent Grant a sympathetic smile. "I'll leave you in good hands, bro. Let me know how you make out at the clinic."

That's when it hit him that he'd be relying upon Abby's fiancé to stitch him up. "Never mind," Grant said. "I'm not going there."

"The hell you aren't," his bossy older brother said. "You want me to call Mom and sic her on you?"

"You wouldn't do that."

"Wanna bet? You need stitches and probably a tetanus shot. Don't be a fool."

"I've got him." Stephanie manhandled him out of the chair and had him on the way to his father's truck before Grant even knew what hit him. She was awfully strong for such a skinny chick. Rummaging around in his shorts pocket for the keys, she rubbed against his package, startling him.

"Watch what you're grabbing, will ya?"

"Nothing I haven't already seen."

"Don't remind me," he muttered and then wanted to shoot himself for being so flippant as a flash of pain darted across her face. It was gone as fast as it came.

She slammed the car door, narrowly missing his foot. The wind and rain followed her into the driver's seat.

"Just take me back to Janey's. I don't need to go to the clinic. I can take care of it at home."

Stephanie didn't say a word as she started the truck, adjusted all the mirrors and cautiously shifted the truck into drive.

"You do have a license, don't you?"

"Of course I do."

"Then why're you driving like an eighty-year-old?"

"Because we're in the midst of a tropical storm, in case you failed to notice, and this is your father's truck. I don't want anything to happen to it."

"He's used to things happening to his trucks. He had five kids driving them at one point or another."

"Nothing will happen to it while I'm driving. Now be quiet so I can concentrate."

Grant wanted to remind her that his family employed her, but since he'd already acted like enough of a jerk around her, he kept his silence—until she took a right toward the clinic rather than a left toward Janey's. "Wait a minute! I said I want to go home!"

"And I said you need stitches."

"You're not the boss of me!"

"What're you? Three? Did Thomas teach you that?" She referred to Mac and Maddie's three-year-old son. "I heard him say that to his father at the wedding."

Fuming, Grant had to force himself to stay calm. "I'm not going in the clinic."

"I'll call your mother."

He spun around in the seat to stare at her. "You wouldn't dare."

"Try me. I love Linda. I have her number on speed dial."

"You're the devil."

"Sticks and stones . . ."

Grant had never had a more ridiculous conversation. He was about to make a second attempt to talk her out of going to the clinic when the wound bled through the cloth and quickly turned the white fabric red.

Stephanie noticed and pressed harder on the accelerator.

"Easy does it. I think you're going thirty now."

"Shut up."

"You shut up."

She shook her head, seeming regretful. "I told you it was a bad idea to sleep together."

"*When* did you tell me that?" Of course he had no recollection of *that* but had plenty of other vivid memories torturing him all morning.

"Before we slept together. We got along just fine before."

"We did not. We've never gotten along."

"We got along pretty well in your sister's bed last night, but you probably don't remember that."

"I remember it," he snapped.

"You don't need to bite my head off just because you're pissed with yourself." Before Grant could begin to process that audacious statement, she let out a curse.

He looked out the windshield and saw a tree down across the road that led to the clinic. "See? Wasn't meant to be. Hang a Uey and let's get out of here."

The words weren't even out of his mouth when she was marching around to his side of the truck. She yanked open the door, grabbed his arm, and pulled him out. "Walk."

"In case you haven't noticed, there's a huge tree in the way."

"No, really?" She clamped down on his arm and propelled him toward the fallen tree. Her thin jacket was no match for the icy rain and whipping wind. In no time at all, her lips were blue, but she pressed on until they had no choice but to climb over the tree. "Let's go."

Grant was about to protest when she gave him a little shove that sent him stumbling toward the tree. His foot got hooked around hers just as they hit a slick patch of mud. They flew over the tree and landed with a thump in a mud puddle on the other side. Somehow, she ended up on top of him, both of them dripping with mud.

She looked down at him and burst into laughter.

As he watched the laughter transform her face, the tight ball of tension he'd carried around all morning uncoiled, and he realized he didn't dislike her at all. Rather, it was quite possible he could end up liking her far too much.

Chapter Three

Laura McCarthy stood on the sidewalk outside the Sand & Surf Hotel, letting the wind and rain pummel her as she studied the weathered Victorian structure. The old gray lady had gotten tired since the last time Laura visited the island. Her gray shingles were worn and stained, the windows dingy from salt water, and the white paint on the trim was peeling in places.

Located across the street from the Beachcomber, the Sand & Surf had been closed for a couple of years now as the owners looked for someone to buy the place. It overlooked downtown on one side and the Atlantic Ocean on the other, with beach access and a sweeping porch made for watching sunsets. Laura wished she had an extra thirteen million in the bank so she could take it off their hands.

The thought made her laugh softly to herself. Ever since the first time she'd come to the island as a child to see her aunt, uncle and cousins, the sprawling hotel had called to her. She could picture high tea in the salon, cocktails on the porch and rooms filled with guests who returned year after year.

Pipe dreams.

Laura drew her coat tighter around her as rain seeped inside and her hair escaped from the hood.

"Not exactly a sightseeing kind of day."

Startled, Laura spun around to find a tall man wearing oilskin and a wry smile. Wet dirty-blond hair stuck to his forehead, but he didn't seem to notice. Something about him was familiar, but she couldn't place him.

He sized her up with gray eyes full of amusement, as if he was in on a joke and trying to decide if he was willing to share it. "You were at the wedding last night."

"Did we meet?"

"I was the entertainment." He extended his hand. "Owen Lawry."

Laura reached out to shake hands. "Oh! Of course. You and Evan were so awesome!"

"Thanks. We haven't jammed together in ages. Felt good."

"Sounded good, too."

"I'm glad you enjoyed it. Friend of the bride or the groom?"

"Cousin of the bride."

"Is that right?" He took a closer look. "Now that you mention it, I can see the resemblance."

Laura laughed. "Sure, you can. Janey is petite and perky, and I'm tall and gawky."

"That's not true. Don't forget I had a front-row view of the dancing last night."

Despite the wind and icy rain, a rush of heat settled in her face. Was he *flirting* with her? And then reality returned to remind her she had no business flirting with anyone. A shiver traveled through her, and suddenly she wanted to be warm and dry again.

"Do you have a name, or should I call you Janey's cousin?"

His teasing tone confirmed her suspicions that he was

indeed flirting—that and the fact he continued to hold her hand.

"Sorry," she said, withdrawing her hand. "I'm Laura McCarthy."

"You like the Sand & Surf, Laura McCarthy?" he asked, gesturing to the hotel.

She shifted her gaze to the hotel and nodded. "It's nice to play pretend."

"It's a great place."

Even though she was more than ready to get out of the elements, curiosity got the better of her. "Have you been inside?"

"Yeah. You?"

She shook her head wistfully as she took in the grand old hotel. "Never."

"Would you like to?"

Laura drew in a breath of surprise. "Now?"

"If you want."

She hesitated, aware that she was about to step into an abandoned hotel with a man she'd only seen for the first time the night before.

"I'd understand if you wanted to call your cousin Evan to vouch for me. I've known him since I was ten." He withdrew his cell phone and held it out to her.

Laura contemplated the phone as she remembered the genuine friendship she'd witnessed between this man and her cousin the night before. And even though she'd vowed never to trust another man for the rest of her life, her desire to see the inside of the Sand & Surf won out.

"I'll trust you," she said.

He flashed a satisfied—and extremely engaging—grin and gestured for her to follow him to the porch, where he reached into the mail slot, rooted around and pulled out a key.

Astounded, Laura stared at him. "How'd you know that was there?"

"I know the owners." Using the key, he pushed open the main door and ushered her inside.

Walking past him into the musty interior, she cast him a suspicious glance, wondering just how well he knew the owners.

Ned Saunders made a complete loop around the island in his cab and concluded not much of anything was going on beyond wind, rain, high surf and downed trees. With the ferries stopped for the day, the taxi business would be deader than a doornail. No reason he couldn't take a rare summer day off to spend some time with his lady. Elated by the idea, he drove over to the Sturgil place, where Francine lived in an apartment behind her daughter Tiffany's house.

Things had been tense lately between Tiffany and her husband, Jim Sturgil, and Francine had been doing a lot of babysitting for their daughter Ashleigh. Poor Francine had been distressed by her daughter's marital troubles, but he'd had no luck convincing her to come stay with him while her daughter and son-in-law tried to work things out.

In fact, he'd had no luck whatsoever convincing her to do anything more than kiss him once in a great while. Maybe he'd been fooling himself when he tried to rekindle an old love earlier in the summer. The first time around— more than thirty years ago—she'd walked away without a word when sweet-talking Bobby Chester came to Gansett Island for a bachelor party weekend and caught her eye. A couple of years of marriage and two daughters later, Bobby got on a ferry to the mainland and never looked back. As far as Ned knew, none of them had ever heard from Bobby again.

Foolish pride had kept Ned away from Francine until his young friend Luke Harris had reconnected with Sydney Donovan and put ideas in Ned's head. But Luke wasn't an old fool. No, he was a young, handsome guy who had everything in the world to offer his lady.

"Yer bein' an ass," Ned muttered. "Ya got plenty ta offer her. Ya got a nice house and plenty a room. Hell, ya got a bunch of houses on the derned island. She can pick out whatever one she wants."

He drove into Tiffany's driveway and went past her house, grateful to see that things seemed quiet there for once. Parking at the foot of Francine's stairs, he pulled up the hood on his raincoat and dashed into the storm. At the top of the stairs, he knocked on the door and waited, his heart doing that happy, skipping thing it did whenever he was about to see her.

Wearing a robe with her hair wrapped up in a towel, she gasped when she saw him. "I thought you were Tiffany!"

While he could tell she was dismayed to be caught un-prepared to greet him, Ned was dumbstruck by how pretty she was with her hair pulled back off her face. It brought back memories of a fresh-faced girl just off the ferry to work the summer at the Beachcomber, reminding him of the day he'd rushed to help with her bags and lost his heart in the process. Despite her obvious discomfort, he stepped inside and closed the door.

The hand she raised to cover where her robe came to-gether over full breasts trembled ever so slightly, but Ned saw it. She was nervous. For some reason, that pleased him. He took another step toward her.

She retreated until her back met the wall. "What . . . what're you doing?"

He reached up to caress her face. "Saying a proper hello." Leaning in, he touched his lips to hers. "Kiss me,

Francine." Only for her would he have shaved off the beard he'd worn his entire adult life and trimmed back the mustache that she'd called prickly the first time he kissed her. Hell, he'd even started combing his hair once in a while— also for her.

Her lips closed and puckered, which made him laugh.

Brows narrowed over green eyes. "What's so funny?"

"You are." Raising his other hand, he framed her face and held her in place for a better kiss—a much better kiss. "Mmm, that's more like it." When he drew back, he noticed her face was flushed, her eyes were wide and she was breathing funny. Maybe he was pushing his luck, but he kissed her again.

This time, he felt her hand in his hair, seeming to want to keep him there.

Encouraged, he tipped his head and brought her in tighter against him. "Do ya remember," he asked, as he shifted his focus to her neck, "how it was between us all those years ago?"

"No."

Chuckling, Ned rested his hands on her hips and continued to kiss her neck. "Ya do, too. Ya can't fool me." They'd only just begun to sleep together when Bobby came along and ruined everything.

Her hand on his chest stopped him cold. "Please don't."

He was surprised to see tears in her eyes. "Aww, honey, what's a matter?"

"Nothing." She stepped around him. Over her shoulder, she said, "I'm going to get dressed."

"Not on my account, I hope. I kinda like ya the way ya are."

She scurried away, but not before he caught the blush that flamed her cheeks.

Frustrated by the walls she'd built up around her heart,

he flopped into a chair to wait. Fifteen minutes later, she emerged made up and put together—even though her red hair was still wet—and displeased to see him still there.

"What's going on here, Francine?"

"What do you mean?" She got busy making coffee, apparently forgetting the power was out. When she remembered, she gave the coffeemaker a frustrated shove, causing water to spill from the top.

Unable to sit still, Ned got up and went to her. From behind, he reached around for her hands, which were still trembling. "Whatever it is, we can figure it out. But ya gotta tell me what's got ya so wound up."

"I said it's nothing." She shook him off and started cleaning up the mess from the coffeemaker.

"Ya want me to go away and leave ya alone the way I did for thirty-something years?"

"No," she said softly.

With his hand on her shoulder, he compelled her to turn to face him. "Then ya gotta tell me what's going on. Why don'cha want me to kiss ya or hold ya? I know ya like it."

Tears spilled down her cheeks, every one of them a spike to his fragile heart.

He brushed them away and bent his knees to bring himself to her eye level. "Will ya talk to me? Please?"

She wanted to. He could see that. But rather than share what had her so tortured, she rolled her bottom lip between her teeth and shook her head.

"Francine . . . Yer killing me here."

"I'm sorry. Maybe we shouldn't see each other anymore."

Ned's mouth fell open in shock. "Ya don't mean that."

"It's probably for the best."

Staring at her, he could barely form a clear thought. The weeks they'd been back together had been the happiest of his life. It couldn't be over. It just couldn't. "It's not fer the best. How can ya say that?"

New tears leaked from her eyes, telling him that she didn't want to end this any more than he did.

"Francine, honey, come on."

She shook her head and turned her back to him.

Even though it pained him deeply, he took a deep breath and walked away. As he headed to the door, every step hurt worse than the one before. With his hand on the doorknob, he said, "Ya know where I am if ya change yer mind."

In a daze, he somehow managed to get down the stairs and into his car. He sat there for a long time staring out the windshield. Finally, he started the car and backed out of the driveway.

Listening to him leave, Francine sank into the closest chair and let the tears come. Sending him away had been, without a doubt, one of the hardest things she'd ever done. But she couldn't continue to deceive him or lead him on. She'd done that once before, and no way would she be responsible for crushing him a second time. It had already gone on longer than it ever should have.

That was her fault. She'd been so darned happy to see him that day he popped up on her doorstep, asking her to dinner as if the more than thirty years since their last date had never happened—as if she hadn't left him for another man without so much as a how-do-you-do for the boy who'd been so sweet and kind to her.

Better to break it off now than later when things would no doubt be more complicated. Knowing it was the right thing to do didn't make it hurt any less. After so many lonely years, being with Ned again had been amazing. And fun. And exciting. Her shoulders slumped as it dawned on

her that there'd be no more dinners out or sunsets at the
bluffs or cookouts with their family and friends.

Francine had no idea how long she sat there before
Tiffany poked her head in the door. Her long dark hair was
in a ponytail, and her lean dancer's body vibrated with
energy—as usual.

"Hey, was Ned here before?" Tiffany came in and
stopped short when she saw her mother crying. "What's
wrong?"

Francine forced herself to meet her younger daughter's
worried gaze. "I need to ask you something."

"Of course. What is it?"

Wiping the tears from her face, Francine said, "Remember when you told me a couple of months ago that you
were trying to find your father?"

Tiffany's blue eyes widened with surprise. "You said
you didn't want to know about it."

"I didn't. I don't. But I wondered . . . Did you ever
find him?"

"No, but I found his sister. Marion."

Francine bit back a gasp. The last person on earth she
had any desire to see was Bobby Chester, but since there
was a very good chance she was still married to him, she
needed to know where he was. "Have you spoken to her?"

Tiffany shook her head. "I got as far as finding her
number, but I knew how you felt about it, and Maddie has
no interest in seeing him." She shrugged. "I didn't want to
upset everyone, so I dropped it." Glancing toward her
house, she added, "Besides, I've had enough crap on my
plate lately without inviting in more."

"I hate to see you so unhappy."

"Jim's moving out," Tiffany said in a dull, flat tone.

"I'm sorry, honey."

"Been a long time coming."

"Still . . . whatever I can do."

"Thanks. I've got to get back to Ashleigh. Jim's leaving soon."

"I'll see you later."

Tiffany was already through the door when Francine ran after her. "Tiff!"

At the bottom of the stairs, Tiffany turned to look up at her mother.

"You said you have Marion's number."

"What about it?"

"I think I'd like to have it."

"You sure about that?" Tiffany asked, her expression wary.

Francine thought of Ned and how devastated he'd been earlier when she called off their relationship. "I'm sure."

Chapter Four

Covered in mud and shivering from the chill, Grant and Stephanie made their way to the clinic on foot. Stephanie had decided he was the most confusing man she'd ever met. One minute he was pushing her away with his surliness, and the next he was lying beneath her, looking up at her with a dazed expression on his face and a substantial bulge in his pants.

Which version was she supposed to believe? The Grant who made it clear he still wanted his ex-girlfriend, or the Grant who'd made passionate love with her the night before and clearly wanted to again, if the erection pressing against her in the mud puddle had been any indication.

Once he'd returned to his senses, he'd disentangled himself from her, helped her up and acted like nothing unusual had happened.

A smart woman would steer clear of him altogether. His heart was obviously still committed elsewhere, and the last thing she needed was a big complication right now. She had her plan in place with no desire to deviate from it. After the summer on the island, she'd be returning to Providence and getting back to work on the most important thing in her life. Nowhere in that plan was there room for the kind of trouble Grant McCarthy could bring.

Stealing a fleeting glance at him, she sure did wish he wasn't so insanely hot. With his thick, wavy, jet-black hair, brilliant blue eyes, prominent cheekbones, sensuous lips and a to-die-for muscular frame, Stephanie could stare at him all day and never get tired of the view. Even covered in mud with wet hair clinging to his scalp, he still maintained that aura of elegance and class that had drawn her in from their first meeting. Too bad he was such a pain in the ass—and madly in love with someone else.

If she were being honest with herself, she'd admit to being seduced long ago by his amazing words in *Song of Solomon,* the movie he'd written. She'd watched him accept the Academy Award for best original screenplay and had been dazzled by his handsome face, self-deprecating wit and touching acceptance speech in which he gave his parents credit for encouraging him to follow his dreams.

Stephanie vividly remembered thinking at the time how lucky he was to have the kind of parents who stood behind their children the way his clearly had. Imagine her surprise when those same parents showed up one day last winter at the Providence restaurant where she worked and struck up a conversation that led to the job offer to run the restaurant at McCarthy's Gansett Island Marina for the following summer.

It had been a gamble, of course, to leave the year-round job in the city for five months on Gansett, but the change of scenery had done her good, and the money was fantastic. She'd made as much in a summer on Gansett as she did in a year in Providence—and she'd been able to live for free at the marina. However, the uncertainty of what awaited her when she went home after the Columbus Day holiday weekend weighed on her, but she'd figure something out. She always did.

Grant seemed to falter as they reached the clinic parking lot. Stephanie knew the last thing in the world he wanted was to rely on his ex-girlfriend's new fiancé to stitch him up, but since Dr. Cal was the only game in town—other than Doc Potter, the vet—Grant had little choice.

"Just go in, get the stitches and keep your mouth shut," Stephanie said.

"What else would I do?"

She sent him a withering look. "Remember when I told you not to get into it with Abby when your father was in the hospital? Did you listen to me then? *No*. You had to get all hot and bothered with her and show her how insanely jealous you are that she's with someone else now."

That made him mad, as she'd known it would. She couldn't say, exactly, why pushing his buttons was so much fun. It just was.

"What the hell would you have me do? Let the love of my life walk away without a fight?"

Stephanie swallowed her own burst of unreasonable jealousy and fought to keep her voice calm and rational. One of them had to be. "Did it ever occur to you that maybe you haven't met the love of your life yet?"

That stopped him in his tracks, and he spun around to face her. As luck would have it, anger only made him more attractive. Life wasn't fair. "You have a lot of nerve saying that. You don't even know me."

He was absolutely right, of course. She told herself to shut up and mind her own business. But before her mouth could get the message from her brain, she was already talking again. "You spent ten years with her, lived with her for what? Five years and never married her. What does that tell you?"

"I don't need you to tell me I'm an idiot. I already know that."

The wind whipped around them, but she couldn't bring herself to walk away from him. "I never said you were an idiot."

"Whatever. How do you even know all that?"

Cornered, Stephanie looked down at the wet blacktop. "I heard your sister and Maddie talking about it."

"Great, so they think I'm an idiot, too, I suppose."

"The word 'idiot' was never used."

"I forgot how much I hate it here," he muttered. "Everyone up in my grill, minding *my* business for me."

"Oh yeah, poor you with the lovely parents and the gorgeous home and the successful businesses, not to mention the brothers and sister and friends who'd do anything for you. It must really suck to be you." As soon as the words were out of her mouth, she wanted to take them back. They were talking about *him*, and she'd shown him a little too much about *her*.

"Stephanie, listen, I didn't mean—"

She held up a hand to stop him. The very *last* thing she wanted from him—or anyone—was pity. "Forget it. Feel free to mope around after Abby. In fact, if you're so all-fired determined to get her back, let me help you. It's painful watching you do it your way. You went beyond clueless about two weeks ago."

"What the hell is that supposed to mean?"

"For one thing, you have to stop looking at her with those sad hound-dog eyes. It's nauseating to watch, and she doesn't even notice."

"I have not been doing that!"

"Oh please, here's you at the wedding." She imitated his pathetic expression.

"If I ever look that ridiculous, please shoot me."

"Where can I get a gun around here?"

"You're seriously starting to irritate me."

She suspected she'd been irritating him since the second he woke up and realized she was in bed—naked—next to him. And yes, she'd known he was awake the whole time she was sneaking out of Janey's bedroom. "You ought to see the way you look at Cal, like you want to gut him and feed him to sharks." Furrowing her brows, she attempted to mirror his I-hate-Cal face. She wasn't sure she could do it justice, but she gave it a hell of an effort.

He shook his head. "You're full of shit."

"He hasn't done anything to you."

"He *stole* her from me!"

"Jesus Christ, Grant. Are you stuck in middle school? She's thirty-something years old. She wasn't *stolen*. She *chose* him."

"Only because he was here and I wasn't."

"If that's what you think, the situation is worse than I thought." Stephanie paused, choosing her words carefully. While she wanted to help him extract his head from his ass, she wasn't looking to purposely hurt him. "You've been back a month now, and she hasn't changed her mind. At what point do you have to accept that she isn't going to?"

Apparently, he had no good answer to that. At the main door to the clinic, he stopped and turned to her. "Thanks for getting me here," he said tersely. "I can handle the rest."

"I'm not leaving until you're stitched up."

"I don't need to be babysat."

"On that we disagree."

"You're a pain in my ass, you know that?"

"It seems I've heard that somewhere before." She pushed past him, activating the clinic's automatic double doors. As they stepped inside, Abby came rushing down the hallway. Fabulous.

"What's wrong?" Grant asked her. All his anger toward Stephanie morphed into concern for Abby.

"I need to go home and pack for Cal. He just got a call that his mother had a stroke in Texas."

"He can't go anywhere today."

Tears flooded her big brown eyes. "One of his fishing buddies is going to run him over to the mainland. I tried to tell him they're crazy to go out in this, but he didn't want to hear it." She glanced down and saw the bloody, muddy rag around Grant's hand. "What happened?"

"Door slammed shut on my hand at the marina. Needs a couple of stitches, I guess."

"Cal is getting ready to leave, but Victoria, the nurse practitioner, is here. She can probably do it for you."

Stephanie could sense Grant's relief that he wouldn't have to be seen by Cal after all.

Looking harried and undone, Dr. Cal came down the hallway toward them. As soon as she saw him, Abby turned away from Grant and focused all her attention on her distraught fiancé. Wrapping her arms around him, she guided him toward the door. Tall and blond in a rugged sort of way, Cal seemed to melt into Abby's embrace.

"Um, Cal," Grant said, hesitantly. "Sorry to hear about your mom."

"Thanks," Cal said, distracted and clearly anxious to be on his way.

"Uh, I know island life is still sort of new to you," Grant

continued, "but going out on the water today is taking your life in your hands."

Against all odds, Stephanie found that she was proud of him.

"I know it's not the smartest thing I've ever done," Cal said in a deep Texan drawl, "but they're saying the storm will last for days, and my daddy said Mama may not have days left. I can't wait."

Stephanie reached out to squeeze Cal's arm. "We'll pray for your safety and for your mother, too."

"Thanks, y'all." To Abby, he said, "Let's go, baby. I gotta meet Steve down at the docks in half an hour." With his arm around Abby, Cal headed for the door.

Abby never looked back.

Stephanie looked up to find Grant's gaze firmly affixed on his ex-girlfriend. "That was good," she said.

He finally tore his eyes off the retreating couple and looked down at her. "What was?"

"That you warned him about going out on a boat today."

Grant shrugged. "Contrary to what you think, I don't want him dead. I just want him out of her life. Maybe once he gets back to Texas, he'll realize that's where he belongs and that will be that."

Stephanie shook her head with dismay. "You just don't get it, do you?"

"Get what?"

A nurse came down the long hallway to the waiting area. "May I help you?"

"He needs stitches," Stephanie said, *and a lobotomy*, she thought but didn't say.

"Let's get you into an exam room and see what we've got," she said, gesturing for them to follow her.

Grant hesitated long enough that Stephanie gave him a shove to get him moving.

"Ass pain," he muttered.

"Baby," she retorted. He was the most maddening of men, but there was something about him that had her following him into the exam room when her better judgment was telling her to get the hell out of there.

Chapter Five

Since he didn't know where else to go, Ned drove to his best friend's house. "Big Mac" McCarthy was still recovering from the accident at the marina in which he'd suffered a severe concussion and a fractured arm.

He hadn't bounced back as quickly as everyone had hoped he would. Dr. Cal had told them head injuries could be tough that way. Often, the patient's personality could be different as the brain recovered from the trauma of the injury. Ned had been concerned about his friend, and knew the rest of the family had been equally worried.

They'd been friends for so long that Ned couldn't imagine life without the old guy. That day at the marina . . . The memory of the drunk whose poor boating skills had resulted in Big Mac being pulled right off the pier ate at Ned and everyone else who'd witnessed the horror of it.

Big Mac's son Mac had jumped into the water after his father, and Luke Harris had leaped onto the boat, finally getting the boater's attention but suffering a badly sprained ankle in the process.

Ned shuddered just thinking about it. He'd been to see Big Mac every day since, and he'd continue to go every day until his friend was able to get back to his routine of coffee, doughnuts and bullshitting with the guys at the marina in the morning, followed by a day of "work" on the docks. They'd all been relieved when Big Mac rallied to walk his little girl down the aisle. Maybe the wedding would be a turning point in his recovery. They could only hope.

Ned pulled into the driveway at the White House and cut the engine. After what had transpired with Francine, he probably wasn't fit for company, but he wouldn't miss a day with his friend.

The wind and rain beat him up on the way to the door. On the porch, he stomped the water off his shoes, knowing how fussy Linda was about her precious house. He knocked on the door and waited.

Linda came to the door and smiled when she saw him. "Hi, Ned. Come in." She held the door for him and embarrassed him, as she always did, by kissing him on the cheek. Raising five kids hadn't done anything to diminish her petite beauty. Blonde and blue-eyed, she could be formidable and a bit exacting, but she'd made him part of their family, and he loved her for that.

"So faithful," she said, taking his coat. "Even in the middle of a tropical storm."

Ned shrugged. "Nothing he wouldn't do for me. How is he today?"

"He's enjoying having the boys home but a little melancholy after the wedding."

"Probably woulda been that way after giving away his baby girl even without the head bump."

"No doubt. He's in the family room. Go on in."

Ned started toward the kitchen but stopped and turned back to her. "Could I ask ya something?"

"Of course."

"If a gal says she doesn't want ta see ya anymore, but she's crying her eyes out when she says it, what does that mean?"

"Oh, Ned. Oh no! What happened?"

"Wish I knew. Everything was goin' along just fine. Till today. I get the feeling she's keepin' something from me, but damned if I know what."

"Maybe you need to give her some space and let her miss you a little. She'll come around. I told Mac last night that she looks at you like a woman in love."

"Ya think so? Really?"

She reached for him and wrapped him in a warm hug. "I do. Be patient. Let her work out whatever she's got going on. She'll be back."

"I sure hope yer right."

"When have you ever known me not to be?"

Ned threw his head back and laughed. "Not once in dern near forty years."

"There you have it," she said with a smug smile. "Come have some leftover wedding cake and shoot the bull with your buddy. You'll feel better after."

"Already do." He gave her a peck on the forehead. "Thanks, gal."

"Any time, my friend."

Feeling a little lighter after his talk with Linda, Ned let her escort him into a kitchen filled with flowers left over from the wedding and accepted a cup of coffee she proudly told him she'd brewed on the gas grill like a prairie woman. That made him laugh, too, since the last thing Linda McCarthy would ever be was a prairie woman.

He took the coffee with him into the family room, where Big Mac was watching his grown sons Evan and Adam wrestle. Some things, it seemed, never changed.

"Still time to place your bet," Big Mac said to Ned.

"My money's on Adam," Ned said. The smallest of the four McCarthy boys had always been the scrappiest.

The brothers were red-faced and sweating profusely as they struggled on the floor.

"Traitor," Evan grunted out.

"I remain optimistic that they might grow up one of these days," Big Mac said.

"Keep dreamin', old pal. If it ain't happened yet, it ain't gonna."

"There's your opening, Adam," Big Mac said.

Ned was delighted to see his friend engaged in the goings-on. Having his kids around always raised his spirits.

"Is *anyone* on my side?" Evan asked as his older brother got the better of him.

"I am, darling," Linda said from the doorway as she watched with long-suffering patience. "But I'll skin you both if you break anything."

Ned chortled. He loved this rowdy family with all his heart. As much as he wanted to tell Big Mac about picking up Stephanie after she'd spent the night with Grant, he'd never once told tales on the McCarthy kids and wasn't about to start now. He'd kept a lot of secrets for all five of them over the years, earning him favored uncle status with each of them.

"Ya all recovered from the big day?" Ned asked Big Mac.

"Guess so. My little girl sure seemed happy, didn't she?"

"That she did—and she was awfully beautiful, too. It was a helluva day."

"Since they're stuck here thanks to the storm, everyone's getting together at Mac and Maddie's later so they can open their gifts. Hope you can come."

"I'll be there." It occurred to Ned that Francine would probably be there, too. "Wouldn't miss it." He took a quick glance at Big Mac, noting that he seemed tired and still somewhat diminished by his injuries. Wondering if his old friend would ever be the same as he'd once been filled Ned

with fear and determination to see him through this. "Some
pretty big surf running out at the bluffs if ya wanna take a
ride and check it out."

"Maybe after a while."

"Sure. Whatever you want."

Laura McCarthy was in love. Owen had shown her
through all three floors of the Sand & Surf, pointing out
nooks and crannies that made it unique, sharing stories
about the guests who'd once filled the rooms and insights
about the couple who'd run the hotel for five decades.

"How do you know so much about them?" she asked as
they headed down the stairs to the lobby.

"I told you—I know them."

"*How* do you know them?"

"They're my grandparents."

Shocked, Laura stared at him. "Why didn't you say so?"

"I don't know," he said with a delighted grin that told
her he'd enjoyed deceiving her.

"You've obviously spent a lot of time here."

"Every summer of my childhood, from the day after
school got out until the day before it started."

Having spent several summers of her own childhood
with her cousins on the island, Laura couldn't believe
she'd never met him before. "Where did you live the rest
of the year?"

"Here. There. Everywhere."

The vague answer aggravated her. He seemed to be
going out of his way to be an enigma. She must've looked
annoyed, because he laughed.

"My dad is an air force general. We literally lived everywhere. This was the only real home I ever had, the one place
that remained a constant. My mom grew up here, too."

"So you stay here when you're on the island?"

"Yep. My grandparents pay a caretaker to come in and keep a couple of rooms clean and to make sure we don't have any unwelcome guests."

"Like rodents?" Laura took a nervous look around the lobby.

"That and squatters who make themselves right at home."

"They *live* in here?"

"We've had to relocate a few people since my grandparents finally reached the point where they couldn't run it anymore."

"Where are they now?"

"In Florida, hoping someone will fall hopelessly in love with the place and take it off their hands one of these days."

"Why don't you do it?"

Owen snorted with laughter. "Because that would require me to stay in one place longer than a week or two. I don't do roots."

"So where do you live?"

"Here. There."

"Everywhere," she finished for him with another exasperated scowl. "You're very evasive."

"Not really. I go where the gigs are. All I need is my van, my guitar and a clean pair of jeans every couple of days. Works for me."

"Aren't you getting kind of, um, *old* to be living like a hobo?"

"*Old?*" He hooted. "I'm thirty-three!"

"Exactly. When do you grow up and get a real job?" A flash of what might've been anger or even hurt crossed his handsome face, and Laura regretted that she'd been so blunt. "I'm sorry. It's none of my business."

"I hear that a lot—that I need to get a *real* job." His normally laid-back tone of voice had taken on a bitter edge.

"You know what's so funny about that? I probably have more money in the bank than most of the guys my age who went to college, got married, shackled themselves with a mortgage and settled down to pump out two-point-five kids in the burbs. I'll guarantee I'm a whole lot happier than most of them are—and I bet my blood pressure is half what theirs is."

"You don't have to explain yourself to me or anyone. I certainly have no business judging the choices anyone else has made."

"Made some bad ones, Princess?"

Her gaze darted up to meet his, which was once again teasing and open. "Why did you call me that?" That was her father's name for her, and hearing it from someone else was unsettling.

He shrugged. "There's something sort of regal about you."

If only he knew. "No, there isn't."

"Whatever you say. You didn't answer the question."

Laura wanted to pretend like she didn't know what he meant, but acting coy had never been her thing. "I've made a few clunkers. Especially lately."

"Well, if you're looking to regroup, you've come to the right place. Gansett is known for its restorative powers."

"Is that so?"

Nodding, he said, "You might want to stick around for a while."

"Why's that?"

"Because last night, the McCarthys talked me into staying until Columbus Day to play the Tiki Bar at the marina—six whole weeks in one place." He shuddered dramatically. "It'd be a lot more interesting if you're here, too."

Laura eyed him skeptically. "If you say so. Thanks for the tour."

Owen walked her to the front door. "My pleasure. I hope I'll see you again soon."

Unsure of how to reply to that, she put on her hood and zipped her raincoat for the walk back to her aunt and uncle's house. The hour with Owen had been one of the more enjoyable that she'd spent since her life was ripped apart.

He'd given her a lot to think about.

If not for the storm, Grant might've skipped the gathering at Mac's house. Sitting alone in a dark house had given him far too much time to think, so he headed to the marina. Back in the day, he would've used the unexpected free time to work on the screenplay of the moment. But lately, the words just weren't there. He kept expecting them to come back. They'd been so much a part of him for his entire life that the silence of their absence was overwhelming.

If he allowed himself to think too much about whether or not they'd ever come back, he'd lose what was left of his mind. The words had made him special. They'd given him something most other people didn't have. Without them, he was nothing—a thought that filled him with irrational panic. It was definitely better not to think about it.

As he drove, he told himself he was going to refill the generator with gas, check on the boats and make sure the marina was withstanding the storm. But underneath it all, he wanted to check on Stephanie. Thinking of her alone in the dark at the deserted marina bothered him for some strange reason.

She was a pain in the ass, no doubt about it, but his mother had raised him right, and he'd rather not feel guilty about her being alone when she could be with his family and friends. Even though Mac had invited both of them earlier, Grant was quite certain Stephanie wouldn't go to the party on her own.

He parked outside the main building and pulled the hood up over his head to take a quick walk down the main pier. The few remaining boats bobbed and rolled, but they all seemed securely tied, so Grant turned into the wind to hustle back the way he'd come. The rain was almost painful as it beat against his face. Using his key, he let himself into the main building and shook off the wetness in the vestibule.

Still dripping, he stepped into the restaurant and found Stephanie at one of the tables, poring over a pile of papers with a battery-powered light illuminating the vast space. Howling wind had the old wood building creaking and straining, and Grant was grateful that Mac had recently replaced the roof. At least it was dry.

Despite the howling and creaking, Stephanie was completely absorbed in whatever she was doing. Grant couldn't help but notice how vulnerable she seemed as she was nearly dwarfed by the huge stack of papers. She had her head propped in the palm of her hand, and her lips moved as she read, which was oddly adorable. Her neck was long and graceful, which spurred yet another memory from the night before—of worshipping the soft skin on her neck with openmouthed kisses that had made her moan.

Before his body could react to the images that accompanied the memory, Grant cleared his throat and stepped into the room.

She looked up, startled and seeming slightly fearful. What was that all about?

"Hey." Standing so fast her chair toppled over behind

her, she got busy scooping up the papers. "What're you doing here?"

"I thought you might like to go to the party at Mac's."

"Oh. Um." Her gaze darted to the stack of papers. "I have stuff to do here."

"What's all that?"

She shifted ever so slightly, as if she were trying to put herself between him and the papers. "Nothing. Just some work."

Grant closed the small distance between them and leaned over her shoulder, startled to settle his gaze on what looked to be a legal document of some sort. "Are you in trouble?"

"No! Of course not. It's nothing." With a hand to his chest, she fended him off. "It's none of your business."

Grant couldn't help but laugh at that, even though he had never seen her so nervous. "Isn't that rich, coming from someone who's planted herself knee-deep in my business since the day we met."

"That's because you needed my help. I don't. Need yours, that is."

Taking a chair and turning it around backward, Grant straddled it. "Why don't you let me be the judge of that?"

"What're you doing? You can't just plunk yourself down . . ."

He arched a brow. "Like I own the place?" Part of him wanted to cringe as the words left his mouth, since it wasn't like him to play that card, but he was too proud of the zinger to take it back. Let's face it, he owed her a few from earlier.

All the starch seemed to leave her when he said that, and she sagged, which made him feel like an ass for poking at her when she clearly didn't want him to. The Stephanie he knew didn't sag.

"Please, Grant. Leave it alone. I'm asking you as a friend."

"So we're friends now?" He rubbed at the stubble on his chin. "Is that so?"

"It's easier to think of you as a friend than to think of myself as a slut because of what happened last night."

He hated to hear her use that word to describe herself. "So we had sex. Big whoop. People do it all the time."

"I don't."

Something about the way she said the two little words conveyed a world of loneliness that touched him in places he didn't want her touching him. Those places belonged to Abby, and he'd do well to remember that. "So what is all this?"

"I told you I don't want to talk about it."

"And I told you earlier I didn't want to talk about Abby. Did you listen to me? Nope."

"This is different."

"Because we're minding your business instead of mine?"

Glowering at him, she let out a deep sigh. "You are *so* aggravating."

"Likewise." He felt sort of bad for pushing her, but why should she be able to dig into his crap if he couldn't dig into hers? Not that he cared about her crap, but for some reason it was fun to provoke her.

"If you must know, I'm doing some research."

"What kind of research?"

"The kind you do when you want to know more about something."

That's when he realized she was humoring him and had no intention of actually leveling with him. Grant snatched one of the pages off the table. The top line read *The People v. Charles Grandchamp*. The name was familiar to him, but he couldn't say why.

"Give that to me!" She grabbed the paper from him and clutched it to her chest.

Grant glanced up at her and was shocked to find tears forming in her expressive eyes. "Stephanie . . ." He felt like a total creep for pushing the issue, even if he'd only been intending to give her a bit of her own medicine. "I'm sorry."

With her jaw set in that mulish expression she did so well, she looked away from him.

"I was just fooling around. I didn't mean to upset you." Berating himself for going too far, he reached for her chin and forced her to meet his gaze. "I'm sorry, okay?"

She shrugged him off and returned the paper he'd taken to her stack.

"Tell me," he said, not sure why it mattered so much.

Shaking her head, she said, "I can't." The helpless tone to her voice was so wildly removed from her usual sauciness that it further saddened him.

"Maybe I can help."

That drew a bitter-sounding laugh from her that was so different from the laughter he'd experienced in the mud puddle that he would've thought it came from someone else if he hadn't been watching her closely both times.

"No one can help."

"Stephanie—"

"Fine!" The word seemed torn from her very soul as she spun around, her eyes wild with rage and fear and pain unlike anything he'd ever seen in his life. "If you want to know so bad—here it is. Charles Grandchamp is my stepfather—the one person in my whole, entire, miserable life who was ever good to me, who ever loved me or gave a shit about me. And guess where he is?" Before Grant could begin to form a coherent statement, she answered her own question. "In prison, serving a life sentence with no chance of parole, for kidnapping and assault of a minor." Her chest heaved, and tears fell freely down her face.

Riveted by her outburst, Grant couldn't seem to move as he absorbed what she'd said. "Who did he kidnap and assault?"

"Me," she said so softly he almost didn't hear her over the howling and creaking.

Chapter Six

Grant dropped into the chair he'd recently abandoned. He had no idea what to say.

"Except it wasn't a kidnapping," she continued, "and he never laid a hand on me with anything other than love or affection. He saved my life by getting me away from my abusive, drug-addicted mother and has paid for that with fourteen years in prison for a crime he didn't commit."

"If he didn't kidnap or assault you, how'd he end up in jail?"

"Well, technically, he did kidnap me, but no one wanted to hear that a fourteen-year-old went willingly with him rather than spend another second waiting for her mother to get high and either beat the shit out of her or forget about her altogether. She's the one who actually beat me. He paid for the bruises she left on me."

"They didn't let you testify?"

"They did, but the prosecution twisted every word I said to make him look bad, and the jury believed them. I've devoted my life to trying to get him a new trial. Every dime I have goes to lawyers." She glanced at the stack of paper on the table. "I've probably learned enough to sail through law school."

"Does this have something to do with your Fridays off?" She went to the mainland every Friday without fail, even though that was one of the busiest days at the marina in the summer. The first week they'd worked together, she'd told Grant she was off on Fridays and made it clear that was nonnegotiable.

She nodded. "Visiting day at the prison."

"I'm so sorry, Stephanie. I had no idea. I was a jerk—"

"That's all right. I'm getting used to it."

Startled, he glanced at her and found a smile tugging at her full lips. Suddenly, he needed to touch her. All thoughts of Abby and his big plans to get her back fled from his mind in the midst of Stephanie's overwhelming sadness. "Come here."

She recoiled from his outstretched hand. "What?"

"Come here."

"Why?"

Grant swallowed his exasperation. "Just do it."

Rolling her eyes, she took a step toward him.

"Closer."

Another small step.

Grant reached out, grabbed her hand and tugged, causing her to lose her balance—just as he'd intended. He caught her and settled her on his lap with his arms around her.

"What're you doing?" Seeming horrified, she squirmed around on his lap, giving him a whole other problem.

"This," he said, tightening his arms around her.

"Grant—"

"Do you ever stop talking?"

"Really. You don't have to—"

He brushed his lips against her short hair, breathing in the musky, feminine scent of her. "Hush."

It took a minute, but she finally settled and relaxed into his embrace, her head resting on his shoulder.

"There, was that so hard?"

"Yes."

He couldn't help but smile at that. "Have you been fighting this battle by yourself all this time?"

"There's no one else."

"You know," he said tentatively, "as I writer, I'm pretty good at research."

Raising her head from his shoulder, she tried to struggle out of his hold.

"Wait. Let me finish." She didn't relax, but she stopped trying to get free, which he took as a small victory. "All I'm saying is I might be able to help. You've been looking at it for a long time. Maybe I'll see something you've missed."

"That's not necessary."

"I know it's not, but didn't you say before that we're friends? And don't friends help their friends?"

"I appreciate the offer. Really, I do. But it's not your problem." This time when she pushed at him, he let her go. She got up and started sorting her papers into neat stacks.

Grant said nothing as he watched her, but inside he churned. How was he supposed to hear what she'd just told him and not want to help her in some way? She'd said she didn't want his help, but that didn't mean he couldn't look into the case on his own, did it?

"You must want to get to your brother's," she said, obviously wanting him gone after the emotional firestorm he'd started.

"Only if you come with me." No way would he leave her here alone after he'd forced her to talk about her painful past.

"I'm not in the mood for a party tonight."

Grant put his feet up on one of the other chairs, settling in. "We can heat up some chowder or something here, then."

Placing her hands on her hips, she stared at him, incredulous. "You're missing a golden opportunity to talk to Abby without Cal around."

He shrugged as he realized the idea of talking to Abby had lost its luster in the last half hour. "He'll be gone awhile. There'll be other opportunities."

She threw her hands up in dismay. "This is why you need constant supervision. You have no idea what you're doing!"

Relieved to see some of her earlier spunk returning, Grant took the insult without comment. Instead, he smirked at her, letting her think she'd won a round. Whatever it took to wipe that demolished, devastated expression from her arresting face.

Glowering at him, she said, "You just want me to go so you can use me to make her jealous."

"Are you saying you're not game? I thought you wanted to help me get her back."

"You do need all the help you can get."

"I guess you'd better come, then. God knows what kind of trouble I could get into on my own if left unsupervised."

He knew he'd convinced her when she growled at him, gathered up the stack of paper and stomped into her quarters off the kitchen. When she returned with the flimsy windbreaker she'd worn earlier, Grant bit back a swear and stood to shrug off his own coat. "Put this on."

"Why? That's yours."

"Actually, it's Joe's, and that thing you're wearing wouldn't keep a flea dry in this weather."

"What will keep you dry?"

"I'll grab one of my dad's coats from the office."

Tentatively, she took it from him. "I'm not used to this thoughtful side of you."

"I can be quite charming when I put my mind to it," he said, amused by her even though he really didn't want to be. She had a way of putting him in his place. He was far more used to women who were solicitous toward him, hoping to catch his eye, but he'd been a one-woman man his entire adult life. Sparring with Stephanie was an entirely new—and not entirely unpleasant—experience.

"Good to know. You might want to show Abby a little more of that and a little less of the pathetic hound-dog thing, if you want my opinion."

And just like that he went from being amused straight back to annoyed. "I don't, but thanks just the same." He brushed past her on his way to the stairs. In the second-floor office that used to be his father's and was now shared by Mac and Luke, he fumbled around in the dark, feeling for the row of hooks that housed a variety of coats and jackets. His hand finally settled on a foul-weather coat that he took downstairs with him.

Stephanie had donned the yellow coat, which was huge on her, making her look even more waifish than usual.

"Ready?" Grant asked brusquely.

She cut the light on the table, plunging them into inky darkness. "Ready." As she made her way toward him, she stumbled.

Grant reached out and somehow managed to catch her, stopping her fall.

Her fingers tightened on his biceps, which sent a charge of desire to his groin.

He choked back a groan. *Why* did he have to react to her every damned time she came near him?

"Thanks," she muttered, moving past him.

Grant followed her out the door, locked it and nearly had himself back under control by the time he slid into the cab next to her.

* * *

All the way to Mac's, Stephanie berated herself. How could she have been so stupid as to tell Grant the whole ugly story? She never told anyone, so why pour it all out to a guy who infuriated her more than anything else? Maybe it was because sometimes the weight of her burden became too much to bear by herself. For a brief moment, it had felt good to share it with someone else.

As the summer drew to a close, she was still a thousand dollars short of the ten thousand she had to pay Charlie's lawyer to keep the appeal process moving forward, but she'd come up with it somehow.

Their only remaining hope was a new trial, and the lawyer they'd recently hired was confident they had a shot. Of course they'd heard that before and had learned not to get their hopes up. There were times, especially during the glorious summer on the island, when Stephanie wondered how she managed to find the wherewithal to press on in the midst of such a seemingly hopeless situation. But as long as Charlie was behind bars for a crime he didn't commit, Stephanie would keep up the fight. What right did she have to beautiful sunsets or crisp, clear island days while he rotted in jail?

Prison had changed him from a sweet, gentle soul to a hardened, bitter man. She'd never rest as long as he continued to pay for trying to help free her from a nightmare.

"You're awfully quiet over there," Grant said, his deep voice puncturing the silent cocoon of the truck's cab.

"Just thinking."

"About?"

Even though it was inky dark, she glanced over at him, conjuring the image of his arresting profile. The strong jaw, the perfectly sized nose, the thick hair, those soft lips . . . "You won't tell anyone about Charlie. Right?"

"Of course not."

Releasing a deep breath, she said, "Good. Thanks."

"Listen, Stephanie—"

"Please. I can't talk about it anymore. I appreciate that you want to help, but there's really nothing you can do."

"All I was going to say is that I'm here if you need a friend."

She was thankful that the overwhelming darkness hid the tears that immediately flooded her eyes. She'd been so alone with this for so long that he couldn't know what his offer meant to her. But then she remembered he was in love with someone else, and his every thought was directed toward getting her back. Leaning on a man who wanted to be with someone else was a recipe for disaster, and she'd already had more than her share.

"I've never seen such darkness," she said, closing her eyes to hold back the tears. The rain had let up a little, but the windshield wipers were still needed to clear the mist.

"It's crazy, isn't it?" He sounded somewhat relieved by the change in subject. "The insane darkness is what I remember most about the time we were without power for ten days when I was a kid."

"So what's your plan for getting Abby's attention tonight?"

"I guess I'll try to talk to her if I can get her alone."

Stephanie scoffed, relieved to be back on more familiar ground with him.

"What?"

"I don't get how you managed to write such a beautiful movie about love when you're so clueless about women."

"I am *not* clueless about women."

"What would you call it, sport?"

"My exposure has been somewhat . . . limited. That's all."

Stephanie's mouth fell open. "So she's the only one you've ever, you know . . ."

The squeak of the bench seat indicated he was squirming over there. "Until last night."

"Oh my God! Just *me and her*? That's *it*?"

"So what? I've been with her since high school."

His use of the present tense was a disturbing reminder that despite what had happened between them, he'd yet to move on from his relationship with Abby. "I hate to break it to you, but you're not *with* her anymore."

"Thanks for the reminder. That really helps."

"You haven't had any luck getting her to talk to you before now, so what makes you think she'll be any friendlier toward you tonight?"

"Cal won't be hanging all over her like a dog in heat."

Stephanie couldn't help the laugh that rang through the small space. "You're seriously messed up, you know that?"

"So you've told me. Often."

"The way I see it, desperate times call for desperate measures." A pain beneath her ribs was the only warning Stephanie had that she was about to make a very stupid move. "You need to make her as jealous as you've been since you saw her with Cal."

"And how do you propose I do that?"

"You know."

"What do I know?"

Stephanie left the question to linger in the air between them.

And then he let out a ringing laugh that hurt her feelings despite her best intention to remain removed from the surreal proceedings. She wanted to believe her outrageous idea had nothing to do with wanting to spend more time with him. Of course it didn't. That would be a fool's errand,

and she'd prided herself on never playing the fool. Until she met Grant McCarthy, that was.

"You're suggesting I *officially* use you to make her jealous?"

She did her best to keep her tone nonchalant. "Have you got a better idea or a more ready candidate?"

"Actually, I don't."

"You can thank me later."

"Don't get smug just yet. You haven't actually *done* anything."

"What do you want me to do?" she asked, reaching over to run a hand up his leg suggestively.

The sharp breath he sucked in as he grabbed her hand to stop her startled them both. She pulled back her hand as if she'd been scalded. In that moment, Stephanie realized two things—one, despite his supposed indifference toward her, he wanted her, and two, she wanted him, too.

Chapter Seven

The yard was full of cars when they arrived at Mac's. Grant scanned the vehicles for Abby's car and saw it tucked between Joe's company truck and Linda's yellow VW bug. "She's here."

"You knew she would be, as one of Janey's bridesmaids. Who was the other one? I never did get her name."

"Our cousin Laura. She just got married herself a couple of months ago."

"So what's the plan, Stan?"

"How should I know? Just play it cool, I guess."

"Cool. Okay. Does that mean play it like we're together, play it like we're hanging out, play it like we're burning up the sheets? What's your pleasure?"

Grant swallowed hard as her words had a predictable effect on him. Why was it that even the sound of her snarky voice could turn him on? Something was wrong with him. There was no other possible explanation for the way he kept reacting to someone who grated on his nerves the way she did.

"I guess the second one. Hanging out."

"Does that entail touching or subtle flirting or innuendo?"

"I can't even see your face, and I can tell you're enjoying this."

"I am not! I just want to understand my assignment."

Filled with exasperation, Grant sighed. He'd been more exasperated since he met her than in his entire life before her. "*Subtle* touching and *subtle* flirting. Nothing too over the top. No mention of what happened last night."

Stephanie opened the passenger door, flooding the cab with light. "Don't worry. I'm not about to go in there and start spewing off to your parents and family that you rocked my world or anything."

He grabbed her arm to stop her from getting out. "Did I?"

Her brows furrowed over those expressive eyes. "Did you what?"

"Rock your world?"

She dissolved into laughter. "I wouldn't go that far, but it didn't *suck*."

Wincing, he said, "Gee, thanks for that ringing endorsement. I was a little drunk, you know. I can do better."

Something akin to panic skirted across her face as she tugged her arm free and got out of the truck.

Grant got out, too, and met her at the front of the truck. "I just want to say . . ."

"What?"

"If I took advantage last night or acted, you know, less than . . . honorably, I'm sorry. I haven't been myself lately, and the last thing I want is to drag anyone else down with me."

"It takes two to tango, sport, so don't be too hard on yourself. Like I said, it didn't suck."

Why was it that this little sprite of a woman could make

him so hot one minute and so damned mad the next? That was something he continued to ponder as they took the back steps to the deck. The house glowed with the soft light produced by candles, creating a warm, cozy atmosphere for a tropical-storm party.

Grant slid the deck door open and gestured for her to go in ahead of him. Since they were among the last to arrive, everyone turned to greet them, including Abby. He took a certain bit of pleasure in realizing she'd noticed he hadn't come alone. Good. Let her see what it was like for a change. Grant pressed a hand to the small of Stephanie's back, which earned him a quizzical look over her shoulder that he ignored as he greeted his brothers and sister.

Ned was there, as were Maddie's mother Francine, her sister Tiffany and niece Ashleigh. Mac's friend Blaine Taylor, the Gansett Island police chief, still in uniform from what had no doubt been a long day, was talking to Joe and Janey. Grant's cousin Laura was helping Abby organize the big pile of wedding gifts while Owen Lawry tuned his guitar to sync with Evan's.

Stephanie stayed close to Grant's side as he talked to his parents and visited with Maddie, who was settled on the sofa in the middle of the big great room.

"How're you feeling?" Grant asked his sister-in-law as he bent to kiss her cheek.

"Fat and cooped up and cranky."

"Yikes. That doesn't sound like much fun."

"Your brother is driving me nuts," she added in a conspiratorial whisper, her gaze settling on Mac, who was across the room tending to their son Thomas.

"What's he doing now?"

"He's been freaked out all day about the storm and the ferry service being shut down. He hates being stuck here when I'm pregnant. He worries about something going wrong."

Grant exchanged glances with Stephanie.

"What?" Maddie asked.

"Oh, nothing," Grant said.

His sister-in-law clutched his arm. "What do you know?"

Surprised by her strong grip, he looked down to find big caramel-colored eyes staring back at him. "Cal left the island today. His mother had a stroke in Texas."

"*Oh my God!* I wondered where he was when Abby came alone. You can't tell Mac that Cal is gone, or he's apt to have a stroke himself." Her eyes took on a wild look that alarmed Grant. "Promise me you won't tell him."

"I won't," Grant said, "but someone else is apt to."

"*OhmyGodohmyGod.*" Maddie's eyes got even bigger, and her free hand landed on her extended abdomen.

"Maddie," Grant said, alarmed by her sudden pallor. "What is it?"

"Just an odd twinge." She took a deep breath. "It's nothing."

He glanced at Stephanie, who seemed equally alarmed.

"You can't stress yourself out," Grant said. "That's how you ended up on bed rest in the first place."

"When Mac finds out there's no doctor on the island . . ." She swallowed hard. "I can't even think about it. He's been a total wreck all day."

"The best thing you can do is relax and try not to worry."

She nodded. "Yes, you're right. But still . . . Maybe I should've listened to Mac and gone to the mainland for the rest of the pregnancy. If something happens to the baby . . ."

Grant squatted to put himself at her eye level. "Nothing's going to happen. Take a deep breath and calm down."

He waited while she did as he asked. "Now take another one. Calm. That is the word of the day."

Maddie released the second deep breath and gripped the hand he'd offered. "Thank you."

"Any time." He leaned in to kiss her forehead. "That's my niece or nephew in there. We won't let anything happen to either of you. I promise."

She nodded, seeming reassured even if her eyes were still glassier than he preferred.

"Can I get you something to eat or drink?" he asked.

"Some water would be good."

"Coming right up."

Stephanie followed him into the kitchen and helped herself to a soda from the cooler while he got the water for Maddie. "You were good with her. Really good."

Surprised by the unexpected compliment, Grant turned to look at her. "So maybe I'm not a complete dolt with women?"

"Oh, no, you are. But apparently you're good with sisters-in-law."

"A guy can't catch a break with you," he said, amused by her even when he didn't want to be.

She shrugged. "Just calling it like I see it."

Abby came into the room and stopped short when she saw them. "Oh. Hi."

Stephanie took the water from him. "I'll get this to Maddie for you."

"Oh, um, thanks." Even though the gathering was still visible from the kitchen, he and Abby had the room to themselves. "So I assume Cal made it to the mainland?"

"Yes," she said, pouring a glass of white wine. Chardonnay, he recalled. Her favorite. She was petite and curvy with long dark hair. Her big brown eyes used to soften with love every time she looked his way. Realizing she no longer looked at him adoringly was yet another loss he was forced to absorb where she was concerned. "I guess it was quite a trip, though."

"I imagine it would be on a day like this."

"He rented a car and was in Pennsylvania the last I talked to him. He was hoping to catch a flight from there since the airports are closed from here to New York."

Grant tried to focus on what she was saying, but his head was spinning. There was so much he wanted and needed to say to her. Where to begin? He cleared his throat. "Do me a favor and don't let on to Mac that Cal is off-island. He's been a mess over Maddie's pregnancy with Cal here. It'd be better for all of us—especially Maddie—if he didn't know Cal is gone."

"Mum's the word." She took a sip from her glass of wine. "So you and Stephanie, huh?"

Grant felt like she'd sucker-punched him. "What? We're friends."

"Uh-huh."

"It's not what you think."

"It's certainly none of my business."

"Of course it is!"

Her brows knitted in confusion. "How is it my business?"

"You and me . . . We're—"

"Over, Grant." She said it so softly, as if it pained her to have to say it out loud. Again. "I'm really happy to see you moving on. That's what we both needed to do. In hindsight, I can see we should've done it a long time ago."

"No." He shook his head. "That's not true."

She stepped toward him and rested a hand on his arm. "It is true. I figured it out a little sooner than you did, but you'll get there, too."

A sense of desperation unlike anything he'd ever known came over him. He cupped her face in his hand and forced her to look up at him. "How can you walk away like everything we had meant nothing to you?"

"Oh, Grant," she said with a sigh, "that's not at all how it happened. If only you knew how I suffered over you. But I found something better, and maybe you have, too. Don't mess it up by wishing for what used to be. There's no sense in that."

Before Grant could think of a reply to that, Luke Harris came into the kitchen, still on crutches from the ankle injury he'd sustained at the marina. "Oh hey. Sorry to interrupt."

"You're not," Abby said with a sad smile for Grant. "We were done."

"Abby—"

She walked away like he hadn't said a word, shoulders squared with determination.

"Son of a bitch," Grant muttered.

"Sorry, man," Luke said.

"Don't sweat it."

"No luck?"

Grant shook his head.

"What can I do?"

Grant shifted his gaze to find his old friend looking at him with concern. "Not a damned thing, apparently."

"I hate to say it—"

"Don't bother. I'm hearing it from every corner as it is."

"Well, then, I won't pile on. I sort of wondered . . ."

"What?"

"You and Stephanie were having a good time at the wedding. I thought there might be something brewing there."

He wasn't quite ready to talk about what might be brewing with Stephanie, even to one of his oldest friends. "Maybe."

"She's gorgeous."

Surprised by Luke's blunt assessment, Grant sought out Stephanie in the next room. She was talking and laughing with Janey and Maddie, and he had to admit she was rather cute when she was relaxed and her claws were sheathed. But gorgeous? "You think so?"

"I do. Seems like a really nice girl, too. I've thought so since she first came to work for us. She's very sweet and accommodating."

Grant stared at Luke as if he'd grown a second head. "Are we talking about the same woman? Stephanie who runs the marina restaurant? *Sweet and accommodating?*"

Luke laughed. "We all think so. She's madly in love with your dad, in case you hadn't noticed." Luke tilted the beer bottle he'd opened to draw Grant's attention to the hug his father was receiving from sweet, accommodating Stephanie.

"Well, if that doesn't beat all. She's mean and nasty to me."

"Come on," Luke said, scoffing. "She doesn't have a mean bone in her body."

Grant watched Stephanie hug his mother. "You don't know her like I do."

Luke raised a brow mockingly. "Is that right?"

"What're you still doing on crutches, anyway?" Grant asked, anxious to change the subject.

Luke's smile became a scowl. "Damned if I know. I can't put a freaking ounce of weight on it. Cal thinks I might've torn a ligament. I was going to the mainland for an MRI tomorrow, but that's been scuttled because of the storm."

"Oh, man, that's a bummer. I hope it's nothing serious."

"You and me both. I'm sick of being a gimp."

Luke's girlfriend, Sydney Donovan, came into the kitchen looking for him. Her long red hair was captured in a high ponytail. "Hi, Grant." She went up on tiptoes to kiss his cheek. "How are you?"

"Great," he said, because let's face it, who wanted to hear that he felt like crap after talking to Abby?

She slipped an arm around Luke's waist. "Want me to get you something to eat?"

"I can do it," he said with uncharacteristic shortness.

His crankiness seemed to roll right off her shoulders. "I know you can, but I can do it easier."

Luke pressed a kiss to Syd's temple. "Sorry, baby. I don't mean to take it out on you."

"It's okay," she said with a good-natured smile. "I can take it."

Watching them, Grant was filled with longing. His gaze shifted to Stephanie, who chose that moment to toss her head back in laughter, exposing the sexy arch of her neck. A surge of lust fogged his brain, adding to his confusion. He'd thought he had it all figured out, but it was becoming rather clear to him that he had absolutely nothing figured out.

Chapter Eight

Watching her cousin and her new husband open their wedding gifts was pure torture for Laura. They were blissfully happy, and Joe was madly in love with his gorgeous new wife. Laura wondered if Janey had any idea how lucky she was to have such a devoted husband.

As the last gift was opened and exclaimed over, Laura had to get out of there. Fortunately, there were enough people in the room that she was able to slip out the sliding door to the deck without being detected. Once outside, she drew in deep breaths of cool air. While the rain had let up for the moment, the wind continued to whip and howl eerily in the big meadow that stood between the house and the shoreline in the distance.

She'd gotten through Janey's wedding, done her duties as a bridesmaid and somehow managed to keep it together when she was falling apart on the inside. But seeing the newlyweds together just now . . . That'd been too much.

Laura was so happy for Janey, who deserved every bit of happiness with Joe. After Janey had spent thirteen years with the wrong man, Joe had swept her off her feet and finally let her see how much he'd loved her from afar for so long. And then he'd rearranged his entire life so he could go to Ohio with her when she realized her lifelong dream of getting into veterinary school. Her sweet cousin had landed herself one of the good guys, and Laura couldn't be happier for her.

If only she could say the same for herself.

"Aren't you cold out here?"

Startled by a deep voice, Laura spun around to find Owen Lawry removing his jacket and handing it to her. She was so numb she hadn't even realized she was cold. Wrapping the jacket around her, she was engulfed in his warm, masculine scent. The thoughtful gesture brought a lump to her throat that Laura cleared away, determined to keep a tight lid on her despair in the midst of such happiness. "Thank you."

"No problem." Like he had earlier, he lowered himself to her height to meet her gaze. The light from inside the house cast a faint glow over the deck, making it possible for her to make out his features in the dimness. "Everything okay?"

"Never better."

"Somehow I don't believe you."

Unprepared for his insight, Laura bundled deeper into the coat.

"I heard you're a newlywed yourself."

She winced at his casually inquisitive tone.

"I guess your husband couldn't make it for the wedding."

What the hell? They'd all find out eventually. "It was more that he couldn't make it for the marriage."

There was just enough light for her to see the shock register on his face. "You wanna run that by me one more time?"

"We were married in May," she said, her heart aching as

she recalled the happiest day of her life. "A big, beautiful wedding in Providence. In June, two of my bridesmaids came to me looking like they hadn't slept for days. One of them had seen his picture on an online dating service and had queried his profile anonymously, thinking he'd tell her he's married now. Except that's not what he did."

"Oh, man."

"Exactly. He made a date with her, and she went to the restaurant just to see if he'd actually show. There he was, my husband, waiting to meet her. She made sure he never saw her." Laura couldn't believe she was sharing her nightmare with a perfect stranger when she hadn't even worked up the nerve to tell her aunt, uncle or cousins yet. No doubt it was easier telling him than it would be to tell them. "When they came to my house, I could tell something was terribly wrong, but I never thought . . . I never suspected . . ."

"Why would you?"

Shrugging, she rested a hand on the rail that framed the deck as the wind whipped at her shoulder-length hair. "Afterward, with hindsight, there were signs. I guess I chose to ignore them because I was so happy. We'd dated for three years, and I finally had everything I'd always wanted. Or at least I thought I did."

His hand landed on her shoulder, offering comfort. "You didn't do anything wrong, Princess. He was the fool who didn't know how lucky he was to have you."

"That's nice of you to say, but you don't even know me. How do you know I wasn't a total shrew of a wife?"

Owen laughed softly. "I guess I don't." Raising a rakish eyebrow, he said, "Were you?"

"I might've been if we'd made it to the second month."

"That's usually when the trouble starts."

"And you know this from experience?"

His face twisted with feigned horror. "Hell, no. I've heard rumors. That's all."

"Ahh," Laura said, amused by his attempts to prop her up. He seemed like someone who'd make for a good friend. "I see. Rumors. Do you believe everything you hear?"

"Hardly. I'm sorry such a shitty thing happened to you. No one deserves to be treated that way."

"You're right about that."

"If it had to happen, at least it was before kids were involved."

"Yeah." Laura stared into the darkness, feeling dead inside. "Thank goodness for that."

"I have some news that might lift your spirits," he said with that effortlessly charming grin he did so well.

"What's that?"

"I talked to my grandmother this afternoon and told her about our tour earlier. She wondered if you might be interested in a job."

Intrigued, Laura folded her arms to tighten the coat around her. "What kind of job?"

"Running the Sand & Surf."

She gasped. "You're not serious."

"I'm very serious, and so is she. I told her how much you've always loved the place, how excited you were to see the inside, and she said you sounded like the answer to her prayers. That's a direct quote, by the way."

Astounded, Laura stared at him. "But I don't know a thing about running a hotel! I majored in history."

"I talked to Libby, who runs the Beachcomber. She said she'd be happy to lend a hand to get you started. Of course, the old girl needs some work after being closed up the last few years, but you'd have the winter to get her ready for next season."

"You're really serious," Laura said, reeling.

"As serious as I ever get about anything."

"Wow. I just . . . Wow."

Owen laughed and tugged on a strand of her hair. "You don't have to decide anything tonight, Princess. Think about it for a couple of days."

Laura wondered how she'd manage to think of anything else now that the possibility had been presented to her. "What's in it for you if I agree to this?"

"Nothing more than knowing my grandparents have some peace of mind. They mean a lot to me."

Evan stuck his head out the door. "Hey, O. You wanna play?"

"Be right there."

"Cool."

Owen returned his attention to her. "So you'll think about it?"

"I will. Thank you for the offer."

"Sure thing. You know where to find me when you decide."

"Oh, your coat."

He stopped her from removing the jacket. "You need it more than I do."

"Um, don't say anything. About what I told you. I haven't gotten around to telling my family. Not only is it embarrassing and humiliating, I didn't want to bring my crap to Janey's wedding."

Owen surprised her when he leaned in and pressed a kiss to her forehead. "They won't hear it from me."

Nodding, Laura bit her bottom lip to contain a sudden rush of emotion brought on by the kindness of a stranger.

"Any special requests?"

Confused, she looked up at him. "What do you mean?"

"A song," he said with an indulgent smile.

Without hesitation, she said, "Anything by James Taylor."

"You got it, Princess."

He left her on the porch, and through the screen door, she heard him talking to Evan as they set up. A hush fell over the room as the two guitars found perfect harmony. When she heard the opening notes of "You've Got a Friend," she couldn't contain the smile that spread across her face.

Ned's heart ached as he watched Francine play with her grandchildren on the other side of the big room. Owen and Evan were keeping the group entertained with their music, but Ned couldn't seem to pull his gaze off her and the babies.

As if she sensed him watching her, Francine looked up all of a sudden and locked eyes with him.

Ned felt the impact in every cell of his body. Damned if he hadn't reacted to her the exact same way from the first time those green eyes connected with his at the ferry landing the day she first arrived on Gansett. He knew he should look away but couldn't seem to.

Normally, he'd be over there with her, playing with the babies, enjoying the party together. Normally, she'd be whispering pithy comments in his ear that made him laugh even when he didn't mean to.

Little Ashleigh tugged on a lock of her grandmother's hair, and Francine finally looked away from him.

A piece of him died at the loss of the brief contact. It took all he had to remain seated, to pretend he was engrossed in the music, that he cared about anything other than why she'd pushed him away when everything about them together worked. It worked just as well now as it had more than thirty years ago, before Bobby Chester showed up and ruined everything.

While he nursed a beer and pretended to keep his focus on Evan and Owen, Ned was keenly aware of Francine's every move. That's how he saw Mac scoop up Thomas and take him to kiss his mother on their way upstairs, presumably to put the little guy to bed. A minute later, Tiffany came to claim Ashleigh, who kissed her grandmother good night. They made a stop at the sofa so Ashleigh could hug and kiss her Aunt Maddie before they left to go home.

Sitting by herself, Francine's hands twitched nervously in her lap as if she had no idea what to do with them. When Ned realized she'd gotten up and was walking toward him, his heart beat funny and his hands got all sweaty. He waited until she was standing right in front of him before he bothered to glance up at her.

"Something on yer mind, doll?" He was rather proud of the nonchalant tone, if he did say so himself.

"I, um, I wanted to, um, tell you . . ."

Ned reached up to link their fingers. "Whatever ya gotta say, just say it. Ya'll feel better after."

"I have some things . . . I need to take care of."

"Anything I can help ya with?"

She bit her lip and shook her head.

Even though he wanted to drag her out of there and force her to tell him what had her so distressed, he squeezed her hand and released it. "Ya know where I am if there's anything I can do for ya."

"I'm sorry . . . for—"

"Don't be sorry 'bout nothin'. Take care of what ya

gotta take care of and then come find me. Don't be a stubborn old cuss and think I won't want ya because of whatcha said earlier. I'll always want ya."

Tears filled her eyes, and she looked away. "I never was good enough for you."

"Now yer just trying to piss me off, doll."

That drew a reluctant smile from her. "Thanks for understanding."

He wanted to tell her he didn't understand anything, but he kept the thought to himself. Rather, he nodded because he didn't trust himself to speak. Maddie waved to get his attention and pointed to her mother. "Looks like yer girl wants to see ya."

Francine turned to look at Maddie. "I guess I'd better go check on her."

"Don't let me keep ya."

"I'll be back, Ned."

"I'll be waiting, doll."

His heart about stopped when she bent to press a kiss to his forehead. He watched her walk away, filled with hope that whatever had her worked up wouldn't be the end of them.

Maddie had tried to ignore it all night. Braxton-Hicks contractions, she'd told herself. Everyone had them in the last trimester. Except, as the night wore on, she could no longer deny the truth. The tightening in her abdomen, the regular waves of increasingly sharp pains, the growing urge to push . . . She was in labor, two months early, on an island that was currently cut off from the mainland by a slow-moving tropical storm, and not a doctor to be had.

She wanted to weep with regret for being so mule-headed

about staying on the island after the first early-labor scare. How could she have been so foolish to risk her baby and herself this way? Why hadn't she listened to Mac when he'd tried to convince her to move to the mainland and live at Joe's place until the baby was born?

"None of that matters now, you fool," she whispered to herself as a new pain stole her breath and caused her to break into a cold sweat. Her eyes darted around the room, and she was relieved to see no sign of Mac, who was still upstairs with Thomas. She had to figure out a plan before he returned.

She tried to get Janey's attention, but her sister-in-law was wrapped up in Joe and talking to Laura. Her mother was having an intense conversation with Ned, and Tiffany had left to take Ashleigh home to bed.

"Everything okay?"

Maddie looked up to find Stephanie standing beside the sofa.

"Ah, well . . ." Another sharp pain stole the words and the breath from her lungs.

Stephanie squatted next to the sofa. "What's wrong? You're pale as a ghost and sweating."

"I think I'm in labor," she whispered.

"Oh my God!"

Maddie clutched the other woman's arm. "Please, before Mac gets back, go tell Abby to find Victoria. She's the midwife who works for Cal. Abby might know where she is. Tell her to hurry."

While Stephanie, wide-eyed and panicked, scurried off to find Abby, Maddie focused on the breathing exercises she'd been taught before she had Thomas. His birth had been easy and uncomplicated. This one would be the same.

She was sure of it. The baby might be coming early, but he or she would be just fine.

Tears burned her eyes as a wave of overwhelming fear was upstaged by another strong contraction that had her biting back the need to push. As Abby came over to her, Maddie's water broke in a gush of liquid that soaked the blanket she'd put under her, just in case.

"Oh my God," she whispered. "*Oh my God.*"

Chapter Nine

Mac helped Thomas into his new "big-boy" bed and tucked the covers in tight around him, the way he did every night.

"Now remember, no getting out of bed unless you have to go potty," Mac reminded him. Since Thomas moved from the crib, they'd woken to a visitor in their bed on many a night and were trying to get him used to staying in his own bed.

"Okay, Dada." He reached his chubby arms up for a hug, and Mac melted into his sweet embrace. Blowing kisses on the boy's neck that made him squeal with delight, Mac tried to remember what it'd been like to be a confirmed bachelor with no plans for a family of his own.

Then he'd knocked Thomas's mother off her bike in an accident that turned out to be the best thing that ever happened to him. Now he couldn't imagine life without Thomas or his mother. That another child would soon join their little family filled Mac's cup to overflowing.

"Love you, buddy," he said, giving Thomas one last noisy kiss.

"Love you, Dada."

His speech reverted to baby talk when he was tired, and

his blue eyes were struggling to stay open at the moment. "See you in the morning." From the doorway, Mac watched Thomas roll to his side and pop his thumb into his mouth. He'd be out cold in under a minute. Hopefully, he'd stay that way until at least seven the next morning, which was probably wishful thinking. His son was an early riser, and Mac had adjusted his own internal clock to match Thomas's, especially since Maddie had been stuck on bed rest.

Anxious to check on her, he headed for the stairs, set the gate that would keep Thomas contained if he got up, and stopped short when he realized the music had stopped and everyone was gathered around the sofa.

Sensing trouble, Mac couldn't quite seem to make his feet move to take him down the stairs, where he'd no doubt learn something he didn't want to know. His sister looked up, saw him there and gestured for him to come. The urgency in her gesture and the expression on her face stopped his heart.

"Maddie." On shaky legs, he raced down the stairs. The group parted to let him in. He took one look at her pale face and caramel-color eyes wide with fear and knew his worst nightmare had come true. Dropping to his knees next to her, he took her hand.

"I'm so sorry," she said as tears spilled from her eyes. "I should've listened to you."

"What do you mean—"

Her sharp cry sent a bolt of fear racing through him as she released his hand to brace her extended abdomen.

Janey squeezed his shoulder. "She's in labor, Mac. Her water broke a few minutes ago."

"Did someone call for Cal? We need him!" He spun around, looking for Abby. "Did you call him?"

Abby looked down at the floor. "He's . . . ah . . ."

"He's off-island," Joe said. "He left earlier today because his mother had a stroke in Texas."

Mac's mind went blank as Joe's words registered. When Cal hadn't come to the party, Mac had assumed he was working. *Jesus* . . . No doctor. A tropical storm. No way off the island. This was far worse than all the dramatic scenarios his overactive imagination had conjured in the last few weeks.

"Victoria, the nurse midwife, is on her way," Abby said. "She'll be here any minute."

"It's time for everyone to go home," Linda said, taking charge. "We'll let you know as soon as we have some news to share." She ushered the subdued group from the house.

"Janey!" Maddie panted her way through another contraction. "Stay. Please."

"I'm not going anywhere, honey," Janey said, smoothing the sweat-soaked hair off Maddie's forehead.

Mac's brothers squeezed his shoulder in support as they departed. His mother told Evan to take their father home because she was staying. He heard Joe say that he'd stay, too, in case they needed him.

"I'm not going anywhere until my grandbaby is born," Big Mac bellowed, sounding more like his old self than he had in weeks. "It'll be okay, son," he said, bending to embrace Mac's shoulders. "She's young and strong, and everything will be fine."

Though he clung desperately to his father's reassuring words, Mac's heart raced with fear, and his eyes were glued to Maddie.

"Mac . . ." Her voice was tense and her breathing erratic. "Need you."

Those two small words punctured the layer of shock, snapping him out of the stupor. It didn't matter if they were stuck on an island in a storm or the doctor was gone or that she hadn't listened to him. Right now, the only thing that mattered was that she needed him, and he wouldn't let her down.

"I'm here, baby," he said.

"So sorry," she panted. "Should've listened to you. You were right."

"Doesn't matter now." He pressed kisses to her face and neck. "We'll get you through this. I promise."

"The baby. What if—"

Mac swallowed his own panic. "She'll be just fine."

"How do you know it's a she?"

He forced a smile for her. "Only a woman would create this kind of drama."

The Maddie he knew and loved would've had a smart comeback for such a sexist statement, but Maddie in labor grimaced as another pain required her full attention. "I need to push."

"Not yet, honey." Where this calm resolve was coming from, he couldn't have said. "Wait for Victoria." He twisted around, looking for some sign that help was on the way.

"She's coming," Janey said. "Let's get her upstairs and out of these wet clothes."

Grateful to have something to do, Mac slid his arms under his wife and lifted her.

She linked her hands around his neck and rested her head on his shoulder.

Holding his whole world in his arms, he took her upstairs, determined to do whatever it took to get her and their baby through this safely.

Stephanie ran with Grant through torrential rain to his father's truck. Even though they were both getting soaked, he held the passenger door for her before he went around to the driver's side.

He sat there breathing hard and gripping the wheel.

"Are you okay?" she asked after a long period of silence.

"I feel weird about leaving. Maddie . . . God, Steph, if something happens to her, what'll he do?"

His use of her nickname and his concern for his brother and sister-in-law made her go soft inside. Pushing aside all the reasons why it wasn't a good idea to continue this odd involvement with him, she reached for his hand, mindful of the bandage covering the stitches in his palm. She cradled his hand between both of hers. "I don't know her very well, but Maddie seems strong and determined."

"Of all days for there to be no doctor on the island." She felt a shudder go through him. "Mac has to be freaking out."

"I'm sure he's focused on taking care of her. He'll have plenty of time to freak out when it's over and everyone is fine."

"I would stay, but my parents are there, and Janey and Joe . . ."

"They have everyone they need most. There's nothing you can do here except get in the way and add to the anxiety."

"True." He blew out a deep breath. "People who get married and have babies are crazy."

Stephanie laughed. "Certifiable."

"Thanks for calming me down," he said, withdrawing his hand from hers to start the truck.

"No problem." Her hands grew chilly without his warmth.

From the faint glow of the headlights, she could see him concentrating on the road, which was littered with leaves and sticks and other debris. His knuckles were white from the grip he had on the wheel. "The storm seems to have regrouped."

"Yeah," she said, gnawing at her lip as she imagined a long night alone in the dark at the marina. She wasn't a big fan of dark places or being alone in dark places. *It's just one night, and I'm sure the power will be back on soon.*

Grant navigated the twists and turns that led to the marina. As he approached the three-way stop, he angled the truck to the right rather than the left that would take them to the marina. He made a full stop and then took the right toward town.

"Um, hello," she said. "You forgot to drop me off."

"No, I didn't."

Her stomach quivered. "Where're we going?"

"To Janey's. I'm not letting you stay at the marina alone in a storm with no power."

Why, oh why, did her heart have to do a happy little jig when he said that? He was just being the gentleman Linda McCarthy had raised him to be. It didn't *mean* anything, and she'd do well to remember that. He was too busy mooning over Abby to even notice her.

"It's okay. I don't mind staying there." She suspected the more time she spent with him, especially the time they spent alone, would only make it harder for her to remember that he was in love with someone else.

"I mind."

She wanted to call him out on that, accuse him of starting to care about her, but she couldn't bring herself to risk whatever he might fire back at her. He might want Abby, but for right now, tonight, she had him all to herself. He'd been moved by what she'd told him earlier. He had comforted her and offered to help. Was it possible he was coming to care for her?

Don't be ridiculous. Don't be a fool and confuse friendship for romance. The closer they got to Janey's cozy cottage, the more nervous Stephanie became. There was only one bed. The second bedroom was full of dog beds for Janey's menagerie of pets. The living room contained two love seats. Where did he expect her to sleep? Surely not with him. Not again.

Her heart fluttered, and her palms were damp. Despite the chill in the air, she was warm from head to toe. The pervasive darkness that enveloped the island only added to the feeling of being isolated, completely alone with the man who'd made her mouth dry and her stomach flutter from the day she met him.

After spending last night in bed with him, she only wanted him more than she had before. While she remembered every detail of what had occurred between them, he didn't, and that bothered her more than it should have.

For the life of her, she couldn't come up with a pithy comment or an insult that would put things back on track. The strain of trying to think of something—*anything*—she could say to break the silence that hung between them like a living, breathing being was killing her.

What did it mean that he was bringing her home with him? Was it really about concern for her safety, or did he want a repeat performance of the night before? If he did, would she be willing? She released a deep, rattling breath, trying to calm her rampaging nerves. Even knowing it was a huge mistake to get more involved with a man who still pined for his ex-girlfriend, she couldn't help but wish the intense attraction she felt toward him might one day be reciprocated.

Since her head was about to explode from overthinking this situation, she should've been relieved when Grant finally pulled into the driveway at Janey's place. But now that they'd arrived, she couldn't seem to move.

He solved the problem for her by leaping from the car and jogging around to her side. When he opened the door, the wind and rain required her immediate attention. Grant tugged the hood up over her head and reached for her hand. "Come on!"

Propelled by him pulling her along, Stephanie followed him into the house even though everything in her resisted the powerful force that drew her to him. Inside, he helped her out of the wet jacket and told her to stay put for a minute. With tension vibrating through her, she linked and un-linked her fingers, waiting to see what he would say or do.

When he struck a match, she startled from the sound and the sudden flash of light in the inky darkness. He bent and used the match to ignite the wood in the fireplace, sending a cozy glow over the small room. Fabulous.

"That's better than the dark," he said as he turned to her.

The sight of him in the firelight—tall, dark, lanky, elegant in a fully masculine way—stole the breath from her lungs. Her face heated with shame and dismay and lust. Mostly lust. She licked her lips and tried to force the memories from last night from her mind, but all she could see was how that fine body had looked without the bulky sweater and damp jeans.

She'd never known a more perfectly beautiful man, and she had no idea how she'd resist him if he wanted a repeat of last night.

Janey helped Mac get Maddie cleaned up and into a fresh nightgown. They layered the bed with towels and blankets and got Maddie settled. Her contractions were about seven minutes apart and growing more intense. Janey could tell her brother was working overtime to hide his panic from his wife. Since her own hands were shakier than usual, Janey could only imagine how Mac and Maddie must be feeling.

"I need to run downstairs for a quick second, but I'll be right back," Janey said.

"See if you can find out what's keeping Victoria," Mac said as he wiped Maddie's face with a cool washcloth in the aftermath of a contraction.

"I will."

Janey dashed down the stairs and signaled for Joe to join her in the kitchen.

"How is she?" he asked.

"Not great. She's in a lot of pain, and it's happening really fast."

"Jesus." He glanced at the stairs, tension pulsing in his jaw. "It's so early . . . The baby . . ."

"I need to tell you something."

That brought his attention back to her. "What?"

"David called me the day before the wedding." She referred to her ex-fiancé, the man she'd been with for thirteen years until she caught him in bed with another woman. She and Joe had married on the day that had once been intended for her wedding to David.

Joe's face went slack with shock. "Okay . . ."

"He knew we were getting married, and he wanted to wish me well."

"Why didn't you say anything?"

"Because it didn't matter. It was a two-minute conversation."

"I'm surprised you took the call," he said, trying—and failing—to hide his annoyance.

She went up on tiptoes to kiss the pout off his lips. "I took the call because it came from a local number I didn't recognize." That seemed to appease her new husband—somewhat.

"Why're you telling me this now?"

"Because he's here—on the island for a few days visiting his mother. I want to call him. To help Maddie."

"Do it," Joe said without hesitation.

"Are you sure?"

"Of course I am. He's a goddamned doctor, and we need a goddamned doctor. Get him the hell over here."

Janey smiled and kissed him again, hoping to remind him of who owned her heart. "Do you promise not to punch him?" she asked, referring to how he'd reacted to David's infidelity.

"Only if he behaves and doesn't say or do anything to provoke me."

"What would count as provoking?" she asked in a teasing tone. "Saying hello, perhaps?" That's all it had taken from David to send Joe over the edge after witnessing Janey's despair at her fiancé's deception.

Joe scowled at her. "Make the call, Mrs. C, and stop trying to provoke *me* so you can have make-up sex later."

Laughing at his stormy expression, she withdrew her cell phone from her pocket. "Why don't you go check on Mac or something?"

"That's okay." He crossed his arms and sent her a mulish look. "I'll stay."

Janey rolled her eyes at him. Her normally low-key husband turned into a jealous fool whenever David Lawrence's name was mentioned. "Hi, David, it's Janey."

"Why do you still have him on speed dial?" Joe whispered.

Janey held him off with a hand to his chest.

"Janey," David said, sounding surprised to hear from her. "I thought you'd be on your honeymoon."

"It's been delayed due to the storm. I know I have no right to ask you for anything—"

"What do you need?"

"My sister-in-law Maddie is in labor, and Cal Maitland is off-island. Victoria, the nurse midwife, is on her way, but the baby . . . It's two months early. We need a doctor, David."

"Where are you?"

She gave him Mac's address on Sweet Meadow Farm Road.

"I'll be there in a few minutes."

"Thank you so much." She closed the phone and looked up at Joe. "He's coming."

"Good. So why do you still have him on speed dial?"

Chapter Ten

"I need to take care of Janey's pets," Grant said, glancing toward the hallway that led to the bedrooms.

"Could I help?"

Surprised that she'd asked, he said, "Um, sure, if you want to." He grabbed a flashlight and led her to the bedroom across the hall from where they'd spent last night together. When Grant opened the door, a scurry of paws greeted them.

"Oh!" Stephanie said, sucking in a sharp breath. "They're . . . What's . . . Oh."

"They've all got special needs."

Stephanie dropped to her knees and was mobbed by furry creatures. "Introduce me," she said, scooping up Pixie, a Jack Russell with a skin condition. Over her shoulder, she looked up at him. "You do know their names, don't you?"

"As if my sister would leave me with them for more than a week if I didn't have every one of their names as well as each of their unique conditions and accompanying medications fully memorized."

"Is your mama particular?" Stephanie asked Pixie in a little-girl voice that got the attention of Grant's cock. Again.

"That's Pixie, Dexter, Sam, Muttley and Riley."

As Pixie kissed Stephanie's chin, she giggled.

Dexter, the cocker spaniel, nudged at her leg.

"Oh, God, Grant. His ears!" This time when she looked up at him, her eyes were bright with tears. "Did someone do that to him?"

When Grant lowered himself to the floor, Sam, a white ball of fur, scurried into his lap. "Janey isn't sure how he lost his ears. He was like that when they found him."

Stephanie pressed her lips to Dexter's snout. "Poor baby. I'm so sorry someone hurt you."

Touched by her compassion, Grant propped the flashlight to better illuminate the room.

She reached out to pet Muttley, a black-and-brown mongrel who was missing his tail, and the dog shied away from her.

Grant suddenly remembered Stephanie doing the same thing the day they met. They'd been standing outside the clinic where his father was being treated after the accident at the marina. She'd been upset about his father, and Grant had intended to comfort her. When his hand landed on her shoulder, she'd flinched. He'd forgotten about that until right now.

After hearing that her mother used to beat her, at least he knew why. Imagining Stephanie as a helpless child being beaten by the mother who was supposed to care for her filled him with rage and made him want to personally ensure that no one ever hurt her again.

"He thinks I'm going to hit him," she said softly.

"It takes him a while to warm up to new people."

Stephanie held out her hand, encouraging Muttley to approach her.

The dog took a tentative step and then another.

Stephanie stayed perfectly still, giving him all the time he needed to get comfortable with her.

When Muttley finally nuzzled her outstretched hand, a victorious smile stretched across her face.

Watching her pleasure at the small victory, Grant felt something inside him shift and open to make room for the possibility . . . Desperate to keep his thoughts where they belonged, he reached a hand out to Muttley. The dog zeroed in on the wound on his palm and licked the bandage that covered it. When Grant started to withdraw his hand, Stephanie stopped him.

"Let him tend to you." The heat of her hand on his arm burned through his thin T-shirt. "He's showing you he trusts you not to hit him."

Moved by her understanding, Grant stared at her as she kept her attention on Muttley, stroking his back and ears.

"Are you sure dog germs are good for the cut?" he asked.

"His mouth is cleaner than yours."

"Um, I've seen where his mouth has been."

"If you could put your mouth where he can put his, you'd probably never leave the house."

Grant went instantly hard at the thought of her mouth in places he couldn't reach. Why was it that his body responded so predictably to this feisty woman with the fresh mouth, but not all the hundreds—if not thousands—of other less prickly women he had known? "That's a lovely visual. Thank you for that."

Stephanie laughed at his haughty tone, and he thanked God for the murky darkness so she couldn't see what her suggestive comment had done to him.

"What's his name again?" she asked, nodding to the German shepherd who stood at the periphery, watching the others cuddle up to them.

"That's Riley. He's the boss."

A three-legged cat sprinted from the corner and out the door.

"Whoa," Stephanie said, startled by the cat.

"That'd be Trio," Grant said.

"What's wrong with Riley?"

"He's missing his hind legs."

Stephanie whimpered. "I can't imagine how anyone . . ."

"I know."

She raised Sam, the blind fur ball, to her chest for a snuggle. "It's good of your sister to take them in."

"She's been taking in strays since she was a little kid." Grant glanced at her black shirt. "Sam has you all covered in white hair."

Stephanie's eyes were closed, her lips parted. "I don't care."

Grant swallowed hard as another burst of lust hit him like a punch to the gut. "I haven't had much luck getting them to go outside today. They don't like the storm."

"Of course they don't." She kissed Sam and put her down with the others. "Come on, guys. Let's go out."

Grant watched in stunned amazement as she herded the menagerie out the bedroom door. They scurried after her like they'd known her forever. He wondered if they recognized a fellow traveler, someone who'd been mistreated herself.

Riley, bringing up the rear, scooted himself along. He stopped to give Grant a searching look.

"I know, man. She's special. Don't worry, I get it."

Seeming satisfied, Riley continued on his way to the back door.

Grant felt like he'd been standing on a chair and someone had kicked it out from under him. His equilibrium was all out of whack, and he had a sudden, uncomfortable feeling that the young woman with the difficult past and a way with animals might be the only one who could help him recover his balance.

Even though it was pouring, Stephanie stayed outside until each of the dogs had at least peed. She came in the back door and removed her coat, hanging it on a hook to dry. The obedient animals trooped into their room and took to their beds, probably relieved to be out of the storm.

Running her fingers through her damp hair, she contemplated the shadows in the dark hallway. The light from the fireplace flickering in the living room was all that kept the house from being totally dark.

Stephanie was struck by a memory of being alone in the apartment she'd shared with her mother. The power had gone out because her mother hadn't paid the bill—again. There'd been a storm, a lot like tonight, with wind and rain. Howling wind that had scared her. She'd been about six then.

Her mother had been gone a long time that night. Hours. She could still remember the raw fear of the dark, the storm, the loneliness, the wondering if she might die there all alone.

"Stephanie?"

Grant's voice startled her out of the reflection. Where had that memory come from? She hadn't thought of that night in years.

"Are you okay?"

"Yes. Of course. I should probably go back to the marina."

"I couldn't stand to think of you all alone in that big dark building with this insane storm going on."

"Why?" The second the word left her lips, she wanted to reach out and take it back.

The question clearly took him by surprise, too. "What do you mean, why?"

Stephanie cleared her throat and forced her gaze to meet his. "I mean why do you care if I'm there alone? You don't even like me."

Exasperated, he glanced up at the ceiling before he looked at her again. "I never said I don't like you."

"All we do is fight."

"That's not *all* we do."

The veiled reference to what had transpired the night before once again filled her with heat. Even though she was under no illusions that he was suddenly over Abby and interested in her, she still found him to be the most interesting—and attractive—man she'd ever known.

"Where exactly am I supposed to sleep here?" she asked, giving voice to her most pressing question.

"You can have the bed. I'll take one of the sofas."

"They're only like four feet long, and you have to be six-foot something."

"Three," he said with a small grin, seeming amused by her discomfort with the sleeping arrangements conversation.

She swallowed hard. "You can't sleep on a four-foot sofa."

Shrugging, he said, "I'll make it work."

Still holding the flashlight, he studied her with those eyes that made her feel naked even when she was fully dressed, as if he could see all her secrets and was having a laugh at her expense. No, that wasn't fair. He wasn't unkind. Clueless sometimes, but never unkind.

"Let's go sit by the fire for a bit." He gestured for her to follow him into the living room and sprawled on one of the love seats. "I don't know about you, but I'm freezing."

"I'm kind of cold, too." Why, she wondered, was she

suddenly so nervous around him when she'd managed to hold her own with him all day? Maybe it was because he knew her secrets now, and hearing what she'd been through had seemed to change something for him. But what? Anxious to end the introspection that was making her nuts, she settled on the other love seat and decided to ask the one question that would take the focus off her. "So how'd it go with Abby?"

"Fine."

Stephanie waited to see if he'd elaborate.

He ran his hand up and down the faded length of denim that covered his thigh. "We had a nice chat. I think I'm finally getting that it's over with her."

"Sorry."

He zeroed in on her with intense blue eyes. "Are you?"

Stunned by the direct question, she stared back at him. "I, um . . ."

"Tell me the truth. Are you really sorry that Abby and I are done?"

"Why do you want to know?"

"I asked first."

Stephanie had no idea what she should say or do. Would it be wise to tell him the truth? That she was glad his relationship with Abby was officially over? Or should she tell him she had no interest in being his rebound girl? Was this her chance to have something more with him? Or was he just trying to get her to admit she liked him as more than a friend so he could let her down easily?

And why was she even contemplating "more" with him—whatever that would entail—when she had no business looking for more with any guy? She already had enough to deal with.

"No need to overthink it," he said. "It's a yes or no question. Are you really sorry that Abby and I are done?"

"No."

"Why?"

"*That's* hardly a yes or no question." In need of fortification, Stephanie yearned for a stiff drink. "The more important question is whether *you're* sorry that you and Abby are done."

"Of course I'm sorry. I had a good thing with her, and I was too stupid and self-absorbed to realize it until I didn't have it anymore."

"I think—" Stephanie stopped herself before she ventured into territory that qualified as none of her business.

"What?"

She shook her head.

"Just say it, Steph. You've shared every other thought that's popped into your head where I'm concerned."

Oh no I haven't, she thought, affected once again by his casual use of her nickname. "It's just . . . if she was 'the one' for you, the one you were meant to be with, don't you think you would've noticed she was unhappy?"

"Probably," he said with a grim set to his mouth. "It bothers me that she was unhappy enough to pack up and move back here after years with me in LA—and I didn't *get it* until she was gone. And even then it took me another year to fully wake up and realize she was truly gone. By then, she was already engaged to Cal."

"It bothers you that you hurt her like that."

"Hell yes, it bothers me. I took her and our relationship totally for granted. I expected that once I pulled my head out of my ass, she'd still be there waiting like always. It was a bit of a shock to wake up a year ago and discover she wasn't waiting around anymore for me to get a clue."

"I suppose all you can do now is learn from it and move on. She hasn't given you much choice about that."

He studied his folded hands for a long moment before he shifted his potent gaze to her. "You still haven't answered my question."

"Which one?"

"Why aren't you sorry that Abby and I are done?"

"Oh, that one."

"Yes, that one." The quirk of amusement that touched his sexy mouth told her he was enjoying putting her on the spot. "Everyone thinks you and I are together, you know."

Stephanie nearly choked on her own spit. "Who's everyone?"

"My brothers, Luke, Ned, Abby . . . They all said something about us dancing together last night and showing up at the party together tonight."

"That's what you wanted, right? To make Abby jealous?"

"She didn't really seem to care. In fact, she thinks you'd be good for me."

"Ahh, I get it. You need someone to fill the void now that it's finally registered that your girlfriend isn't coming back."

His relaxed, amused expression turned dark so fast it startled her. "That is *not* why it matters to me what you think."

Stephanie hated that his anger made her nervous. She was years past the point where anyone had raised a hand to her in anger, but it still had a profound effect on her.

Seeming to sense her dismay, he straightened out of the slouch he'd slipped into and leaned forward. Elbows on knees, he studied her. "Did I scare you just now?"

His insight rattled her as much as his nearness. "Don't be ridiculous," she said with a scoff. "I'm not afraid of you." More like terrified, not that she'd ever tell him that.

"I think you are."

"Don't flatter yourself, McCarthy."

He shifted from his love seat to hers so smoothly that Stephanie had no time to prepare. "Don't be scared of me, Stephanie. I'd never raise a hand to you in anger. It kills me to know that someone else did."

As his softly spoken words and masculine scent filled her senses, her heart beat fast and hard. She struggled to draw air into her lungs. "What're you doing?" The words came out as a nervous squeak that infuriated her. No one had ever had such an effect on her. Ever.

"I want to show you why it matters to me what you think." He reached for her hand and shocked the living shit out of her when he pressed it to his erection. "I've been dealing with this problem all day as images of last night ran through my mind. Every time you come near me, I get hard. Every time you insult me, I get hard. Every time you tell me what to do, I get hard. Every time you freaking look at me, I get hard."

Stunned and aroused and confused and annoyed by his audacity, Stephanie stared at him.

"That's never happened to me before."

"Oh. It hasn't?"

He shook his head. "It's starting to seriously irritate me."

She tried to pull her hand free, but he only tightened his grip. "It's not my fault you have the self-control of a fifteen-year-old."

"It is absolutely your fault."

She forced herself to meet his gaze head-on. "*How* is it my fault?"

"Ever since I watched you get dressed this morning, all I've thought about is getting you undressed again."

"I knew you were watching me."

His cock surged under her hand. "Is that why you made getting dressed into the sexiest thing I've ever seen?" His free hand landed on her leg, heating her through her jeans.

Refusing to be the first to break the intense eye contact, she licked her lips and notched a victory when his eyes shifted to her mouth. "I have no interest in being your rebound girl, Grant."

His gaze shifted back to her eyes. "And I no longer want to be that clueless idiot who doesn't know a good thing when it's staring him right in the face."

"How can you think this is a good thing when all we do is fight?"

"We're not fighting right now."

She was fighting all right—she was fighting the magnetic pull that drew her to him so forcefully she could no more resist him than she could avoid taking her next breath. Maybe this was the stupidest thing she'd ever done. No doubt she would regret it before it was over, but right here, right now, she wanted him more than she'd ever wanted anything. Taking a deep breath for courage, she raised her hand to caress his face.

His eyes darkened with desire and what might've been confusion. He didn't get why this was happening between them any more than she did, and knowing that comforted her.

"Steph—"

Her hand shifted to the back of his neck, bringing him closer—close enough to kiss. Even though they'd done much more than kiss last night, this felt like the first time all over again. With both of them fully aware of what they were doing, this kiss would signal the start of something.

"Are you sure?" he whispered.

She shook her head. She was sure of nothing where he was concerned.

A grin tugged at his sinfully sexy lips. "That makes two of us." And then he tilted his head ever so slightly and captured her lips in a light, undemanding kiss that blew through her in a flashpoint of desire and need and want. Her reaction was so powerful that she immediately sought to defuse the tension the only way she knew how. "Are you writing this whole seduction scene just so you won't have to sleep on the love seat?"

He threw his head back as laughter seized him, and sure enough, under her hand his erection throbbed and surged. "Apparently, there's only one way to silence that saucy mouth of yours." His eyes still danced with amusement as he came back for another kiss that rocked her just as completely as the one before. "Open for me," he said against her mouth as his tongue traced the outline of her bottom lip.

Her fingers found their way into his silky hair as she opened her mouth to accept the deep thrusts of his tongue. A groan rumbled through him, firing her own desire as she pulled her hand free and pushed her core tight against his erection. His hands seemed to be everywhere at once. Discovering she was braless under her sweater generated another deep groan.

All at once, he broke the kiss, lifted his head and found her eyes in the light of the fire. "I want a do-over of last night," he said, pressing kisses to her forehead, cheeks and nose. "This time I want to remember every detail." As he spoke, he shifted off the love seat, pushed the table away and knelt before her. With his hands on her hips, he tugged her closer to the edge and settled himself between her legs. Pushing up her sweater, he bent to kiss her quivering belly.

Stephanie closed her eyes and surrendered to the overwhelming sensations. It'd been so long since she'd taken anything for herself that she was determined to have one

more perfect night with him. Tomorrow was soon enough
to face reality again.

He tugged at the button to her jeans and had them off
before she could process his intentions. His lips were soft
against her leg as he moved from her calf to her knee to the
inside of her thigh. Her entire body burned for him, and
he'd done little more than kiss her.

"Wait, Grant—"

"Shh, relax. It's okay."

She let her head fall back against the cushion as he
tongued her through the silk of her panties. He had her on
the verge of climax with just a few determined strokes of
his tongue. And then he pushed aside the cloth to zero in
on her throbbing clit, sending her screaming into an
orgasm she felt from her scalp to the soles of her feet.

"Mmm," he said, "very hot." He slid his fingers through
her dampness, teasing and tormenting until he finally
pushed two of them into her.

Stephanie wouldn't have thought it possible to come
again so soon, but he had her on the razor's edge with only
the slow movement of his talented fingers. *God*, she
thought. If he'd rocked her world the night before when he
was half drunk, she wondered if she'd survive him when
he was sober.

Grant used his free hand to raise her sweater and tug it
over her head, revealing small, pretty breasts. He zeroed
in on the tattoo on her belly and kissed his way up for a
better look. Was that . . . Winnie the Pooh? Despite her
outer toughness, the Pooh tattoo told the truth about
who she might be on the inside. She was a never-ending
contradiction—full of attitude, yet the vulnerability she'd

shown him when talking about her beloved stepfather had touched him deeply. She fascinated him and turned him on like no one else ever had.

He pressed his lips to the image of the bear and looked up to find her watching him. "You surprise me," he said.

"Because I like Pooh?"

"Among other things." He continued to kiss his way up, bewitched by her musky, feminine scent. Keeping his gaze fixed on hers, he tugged a tightly budded nipple into his mouth while continuing the gentle slide of his fingers. She was so wet and tight that the thought of sinking his cock into her made him ache from the effort of holding back.

Her fingers combed through his hair, tightening to keep his focus on her breast. Gasping and panting, she arched her back, responding to the tugging suction of his mouth. "Grant."

"What, honey?" He loved the way she responded to him.

"I want you. Now." She pulled at his shirt, her movements clumsy and awkward and incredibly provocative.

Grant withdrew from her only long enough to shed his own clothes and roll on the condom he pulled from his wallet with fumbling hands.

"How old is that thing?" she asked, her brows furrowed.

He laughed and scooped her up as if she were weightless. "Brand-new and acquired with you in mind."

Her eyes widened, and her lips pursed in surprise. "When?"

"Never mind," he said, kissing the pucker off her mouth as he carried her to the bedroom, tripping over a dog toy on the way.

"I want to know."

Grant sighed and lowered her to the bed. Hovering over

her, he tried to silence her with another heated kiss, but she turned away from him. He dropped his head to her shoulder, which drew his attention to the small, tight nipples that brushed against his chest.

"Everything was closed today," she said.

He uttered a growl of frustration. "I bought them a week ago, all right?"

Her mouth fell open in shock.

Reaching for her hand, he curled it around his erection. "This problem I seem to have around you didn't start today—or yesterday."

"Oh."

Damn, she was cute and sexy and apparently baffled by his confession. "So are we going to let this condom I bought for you go to waste?"

With her free hand, she reached up to bring him in for another kiss while directing his erection to where she wanted it.

Grant didn't need to be told twice. He flexed his hips and entered her in one smooth thrust. God, she was tight and hot and so sexy.

She gasped and pulled her lips free of his.

"Does it hurt?"

"No." Her hands on his back urged him to move.

When she wrapped her legs around his hips, he almost lost it. "Even better than last night," he whispered as he pushed into her again. "I didn't think that was possible."

"You don't remember last night."

Laughing, he said, "Oh, honey, trust me. I remember." As Grant gathered her in close to him, it occurred to him that at some point during the long day that began and ended with her, she'd managed to worm her way into his heart.

* * *

Afterward, Stephanie slept like a dead woman until her bladder woke her. Shivering in the chilly darkness, she slid back into bed and was surprised when Grant reached for her, bringing her in close to him.

He surrounded her with heat that warmed her inside and out. As she nuzzled her face against his soft chest hair, it occurred to her that she could become rather accustomed to sleeping with him.

"I just got a text from Janey," he said, his voice sleepy-sounding. "Her ex-fiancé is a doctor. Apparently, he's on the island. She called him for Maddie."

"Wow. That must be awkward the day after she married someone else."

"Just a little," he said with a chuckle. "But what a relief to know there's a doctor tending to Maddie and the baby."

"Yeah."

"Janey said it's been pretty rough. Maddie's in a lot of pain, and Mac is half out of his mind with worry."

"I can't imagine how scary that must be. If I ever have a baby . . ."

"What?" he asked, softly.

"Nothing." Her face burned. What was she thinking talking about such things with him?

"Tell me."

She sighed. "I'd want to be in the biggest hospital around with the best drugs money could buy."

That made him laugh. "Do you *want* kids?"

"I don't know. Someday. Maybe." She bit her lip, grateful all of a sudden for the darkness. "Do you?"

"Someday. Maybe."

Stephanie smiled. "I'd think such an *accomplished* writer would be able to come up with his own words."

"I'm not that accomplished."

"Should I remind you about a certain Academy Award?"

"Please don't."

Intrigued, Stephanie wondered if he would say more. Even though she couldn't see him, she could picture him staring up at the ceiling. He was quiet for so long, she'd all but given up on him.

"I haven't written anything in a really long time."

The pain she heard in his voice made her ache for him. "Why not?"

He released a short, bitter-sounding laugh. "Damned if I know."

She didn't want to ask, really she didn't. "Is it . . . because of what happened with Abby?"

"Maybe." She could hear him running his fingers through his hair. "I want to tell you something. It's kind of weird, and you may think I'm crazy."

"I already think you're crazy."

He laughed, which helped to dispel some of the tension.

"What is it?" she asked.

"When I'm writing, when it's going really well, it's like the highest of highs, you know?"

"Not really, but I can imagine it must be quite a thrill."

"Yes, exactly. It's thrilling. That's a good word for it. When something grabs me, an idea or a character or a story, it's like an electrical current travels through me. That's how I know I'm really on to something."

Stephanie sensed he was sharing a part of himself with her that he'd never shared with anyone else. Of course that probably wasn't the case, but under the cover of darkness, she could believe anything she wanted.

"Every time that's happened, every time I've had that particular sense of excitement over a story, something good has come of it."

"That's really cool."

"You think so?"

He sounded so sweet and uncertain that she smiled. "I do."

"Earlier tonight, when you told me about Charlie, about what the two of you have been through, I felt it, Stephanie. The charge of excitement."

As if she was the one who'd been struck by electricity, Stephanie went still. Her heart, which had been beating so fast, slowed. "You . . . you can't."

"I know that. What you told me was in confidence. It's safe with me. I promise."

She couldn't seem to breathe.

He tightened his hold on her. "I'm sorry. I shouldn't have said anything. The only reason I did is because it's been such a long time since I felt the charge that I thought it might've been gone forever. I was relieved to discover it wasn't. That's the part I wanted to tell you."

Stephanie's mind raced as she tried to process what he'd said.

"Do you believe me when I tell you I won't do anything with your story?"

It seemed to matter an awful lot to him. "Yes," she managed to say. "I believe you."

"Good."

"If you felt the charge for my story, then it's possible you'll feel it for another one. Maybe it's a sign that it's coming back."

"That'd be nice. I've missed it."

Stephanie knew she was probably making a mistake

letting him hold her so closely and share confidences with her, but she couldn't seem to bring herself to move away from him, to put distance between them. Her last conscious thought before sleep claimed her was that his arms around her made the dark a whole lot less scary.

Chapter Eleven

Mac couldn't take another minute of watching his beloved wife writhe in pain as she struggled to bring their child into the world. It was, without a doubt, the most excruciating thing he'd ever endured.

Despite the room full of people supporting them, no one could imagine his torment at knowing he was fully responsible for putting her through this.

His mother, Maddie's mother, Victoria the nurse-midwife, Janey and, of all people, Janey's deadbeat ex-fiancé Dr. David Lawrence, were tending to Maddie as she worked through something they called transition. Whatever that was. To Mac, it seemed like pure torture.

From his position behind Maddie, he could feel her convulse when every new pain gripped her body. Sweat had long since soaked through her nightgown, dampening his shirt. Even though he couldn't bear to see her in so much pain, he couldn't bring himself to leave her either.

"Mac," Victoria said, possibly sensing his dismay. She was young and pretty with a ponytail of curly brown hair and hazel eyes that brimmed with kindness and calming energy. "Why don't you get some more ice chips."

Thankful for the generator that was running the refrigerator and freezer during the blackout, Mac eased himself off the bed and settled Maddie against the pile of pillows that had been propping them up. He kissed her forehead. "I'll be right back, okay?"

She nodded, but he doubted she'd heard him. Her eyes were glazed with pain, her face red from exertion, and to him, she'd never been more beautiful. Wanting to get right back to her, he hurried downstairs where his father, Joe and Ned were sprawled out on sofas. One of them had added wood to the fireplace, which cast a cozy glow over the big room.

Mac went into the kitchen and stopped short when the magnitude of the situation struck him once again. Maddie was giving birth—two months early—on the island in the middle of a tropical storm that had cut them off from the mainland. His chest tightened with pain. Fumbling around in the dark, he gripped the countertop and held on as the room spun around him.

Jesus, I can't flake out on her now. Get it together, man!

Strong hands landed on his shoulders and stopped the spinning.

"It's okay, son," his father said. "You're okay."

Mac turned into his father's arms the same way he had at seven when he crashed his first two-wheeler. The embrace was no less comforting at thirty-seven.

"Take a deep breath," Big Mac said as he ran a hand up and down Mac's back.

Their father's effusive love used to mortify his children. Tonight, in the darkness of crisis, it was downright comforting.

"Scariest thing I've ever been through in my life," Big Mac said. "Five times. Never got any easier."

Mac shuddered at the idea of doing this four more times. No way. He was never going near her again. "I'll be keeping my distance after this."

Big Mac let out a great big laugh. "You say that now. Wait until she gets the green light at six weeks. You'll have forgotten all about tonight."

"I don't think I'll ever forget tonight."

Big Mac released him but kept a hand on Mac's shoulder. "She'll be just fine. I know it. That gal is strong and resilient. That's why you love her. That's why we all love her."

Mac glanced up at his dad. "What about the baby? It's so early . . ."

"The baby is a McCarthy. He or she won't give up without a fight."

Nodding, Mac let his father's faith and confidence bolster him. "I need to get some ice chips and get back up there." He set the icemaker on the fridge to crush and filled a plastic cup.

"Mac."

Turning back to his father, he raised an eyebrow.

"I don't know that I've ever said this before, but I want you to know how proud I am of the father you've become to Thomas. It takes a special kind of man to raise another man's child. He's lucky to have you, and this new one will be, too."

Damn if that didn't have Mac blinking back tears. "I've certainly had the best possible example to follow."

Big Mac enveloped him in another tight hug and kissed the top of his head. "Go take care of your wife, son. I'm here if you need me."

Fortified by his father's love, Mac headed for the door. Turning back, he said, "Thanks, Dad."

Big Mac nodded and smiled. "Any time."

On his way upstairs, Mac said a silent prayer of thanks

that his father had survived the accident earlier in the summer. *What would I ever do without him?* Thankfully, he didn't have to find out any time soon. His father had given him the strength to help Maddie through the last stage of labor. Soon they'd have a new baby to love, and all at once, Mac was excited rather than terrified.

"Oh, good, you're back," Victoria said when Mac stepped into the room. "We're ready to push, Dad."

Mac handed the cup of ice chips to Francine so she could feed them to Maddie, and resumed his position behind his wife. He was relieved that she seemed to have lost the glazed look and now seemed more focused and determined. He tucked himself in close to her and put his arms around her.

"Are you ready, baby?" he whispered in her ear.

"I think so."

"I'm right here, and I love you so much."

"Love you, too. Sorry I didn't listen to you. You were right."

Normally, he'd jump all over that. "None of that is important now. All that matters is you and the baby."

"Okay, Maddie," Victoria said from her position between Maddie's legs. "On the next contraction, let's give it a big push."

Janey and Linda were holding Maddie's legs. David was across the room preparing to receive the baby, and Francine seemed to be in charge of pacing from one end of the room to the other.

While they waited for the contraction, Mac ran a cool cloth over Maddie's face and neck.

"Feels good," she murmured, sounding sleepy.

He felt the tension seep back into her body as the next contraction made its presence known. "Here we go, honey."

She gripped his arms so tightly he was sure there'd be

bruises, not that he cared. "Mac," she said, sounding frantic for the first time.

He focused on remaining calm for her. "I'm here, honey. I'm right here."

"Scared. The baby . . ."

"She's a McCarthy," he said, borrowing his father's words. "She'll be just fine."

The next hour was a blur of contractions and pushing and sweating. Mac had no idea how Maddie could withstand the pain. Watching her go through this was beyond unbearable.

"One more good push," Victoria said, endlessly cheerful.

"I can't," Maddie said, her voice noticeably weaker. Tears streamed down her face.

Mac wiped them away with another cool cloth. "Yes, you can. I know you can."

She shook her head, whimpering as the next contraction began.

"Here we go," Victoria said. "Big push, Maddie."

With both arms around her, Mac gave her everything he had, wishing he could do it for her.

Maddie let out an unholy shriek of agony as the baby emerged into Victoria's waiting hands. "It's a girl!"

The room erupted in excitement as the baby's grandmothers and aunt got a first look at her.

"Oh, God, Maddie," Mac said. "Look! There she is! She's beautiful." She was also small and blue and silent. A stab of fear caught him in the belly. They couldn't lose her now. Not after all that Maddie had gone through to give birth to her.

As soon as Victoria cut the cord, David took the baby from her and went to work across the room while the midwife tended to Maddie.

With tears running down his face, Mac held Maddie,

kissing her face and then her lips when she turned into his embrace. "You did it, honey. I'm so proud of you."

"Baby," she said between panting breaths. "Why don't I hear her?"

"David's with her. He's taking care of her." Mac's heart pounded as one minute became two, then three and four, the silence deafening. Desperate to take Maddie's mind off the silence, Mac said, "What'll we name her?" They'd bandied about a variety of names but hadn't settled on one since they'd thought they had two more months to decide.

"How about Hailey, after the storm?" Maddie said.

Even though Mac would prefer to forget about the damned storm, he couldn't deny that the name seemed to fit. "That'd be perfect." He kissed her again, glancing at David, who was bent over the baby. "David? Is she okay?"

After another charged moment of silence, David straightened and turned to them, holding the baby wrapped in a receiving blanket. "She's pink and perfect, with ten toes, ten fingers and from my guess, weighing in at just under five pounds. I suspect you were further along in your pregnancy than you thought. Congratulations, Mom and Dad."

As David put the baby in Maddie's arms, Mac experienced a moment of gratitude so profound it hurt. They were fine. They were both fine. Thank God.

"Oh," Linda said, "she's so beautiful! Welcome to the world, Hailey McCarthy!" She bent to kiss her new granddaughter's forehead.

Wiping away tears, Francine followed suit.

"Let's give the new family some time to get acquainted," Victoria said, ushering everyone from the room.

When they were alone with their new baby, Maddie tugged at her nightgown. "Will you help me get this off?"

Since taking off her nightgown was usually one of his

favorite pastimes, Mac was glad to help out. As soon as she was free of the gown, he watched in stunned amazement as she guided the baby to her breast.

Tiny pink lips rooted around frantically.

Maddie stroked the baby's cheek, whispering words of encouragement until she finally latched on.

"Oh," Mac said, filled with amazement. "Look at that!"

Maddie glanced up at him, a victorious smile gracing her gorgeous face. "We did it."

"*You* did it." He reached for her free hand and brought it to his lips. "I've never loved you more than I do right now."

"Were you scared?"

"Nah. I had complete faith in you."

She rolled her eyes at him. "*Sure*, you did."

Mac laughed at her skeptical reply. He could fool a lot of people, but no one knew him the way his beautiful wife did. "I'm just glad it's over."

"This time."

Her words struck his heart like an arrow laced with fear. "We are never, ever, *ever* doing that again. In fact, we may never, ever, *ever* again do the thing that *led* to it."

"We'll see," she said, full of her own power. "We'll just see about that."

"David," Janey said as the group headed downstairs to announce Hailey's arrival.

He stopped at the landing and turned to her.

She looked up at him, so familiar after thirteen years together. His dark hair was mussed from the long night, his eyes rimmed with fatigue and his jaw rough with whiskers. Seeing him that way reminded her of waking up with him on hundreds of mornings in another lifetime. "Thank you."

The words seemed so inadequate in light of what he'd done for them.

"Sure."

"The baby . . . She wasn't breathing, was she?"

He shook his head.

"You saved her."

"I just did what I've been trained to do. I'm glad I was here when you needed me."

"I won't forget this. None of us will."

"Thank goodness they're both okay."

"How about you? Are you feeling well?" He'd been treated for lymphoma a year ago.

"Still in remission. Fingers crossed."

"I'm so happy to hear that."

"The wedding went well?"

Janey's face heated under his intense gaze. "Yes, it was very nice."

"Good. Congratulations, Janey. I'm happy for you."

"Thank you for coming when I called."

He surprised her when he bent to press a kiss to her forehead. "It was the least I could do after all I put you through."

Catching him in bed with another woman had been among the most shocking moments of Janey's life, but it had led her to Joe, and she could never regret that.

"I'll let you get back to your family," he said. "Take care."

"You, too."

She watched him go down the stairs, where he was thanked with a hug from Linda and a handshake from Big Mac. Even though it no longer mattered, it was still nice to see him gain some redemption with her parents.

After David went out the sliding door to the deck, Janey shifted her gaze in search of her husband and found him looking up at her, his face marked by displeasure. No doubt he'd seen the kiss David had bestowed upon her and was not at all happy. *Time for damage control*, she thought as she headed down the stairs.

She went right to Joe and took him by the hand. "Let's go."

"Where?" he asked, resisting her directive.

With quick hugs for her parents, she led him out the sliding door and down the stairs to his Gansett Island Ferry Company truck.

"Janey—"

"Don't talk, just drive."

He scowled at her but did as he was told.

As they made their way along roads scattered with branches and flooded with deep puddles that slowed their progress, the first inkling of dawn stretched across the sky. The light pink hues did battle with the dark storm clouds in a riot of color over the Great Salt Pond.

After the incredible experience of helping to bring her niece into the world, Janey was filled with euphoria and energy that she planned to put to good use once she got her husband alone in their hotel room. The thought made her giggle.

"What're you laughing about?" he said with a growl that indicated he was still annoyed.

"Nothing. Everything. Life is good."

Joe didn't reply to that as he pulled into the parking lot and turned off the truck. They ran through the wind and rain, using their key to gain access to the back door of the hotel.

She followed him up three flights to the top-floor honeymoon suite.

He took off his coat and started to turn to her, but Janey was one step ahead of him.

Dropping her wet coat on the floor, she launched herself at him.

Joe had no choice but to catch her.

She peppered his face with kisses, her lips skimming the whiskers on his jaw.

"Wait a minute," he said. "I'm still mad at you." His playful tone told the real truth.

"He saved our niece's life," she said between kisses. "She came out blue. She wasn't breathing. So whatever you're thinking or feeling, get over it. I love *you*. I married *you*. He *saved* her."

"Thank God for that," he said, capturing her mouth for a kiss that nearly blew her head off her neck.

She gripped his short sandy-colored hair in a savage hold that had to hurt, but she knew he didn't care. "Take me to bed, Joe. I want you. Right now."

As they tore at each other's clothes, a button came flying off his shirt, making her laugh at the sheer joy of being alive and in love. Her family was safe, her niece was beautiful, and Janey had never been happier in her life.

"God, I love you," he whispered, his tone fierce and sexy against her ear. "I love you so damned much." With his jeans caught around his ankles, he lowered her to the bed and tugged her jeans and panties off with one big yank.

"I love you, too." She dragged him down on top of her. "Now, Joe. Right now."

He plunged into her, and Janey cried out as an orgasm seized her, stealing the breath from her lungs.

"Christ almighty," Joe muttered as he kept up the frantic pace.

Janey wrapped her arms and legs around him, urging him on. And when she bit his earlobe, he came with a mighty roar that sent her into a second, equally intense release.

Breathing hard, he rested on top of her as she soothed him with loving caresses through his hair and down his back.

"Are you still mad at me?"

He grunted out a laugh as he finally withdrew from her. "Maybe."

She pushed him onto his back and went up on one elbow to leave a trail of kisses from his neck to his chest to his belly. "I can't have you mad at me two days after our wedding." As she kissed him and let her hair glide over his belly, she watched him harden once again. Smiling, she turned her attention to his erection, running her tongue over the head. "Forgive me yet?"

"Not quite," he said, sounding breathless.

Janey laughed and set out to ensure that he had no doubt—no doubt whatsoever—that she loved him with all her heart.

Chapter Twelve

Ned waited patiently while Francine talked with Big Mac and Linda, each of them glowing over the arrival of their new granddaughter. As he watched Francine embrace Linda, he thought about how far the two women had come from the days when Linda's complaints about bounced checks had put Francine in jail for three months.

The two kids upstairs were responsible for mending the rift between their mothers. Mac and Maddie had created an atmosphere of family and love and togetherness where there was no room for disagreement. Their mothers had had no choice but to go along and get along.

Francine released Linda and caught him watching her.

Even though his palms were suddenly sweaty, he didn't look away as she came over to him. Lordy, she was pretty.

"What're you still doing here?" she asked.

"I thought ya might need a ride home when all the excitement was over. Ya came with Tiffany last night, right?"

"Yes, I did, and that's awfully sweet of you."

He shrugged off the compliment. Little did she know that he'd lie down on hot coals if he thought it would make her happy. "So can I give ya a ride?"

"I'd appreciate that. Thank you."

Gesturing for her to lead the way, he followed her across the room.

"We'll stick around to help out with Thomas so they can get some sleep," Linda said.

"I'll be back after a while to relieve you," Francine said.

"Sounds like a plan."

The two grandmothers shared another hug before Francine led the way out the sliding door to the deck.

Ned followed her down the stairs. "Nice ta see the two a ya gettin' along so good," he said as he held the car door for her.

"She's all right once you get to know her a bit," Francine said in that snippy tone she'd perfected.

"Seems to me I mighta told ya that at some point."

"Don't gloat. It's not attractive."

Ned hooted with laughter at her sauciness and closed the door. He rounded the car and got in the driver's side.

"So you waited all night just to give me a ride home?" she asked when they were on their way.

"What if I did?"

"You didn't have to do that."

"I didn't mind. It was kinda nice to be there when little Hailey came into the world. Can't wait to see her."

"It was quite something. We were so lucky David Lawrence was there. The baby came out blue and still." She shuddered. "So still. I really thought . . . David knew just what to do."

Reacting to the fright he heard in her voice, Ned reached across the armrest for her hand.

She linked their fingers and held on tight.

"Thank God they're both all right," he said.

"Once Mac is done being grateful, I fear my daughter is in for a major talking-to from her husband that'll begin and end with 'I told you so.'"

Thrilled to be holding her hand, Ned chuckled as he pictured the scene. "I don't imagine he's gonna have to do much convincin' about movin' to the mainland if they find themselves in that predicament again."

"Let's hope it's a few years away. My nerves couldn't take another night like this one for a while."

"Not sure I ever said congratulations, *Grandma*."

"I sure do love those three babies, but that name makes me feel a hundred years old."

"Ahhh, so that's why Thomas and Ashleigh call you Francine."

"That was *their* doing, not mine," she said haughtily.

Amused, Ned brought their joined hands to his lips and pressed a kiss to hers. "Sure it was, doll."

She tugged her hand free, and Ned mourned the loss.

"I was just teasin' ya."

"I know."

The rest of the ride passed in uneasy silence. Ned struggled to find something he could talk to her about that didn't involve begging her to tell him what the heck she had to take care of that didn't include him. Since he was walking such a fine line, however, he held his tongue, even though the curiosity was killing him.

Whenever he thought about what she might have to do, he got a very uneasy—and queasy—feeling in the pit of his stomach. The last time she told him she had something else to do, she'd ended up married to that smooth-talking Bobby Chester.

"I'd offer to buy ya some breakfast," he said as they drove through the deserted downtown, "but I doubt Becky is openin' the diner with the power still out."

"That's okay. I doubt I could eat anyway. My stomach has been in knots all night."

"Ya gonna be all right without any power?"

"Tiff has a generator. She's been taking care of me."

"Glad someone is." Ned drove into the driveway to the apartment behind Tiffany's house. "There ya are."

"I really appreciate this, Ned."

"Not a problem, doll. Try to get some sleep now."

"I will." She surprised him when she leaned over to kiss his cheek. "I'll call you. As soon as I can."

"I'll be waitin'."

"Good." Tugging her hood up over her head, she dashed out into the rain and up the stairs.

He waited until she was inside before he backed out of the driveway, still wondering what the heck she was up to. "I guess ya'll know soon enough. Just gotta be patient." Too bad that was much easier said than done.

Lulled by the crashing roar of the sea outside his window, Grant drifted along contentedly as the squawking gulls announced the start of another Southern California day. Abby's warm, sweet body was tucked against him, his hand was on her back and everything was right in his world.

The crash of a shutter against the window startled him out of the dream state, bringing him back to the reality of a tropical storm hanging over Gansett Island. They hadn't thought to close the blinds the night before, and the faint light filtering in announced the start of another stormy day.

All at once, Grant realized the naked body in his arms wasn't Abby. Stephanie was curled up to him, her hand resting inches above the hard press of his erection. He experienced a twinge of guilt over his subconscious thoughts about Abby.

As he breathed in the alluring, musky scent so unique to Stephanie, his cock surged with renewed interest, obliterating any thoughts of his ex-girlfriend from his mind.

Stephanie stirred, murmured in her sleep and shifted ever so slightly, enough to send his fingers gliding over the smooth silk of her skin. Her hand moved from his belly to his chest, and his heart slowed to a thud as he anticipated what she might do next.

In the murky darkness, he watched her eyes flutter open and awareness register on her expressive face. The instant she realized where she was and what she was doing, she tried to move away.

Grant tightened his hold on her. "Stay." He ran his hand up and down her back, marveling at the softness of her skin. Had he ever felt skin so soft?

Stephanie raised the hand she had on his chest, as if she were looking for somewhere else to put it, and then returned it—almost reluctantly—to his belly.

Grant's cock stood up and cheered, which made him groan.

Startled, Stephanie looked up at him. "What?"

"Nothing," he said through gritted teeth.

"Why do you sound so pained?"

"Ahh, well, take a look for yourself." He watched her follow his gaze to his crotch, where the hard bulge of his erection was visible through the blanket.

"Oh."

Her reaction made him laugh, even if he was in pain.

He turned so he was above her.

As her expressive eyes widened, her mouth formed an adorable pucker that he couldn't resist kissing. Everything about her confused and compelled him, but he couldn't help that he wanted her. That much was plain and simple.

Her hands moved to his back, gliding up and then back down, encouraging him.

"I can't get enough of you," Grant said as he kissed her again.

Her hands moved from his back to cup his ass, drawing him in closer to her. "I seem to have the same problem."

The instant his cock came in contact with the heat between her legs, Grant was lost. His head fell to her shoulder as he pressed harder against her with nothing between them and what they both wanted more than the next breath. He kissed her neck and rolled the tendon at the base of her neck between his teeth, causing her to lift her hips tighter against him.

Dipping his head, he kissed and licked his way to a coral nipple that hardened in anticipation. He drew her nipple into his mouth, sucking and biting in soft nips.

She went wild under him. Her hands seemed to be all over him as she reached between them for his cock. Encased in the warmth of her small hand, stroking, touching, exploring, it was all he could do not to explode as he shifted his attention from one firm breast to the other.

As he received the most enthusiastic hand job of his life, it occurred to Grant that while sex with Abby had been sweet and comfortable, nothing about this was either of those things. Raw and earthy, yes, but certainly not comfortable. He was discovering he rather liked this kind of discomfort.

"Get on your back," she whispered, her voice rough and strained.

He raised his head from her breast. "Why?"

"Just do it."

Unused to his partner issuing orders in the middle of sex, Grant complied and then watched in stunned amazement as she went up on her knees and bent to take him into her mouth—*all the way* into her mouth. Holy shit! "Steph," he said, gasping as she continued the blissful hand job along with the blissful blow job. "*Jesus*."

Her throat closed around the head of his cock, squeezing

and milking. And then she added sweeping strokes of her pierced tongue while applying a light squeeze to his balls with her free hand. The combination sent him tripping into an orgasm so fast and intense he didn't even have a second to warn her before he came harder than he ever had in his life.

She swallowed every last drop and then licked him clean, leaving him a demolished, panting wreck. Every cell in his body quivered with aftershocks as she kissed her way from his belly to his chest. "Are you okay?" she asked in a husky, sexy tone that had his cock twitching like it hadn't just been sucked to within an inch of its life.

"I will be," he said, eyes closed as he forced air into his lungs. "That was . . . just . . . *wow*."

Laughing, she stretched out on top of him, turning her head so she could focus her talented tongue on his nipple. As her piercing rolled over his sensitive flesh, he snapped out of the stupor he'd slipped into. His hands found the firm softness of her ass, kneading and stroking.

"Oh, God, I love that," she whispered.

He squeezed harder. "This?"

She shuddered and sucked harder on his nipple. "Anything to do with my ass sends me straight over the edge."

The way she said that nearly sent Grant straight over the edge—again. He'd never imagined being with a woman who was so open and frank about what she wanted in bed. Abby had always kept him guessing about what she wanted—and what she didn't. She certainly had never almost swallowed his cock. In fact, she'd hated anything oral—giving or receiving. Grant had just been given a firsthand demonstration of what he'd been missing.

Determined to push thoughts of Abby out of his mind, Grant said, "I'll have to remember that."

Her hips moved provocatively over his reawakened erection. "Please do." She squirmed up a little higher and pressed her lips to his, teasing his mouth with darting strokes of her tongue.

Despite his best intentions, he remembered that Abby had always refused to kiss him in the morning until they'd both brushed their teeth. Stephanie didn't seem to give a care about such details as she urged him into a devouring kiss. The sharp points of her nipples dragging on his chest and the press of her pelvis against his dick had Grant as hard as he'd been before she'd destroyed him with her mouth.

"Condom," he said between frantic kisses.

She shifted off him, settling on her side with her head propped on her hand so she could watch him. "Hurry."

On the way to his duffel bag in the corner, he stubbed his toe on a table. "Son of a bitch," he hissed, hopping on his good foot.

Stephanie's laugh was low and sexy. "Quite a view from back here."

After sending her a scowl over his shoulder, he rooted around in his bag, found a strip of condoms, ripped one off and tossed the others on the bedside table. Feeling like a teenager about to have sex for the first time, his hands trembled as he rolled it on. When he turned back to her, she held out her arms to receive him.

"Do you want me to kiss it better?"

His cock surged with hopeful enthusiasm.

"Not *you*," she said, reaching out to stroke him. "I meant your toe."

"It's okay," Grant said, even though it throbbed in time with his erection. He took her by the hips and dragged her to the edge of the bed, dropping to his knees before her.

Without a hint of shyness, she let her legs fall open, inviting him to take whatever he wanted.

He held her gaze for a long, charged moment before he ran his hands over the smooth softness of her inner thighs.

She sighed in anticipation and lifted her hips in encouragement.

Using his thumbs to open her, he bent his head to taste her.

"Oh, God, *yes*," she said, once again surprising him when she pushed his hands aside to hold herself open to him.

With his hands free, Grant slid a finger through her slickness and pushed it into her. Remembering her earlier statement, he reached under her to squeeze her ass with his other hand. That seemed to make her crazy as she pressed harder against him, forcing him to focus on the throbbing bundle of nerves.

"There," she said breathlessly. "Right *there*."

He squeezed and kneaded her cheek as he zeroed in on her clit, sucking it into his mouth as he sank two fingers into her.

She came hard, crying out and pulsing around his fingers.

He couldn't wait to again feel her tighten like that around his cock. With that in mind, he withdrew from her, stood up, arranged her legs around his hips and plunged into her.

Stephanie threw her head back and moaned as he pounded into her.

As if he was outside himself watching someone else, he went at her like this was the last time he'd ever have sex. Fueled by her enthusiasm, he bent his head, drew her nipple into his mouth and bit it lightly, mindful of not hurting her even as he took her fiercely.

"Harder," she said, startling him.

"Which?"

"*Both!*"

He bit down on her nipple as he slammed into her again, the bed moaning and groaning under them.

This time when she came, she screamed, a long, keening wail that had his full attention until her internal muscles clamped down around his cock and drew an equally intense orgasm from him. He came like he hadn't already exploded only a few minutes earlier.

"Oh my God," she said, breathing hard. "That was un*believable*."

After he disposed of the condom, he rested on her chest, feeling as if he'd been hit by a bus. "I can't tell you," he said, sticking his tongue out to taste her sweet nipple one more time, "how sorry I am that I missed the finer points of that the first time we did it."

She chuckled softly as her fingers combed through his hair in a loving gesture that further twisted him into knots. She was a study in contrasts, his Stephanie—shouting out orders during sex one minute and soothing him the next. *His* Stephanie? *Whoa, where had that thought come from?*

"Trust me, it's much better with your full participation."

"We might need to do it again—soon." He reached beneath her to squeeze a supple cheek. "I don't think I gave your sweet ass quite enough attention."

She squiggled and squirmed, encouraging him. By tightening her fingers in his hair, she directed him to her nipple.

He happily obliged, plumping up her breast with his hand and forcing the pebbled tip deeper into his mouth.

"Mmm," she said, arching into him. "That's good."

She made him so hot. He wanted to lick her everywhere, bite her, suck on her soft skin until red welts marked her as his. He'd never before wanted anyone quite so intensely.

They moved together, simulating intercourse. It would be so easy, he thought, to slide into her, but he'd never do that. Not without protection.

"Hold that thought for a minute," he said, kissing her before he sat up to get another condom.

A sharp rap on the front door startled them.

Chapter Thirteen

"Who the hell is out so early in this weather?" Grant asked as he reached for his boxers on the floor, mourning the loss of a first-rate erection.

"Ignore it," Stephanie said, tugging on his arm.

"I can't. It might be about Maddie or the baby." The thought stopped him cold. "What if it's bad news? I don't want to know."

Stephanie came up behind him and kissed his shoulder. "Go find out that everyone's fine, and then get back here. We've got unfinished business." She punctuated the statement by biting his shoulder.

A shudder of lust rippled through him, reawakening his libido. She was a freaking firecracker. "You're going to kill me," he muttered, pulling on his jeans while the person at the front door pounded harder.

"Nah, you're tough. You can take it."

"Be right back." Grant walked through the house with a growing sense of dread. If something had happened to Maddie or the baby while he was rolling around in bed with Stephanie . . . The thought didn't bear finishing. He swung open the front door to find his father there. "Dad? Is it Maddie?"

His father came in and wrapped Grant in a one-armed bear hug since he still wore a bulky cast on his other arm. "Congratulations, Uncle Grant. Hailey McCarthy was born at five fifteen this morning!"

Grant sagged with relief. "And Maddie?"

"Came through it like a trouper. Your brother, on the other hand . . ."

Grant laughed, imagining Mac frantic with worry.

"All kidding aside, he held up rather well. I'm proud of him."

"I'm glad everyone is okay. I can't wait to see the baby."

"Your mother says she's a real cutie. The rest of us will get to meet her later today."

"I'll look forward to that. Thanks for coming by to share the news." A thought occurred to him all of a sudden. "Did you drive yourself here?"

"That I did."

"Are you allowed to do that? Especially in a storm?"

"Cal cleared me a while back. It's all good." His expression suddenly became more serious. "Listen, son, there's another reason I came by."

Something about the way his father said that sent a twinge of anxiety marching down Grant's backbone, the way it had when he was twelve and got caught skipping school. "What's up?"

"Stephanie." Big Mac's brows narrowed in what might've been displeasure.

"What about her?" Grant had no doubt she was listening to their every word since his father's voice had one decibel—boom.

"It hasn't escaped my notice that you're spending a lot of time with her."

"We're . . . ah . . . we're friends."

"And that's all?"

"Dad, seriously, with all due respect—"

"Don't tell me it's none of my business. Your mother and I met her last winter when we were in Providence and she was working at our favorite restaurant in Federal Hill. When we asked her to come spend the summer working with us out here, she seemed real excited. I don't think she's had the chance to travel much or visit new places. We like her very much. The last thing we'd want is to see her hurt, especially by our own son who is confused over another woman and trying to figure out what the devil has happened to his once-promising career."

Ouch! "Wait a minute—"

"I don't want you to hurt her, Grant," Big Mac said more quietly as his expression became one of sincere concern. "I get the feeling she's already suffered through some big hurts in her life. She doesn't need another one."

"I'm not going to hurt her."

"See that you don't, or you'll answer to me."

"You did get the memo that I'm thirty-five years old, didn't you?"

"What's that got to do with anything? You're still my kid. Don't you forget it."

"As if I ever could," Grant said, smiling despite himself. He'd never been any good at staying mad at his irrepressible father.

"I need to get home for a change of clothes for Mom. I'll see you over at Mac's later?"

"I'll be there."

Big Mac left him with another one-armed bear hug. "Love ya, son."

"Love you, too." Grant stood at the door and watched his six-foot, four-inch father fold himself into his wife's yellow Beetle. Laughing, Grant waved him off, closed the front door and returned to the bedroom to find Stephanie dressed and curled up in a chair.

"What're you doing?" he asked, noting that her eyes were different. Gone was the carefree expression she'd worn earlier. In its place was the closed-off, shuttered look that left him out in the cold.

"I need to get back to the marina," she said.

"Why? We won't open today without power and the storm still raging."

"I need to go."

Grant crossed the room and kneeled before her. "I don't want you to go."

"Why? Because you want more sex?"

He ran his hands over her denim-clad legs. "That's not the only reason." Hooking his hands behind her knees, he drew her closer to him and nuzzled her neck. "I like being with you." And the truth of it was that he truly did. Even when she was driving him crazy with her sassy mouth, he liked being with her.

Her hands landed on his shoulders as she tipped her head to give him better access to her neck. "I'm not looking for anything more than this."

"Which is what?"

"Sex. Nothing more."

"Because of what my father said?"

"Because it's all I'm capable of at the moment. I've got a lot on my plate, and I'm going home soon. I don't have the time or the capacity to take on anything else."

Oddly wounded, Grant said, "And here I thought you liked me."

"I *do* like you, and I like having sex with you. But that's all it is—all it's ever going to be. Okay?"

He knew he should've been celebrating that this amazing, sexy woman only wanted him for his body, especially since he wasn't exactly in a position to offer her much more either. Yet he was disappointed by her insistence that it could never be anything more than sex. "If that's what you want."

"It is."

He could tell he surprised her when he scooped her up and carried her back to bed.

"What're you doing?"

"The only thing I'm allowed to do." Unzipping her jeans, he pulled them down over her legs and then returned for her panties and sweater. As he ran his tongue over her nipple, it occurred to him that he could very easily become addicted to the way she responded to him. But then he remembered he wasn't allowed to get addicted.

When she fisted his hair to keep him anchored to her chest, he stopped thinking at all.

Laura was enjoying a cup of coffee she'd brewed on the gas grill the way her aunt Linda had taught her when her uncle Big Mac came in the front door of the White House.

"Good morning!"

Big Mac's ebullient greeting eased some of the worry Laura had carried all night, wondering how Maddie and the baby were faring. "I hope you've come bearing good news."

"It's a girl! Hailey McCarthy arrived at five fifteen!"

Laura stood to hug him. "Congrats, Grandpa."

He kissed her forehead. "Thanks, honey. Auntie Linda stayed over there to help out with Thomas this morning. You doing okay here without any power?"

"I'm improvising," she said, gesturing to the coffee. "Can I offer you some?"

"I'd kill for a cup."

"Coming right up." Pulling on her raincoat, she stepped

onto the deck and did battle with the wind as she retrieved the coffeepot from under the lid of the closed grill. She returned to the kitchen and poured a cup for her uncle. "I hope you don't mind that I used the grill."

"Sweetheart, please. My house is your house. You know that."

Laura was mortified when her eyes suddenly filled with tears.

"Hey, hey!" Big Mac took her by the chin for a closer look. "What's all this?"

"I . . ." Her throat closed, and tears spilled down her cheeks.

"Aw, baby, come here." He drew her in close to him, and she clung to the larger-than-life uncle she adored. "Whatever it is, we can fix it. I promise."

"I'm sorry," she said, pulling back from him to wipe the dampness from her face.

"Have a seat and tell me what's going on."

Embarrassed to have broken down in front of him, she dropped into a chair.

"Does this have something to do with why your new husband didn't come with you this weekend?"

Not trusting herself to speak yet, she nodded.

"Aw, honey. It's not working out?"

Laura shook her head.

Big Mac's huge hand engulfed hers. "I'm so sorry. What happened?"

She cleared her throat, determined to get through this without more tears. Honestly, she was amazed there could still be more tears. "Apparently, he wasn't ready to quit dating."

Big Mac's mouth fell open in shock. "What the heck does that mean?"

Laura relayed the whole ugly tale and watched her uncle become more furious by the minute.

"What kind of guy does that?"

"The kind of guy who's the exact opposite of you," she said, squeezing his hand, amused by his quiet rage on her behalf. She expected nothing less from him.

"Have you told your dad yet?" Her father, Frank, was Big Mac's older brother and a superior court judge in Providence.

She shook her head. "He's in the midst of that big trial. And with everything going on with Shane," she said, referring to her brother, "I didn't want to upset him. I'll tell him when the trial is over. You know he felt so bad about missing Janey's wedding, but with the storm coming, he couldn't take the risk of getting stuck here."

"I talked to him about it. I completely understand, believe me." He gestured to the wind and rain that pounded against the sliding door to the deck. "Looks like he made the right decision."

"It's kind of nice to be marooned here."

"What're you going to do now, honey?"

"When I got here, I had no idea, but I've since been offered a very interesting new opportunity."

"Which is?"

"I met Owen Lawry yesterday, and he gave me a tour of the Sand & Surf. Turns out his grandparents are looking for someone to run the place, and they've offered me the job." Just saying the words filled her with the kind of giddy excitement she hadn't expected to ever feel again after hearing about her lying, cheating scumbag of a husband.

Big Mac seemed intrigued by the news. "Is that so? It's been closed a few years. Probably needs a ton of work."

"It does."

"Are you sure you're up for that? I'd hate to see you make a hasty decision that you'll regret later."

"Well," Laura said, her tone tinged with irony, "I dated Justin for three years before I married him, and look at how that turned out."

"True enough."

"Something about this opportunity feels right to me."

"Then maybe you ought to go for it. We'd certainly love to have you here full-time."

"I'm counting on that," she said with a smile.

"Now that's more like the Laura McCarthy I know and love." He leaned in to kiss her cheek. "Any man who'd treat you the way he did isn't worth mourning over. You know that, right?"

She nodded. "I'm doing better than I was."

"Now how about Shane?" he asked.

"That's another whole story," she said with a sigh. Her younger brother's wife had been hiding a raging addiction to pain medication that had landed her in rehab the week before Laura's wedding. "He's a mess. Nothing we say or do seems to help. I tried like heck to get him to come to Janey's wedding with me, but he wouldn't budge. All he does is sit in that house and brood. Dad and I are at our wit's end over what to do with him."

Big Mac shook his head in dismay. "Maybe you can lure him out here to help you out with the hotel."

"That's actually a really good idea. I could certainly make use of his skills." There was nothing her brother couldn't build, fix, rewire or reconfigure.

"Gansett is known for its restorative powers. Just ask my friend Luke Harris, who works with me at the marina. His lady, Sydney—you met her at the wedding—her husband and kids were killed by a drunk driver a couple of years ago."

Laura gasped. "Oh my God."

"Awful thing," Big Mac said ruefully. "She came out earlier this summer to figure out her next move and reconnected with Luke, who was her boyfriend in high school. Now she's opened an interior design business and found a nice new life for herself here on the island. I'm sure she still does her share of grieving, but she's doing real well now."

"Wow, that makes what happened to me seem so insignificant."

"It's certainly not insignificant, but I believe every time a door closes, a window opens. This thing with the Sand & Surf might be your window."

"I think you might be right."

Big Mac released her hand and stood. "I'm glad you came to us, honey. You know you've always got a place here."

Laura got up to hug him. "The summers Shane and I spent here were the best of our lives. In some ways, this is as much our home as Dad's house in Providence. After Mom died . . ." She shook her head as memories of the dark years that followed her mother's death assailed her. "We loved it here."

"You couldn't pay us any higher compliment." He kissed the top of her head. "I'm in bad need of a shower and a shave. Is there any hot water left?"

"Some, but you better get to it before Adam and Evan get up."

"Good thinking. You'll be okay?"

"I'm much better now. Thanks for listening."

"Any time, sweetie."

After he went upstairs, Laura wandered over to the window to check out the pond, which was churning and frothy with whitecaps. Boats on moorings bobbed in the chop, and on the far side of the vast waterway, two sailboats were aground on the beach.

As she thought about the Sand & Surf and the huge challenge it would be to bring the old girl back to life, she was filled with excitement. A smile stretched across her face as she realized the decision had been made—as if there'd ever been a decision in the first place. From the moment Owen had mentioned it last night, she'd known what she would do.

Tugging on her raincoat, she left a note for her uncle and cousins that she was taking a walk into town.

She needed to see a man about a hotel.

Chapter Fourteen

Maddie woke from a sound sleep to find Mac out cold next to her. Remembering that she needed to check on the baby, she shifted from her side to her back and let out a gasp of pain. Every inch of her body hurt, but the fire between her legs was excruciating.

Instantly awake, Mac sat up. "What? What's wrong?"

"Hurts."

"What does?"

"Everything." She tried again to find a more comfortable position without success. "Check on her, will you?"

He peered into the bassinet they'd put next to their bed. "Still asleep."

"What about Thomas?"

"My mom has him downstairs. Don't worry."

"You should check on them, too."

"I will as soon as I take care of you."

Rubbing a hand over his tired face, he got up and disappeared into the bathroom that adjoined their bedroom.

Maddie heard the water go on in the tub and was filled with anticipation. Somehow, her dear husband always seemed to know exactly what she needed.

When he returned, he seemed full of energy and not at

all like he was operating on two hours of sleep. Moving carefully, he pulled down the covers. "Let's get this off," he said, referring to her nightgown. "Don't try to move. Let me do everything."

Since she didn't have much choice, she let him remove the gown. She couldn't help but wince at even the smallest of movements.

"Sorry, baby." He kissed her brow and then her lips. "Was it this bad last time?"

"Probably."

"You don't remember?"

"The memories fade, which is why women are able to have more than one child."

"I can't imagine how you'd ever forget. Ready for a ride?"

"As ready as I'll ever be."

"Tell me if anything hurts too badly." He leaned in to slide his arms under her neck and legs and lifted her very slowly.

Maddie looped her arms around his neck and rested her head on his shoulder. "Feels like a million years since you carried me upstairs last night."

"More like two million years." In the bathroom, he lowered her into the tub that he'd filled with steaming water and her favorite bath oil. "Good?"

"Heavenly." She crossed her arms over her ridiculously large breasts, which had become even more ridiculously large during her pregnancy. Left to their own devices they would've floated to the surface like grotesque air bags.

Squatting beside the tub, he reached for her arms and drew them away from her chest. "Don't cover yourself from me, Madeline. You know how that irritates me."

"They're hideous."

"They're beautiful. Slide down a bit to get your hair wet. I'll wash it for you."

She did as he asked and was treated to a lovely scalp massage as he washed and conditioned her long hair. "Feels good."

"Have a soak while I check on things downstairs. Do you think you might be ready for something to eat?"

"Not quite yet."

"I'll be right back."

Watching him go, Maddie was so grateful to have such a wonderful husband and father for her children. When he'd asked about how she'd felt after Thomas's birth, she couldn't very well tell him that she'd been lonely, bereft and overwhelmed at the thought of raising a child on her own.

Thomas's father had left her after a brief affair without ever even knowing he'd fathered a son. Once he'd learned of Thomas's existence, he'd quickly signed away his rights to the child in exchange for their assurances that they'd never ask him for money. Bastard. They were certainly better off without him. Mac's adoption of Thomas had been final in June.

As she floated in a sea of contentment, she thought of her sister, Tiffany, who'd spent years unhappily married to a man who rarely made time for her or their daughter. Last night, she'd seen Tiffany having an animated conversation with Mac's friend Blaine Taylor, the Gansett Island police chief.

In all the excitement of Hailey's arrival, Maddie hadn't had a chance to reflect on how happy her sister had seemed while talking to the handsome policeman, who'd hung on Tiffany's every word.

"What're you all smiles about?" Mac asked when he returned.

Maddie opened her eyes and looked up at him. "I never got a chance last night to ask if you noticed Tiffany talking to Blaine."

Mac let out a bark of laughter. "You're totally exhausted and sore as hell but still matchmaking?"

"Can I help it if I want my sister to be as happy as I am?"

He knelt down next to the tub, folded his arms on the edge and propped his chin on his forearm. "Are you happy? Even after what you just went through?"

Maddie reached out to smooth his unruly dark hair. His eyes were rimmed with red from exhaustion, and his face was rough with whiskers. "I've never been happier in my life. You know that."

He caught her hand and brought it to his lips. "That's good to know, because I had no idea it was possible to be this happy. Two years ago, I was all alone, living far from home, doing a job that nearly put me in an early grave because I was stressed out all the time. Now I've got a gorgeous wife and two adorable kids, my family all around and a job I love. All because I knocked a beautiful temptress off her bike."

Maddie smiled at the reminder of how they'd met. "Best day of my life."

"Every day since then has been pretty damned good, too." He squeezed her hand. "We have a very excited little boy downstairs who's dying to meet his baby sister."

"We shouldn't keep him waiting any longer." She raised her arms. "Give me a lift?"

"Any time." By the time he got her out of the tub, dried off, dressed in a clean nightgown and back in bed, her small burst of energy was gone. She felt like she could sleep for a year, but Hailey was awake and crying, and Thomas was waiting to meet his sister.

Mac went over to the baby and stared down at her, a look of wonder on his face. "She's so tiny. I'm afraid to touch her. I might break her."

"You won't break her, Dad. Go ahead. She needs you."

As Maddie watched him lift his baby daughter into his arms, she decided she'd never loved him more than she did in that moment. Hailey McCarthy was a lucky girl to have him for a father, even if he wouldn't let her date until she was thirty.

"She's so pretty, Maddie. Look at her." He turned so she could see. The baby had settled as soon as he picked her up. She had silky dark hair that Mac smoothed with his free hand. "Did Thomas have all this hair?"

She shook her head. "He was born totally bald."

"I wonder if she'll have dark hair like me or if it'll be lighter like you and Thomas."

Maddie reached up to take the baby from him. "Time will tell."

"Let me go get the big brother." Mac went out the bedroom door and returned a few minutes later holding Thomas.

Maddie's heart contracted at the sight of them—one so dark, the other so blond and fair, but father and son in every way that mattered.

Thomas's big blue eyes got even bigger when he caught sight of his mother holding his new baby sister.

"Remember what I told you, pal," Mac said to the boy. "Be very gentle with Mommy and baby Hailey."

"I will, Dada." Thomas squirmed, wanting to get down.

Mac delivered him to the bed.

Thomas crawled right up to take a look at his sister. "She's all scrunched up."

Maddie bit her lip to keep from laughing. "She will be for a week or two, and then she'll be so pretty."

"She's pretty now." Thomas ran a gentle finger over Hailey's downy hair. "Baby Hailey, I'm Thomas, your big brother." He leaned in to kiss the baby's cheek. "I'll take very good care of you."

Maddie looked up at Mac and caught him blinking back tears. She held out a hand, inviting him to join them.

He went around to the other side of the bed and crawled in with them.

"I know it was terribly risky and we got awfully lucky," she said, linking her fingers with his. "But I'm glad it happened the way it did, and we're all finally home together."

Mac kissed her and then their children. "I am, too."

Francine stared at the innocuous piece of paper on which her daughter had written a phone number. She'd met Bobby's sister Marion just twice in the four years they'd been together—once at their wedding and a second time after Maddie was born.

Since she'd had her own young family, Marion hadn't been able to get out to the island to see them, and Bobby had balked at the cost of taking the car on the ferry, which had kept their family tethered to the island—until the day he'd stepped on the ferry and never looked back.

The idea of reaching out to him, even through his sister, made Francine ill. Then she thought of Ned—dear, sweet Ned who'd forgiven her for leaving him for Bobby all those years ago—and everything she wanted with him. None of that could happen as long as she was still married to Bobby.

She took a deep breath and dialed the number on her cell phone.

Marion answered on the first ring.

Francine was struck dumb.

"Hello?" Marion said a second time.

"This is Francine." After a long, pregnant pause, she added, "Chester."

"Oh, my goodness! Well, this is certainly a surprise!"

"I'm sorry to call out of the blue this way."

"It's nice to hear from you, Francine. I've wondered about you . . . and the girls. You're all well?"

"We are. I have three grandchildren now. The third one was born early this morning, in fact."

"Congratulations! That's wonderful. I can't imagine Maddie and Tiffany all grown up and married. They're still little girls in my mind."

The comment was tinged with sorrow, reminding Francine that she and her daughters weren't the only victims of Bobby's selfishness. "I should've tried harder to keep in touch with you."

"I certainly don't blame you for anything that happened."

"That's good of you." Francine's palms were sweaty all of a sudden. "And your family is well?"

"Everyone is good. The kids are all grown up. I'm a grandmother five times over myself."

"Congratulations to you, too." Francine marshaled the courage to get to the point. "The reason I'm calling is I need to get in touch with Bobby."

"Whatever for, Francine?" Marion asked softly. "Certainly you've moved on from him a long time ago."

"Oh, yes, a long time ago," Francine said. Of course, she didn't mention that it'd taken fifteen years not to think of her long-lost husband every day anymore. Her poor Maddie had watched people coming off the ferries for years, hoping her father would be among them. For that alone Francine would never forgive Bobby Chester.

"Then why do you need to reach him now?" Marion asked.

"Well, it occurred to me that I'm probably still married to him. I'd like to rectify that."

Marion was silent for a long time. "I can't believe he never took care of that."

"If he did, it was without my involvement."

"I doubt he bothered. Details aren't Bobby's strong suit."

Nothing that smacked of responsibility was Bobby's strong suit. "I wondered if you might ask him to call me," Francine said, even though there was no one she wished to speak with less than him.

"I haven't talked to him in months, but I'll call him for you."

Francine recited her phone number for Marion. "Thank you very much. I appreciate your help."

"If you think of it, I'd love to see some pictures of the girls and their children."

"I don't have your address anymore."

"Let me give it to you."

As she rattled it off, Francine remembered visiting her sister-in-law's home. "I'll put some in the mail to you this week."

"It was good to hear from you, Francine. Call me again sometime, will you?"

"I will."

Laura was disappointed that Owen didn't seem to be around the hotel when she got there. Her hair was soaked from the rain, and the wind had battered her all the way from North Harbor. As she stood dripping on the hotel porch, relieved to be out of the elements, she had no desire to venture back into the storm. Since she wouldn't dare make use of his secret key, she did what any future innkeeper would naturally do in this situation and started looking into windows, imagining how the lobby might look after some elbow grease and paint.

"Peeking in my windows, Princess?"

Owen's deep voice startled her.

Laura spun around to find him standing right behind her. His close proximity caused her belly to flutter with nerves.

As usual, his gray eyes were filled with amusement as he studied her.

"I wasn't *peeking*," Laura said, embarrassed to have been caught. "I was thinking."

"About?"

"What I might do to spruce up the lobby."

A big smile lit up his face. Judging by the crinkles around his eyes, he did a lot of smiling. "Does that mean what I think it does?"

"Yes, indeed," Laura said, elated by the decision, the challenge and the fact that she no longer had to live in the Providence apartment she'd lovingly furnished for her and Justin.

"My grandparents will be thrilled."

"You can tell them I am, too, and I look forward to talking with them. Please also thank them for the opportunity for me."

He withdrew a cell phone from his coat pocket as he used his badly hidden key to get them into the hotel. "You can tell them yourself." As he held the phone to his ear, he kept his gaze on her. "Damn. They're not picking up. Hey guys, it's Owen. I have some great news for you. Give me a call when you can." He returned the phone to his pocket and took off his wet coat. "Why are you always out walking around in the storm?"

Laura trailed her fingers through the dust on top of an antique table. "Because I don't have a car, and I like being outside."

"Even in a tropical storm?"

"I love a good storm. Thunder, lightning, snow, rain."

He leaned on the mahogany banister and watched her,

his expression open and inquisitive. "What do you love about it?"

"The excitement, the drama, the disruption. People make plans that can't be kept because of the weather. How often these days does anything get in the way of our plans?"

"Something got in the way of your plans, and it wasn't the weather."

Amused by the insightful comment, Laura turned to face him. "Ouch."

"Sorry. I didn't mean to be flippant about what happened to you."

"No, you're right. In my case, I'd equate the storm to a tornado—an F5, in fact. Metaphorically speaking, the wreckage it left was similar to the pictures you see on TV." As she spoke, Laura walked around the room, examining the furniture, viewing the yellowing wallpaper and imagining what it would take to breathe new life into the musty, faded lobby.

"Do you find it exciting to be without power for days on end?"

"In some ways. I made coffee on a gas grill this morning, and it was damned good, if I do say so myself. In fact, my uncle confirmed it."

He crossed his arms over the sage cable-knit sweater he wore. The color made his gray eyes seem green. "Anyone who can make coffee on a gas grill can survive the other stuff, you know."

"I have every intention of surviving." As she brushed the dust off her hands, she realized she'd moved past the fury and into the acceptance stage at some point during her stay on Gansett Island. "What were you doing out in the storm?"

"Looking for coffee, ironically enough."

"Did you find any?"

"Nope."

"Got a gas grill?"

"As a matter of fact I do. I've got coffee, too. But because I'm not as clever as you, I didn't think of combining the two."

The silly compliment pleased her more than it probably should have. "Then allow me." Feeling lighter than she had since the F5 shattered her life, she gestured for him to lead the way.

Chapter Fifteen

After spending most of the day in bed, Grant and Stephanie shared a lukewarm shower and ventured into the storm to visit his new niece and then check on the marina. They refilled the generator's gas tank and battled their way down the main pier to check on the boats.

"I've got some things I need to do here," Stephanie said when they stepped back into the dark building that housed the restaurant and office. She flipped on a flashlight. "Would you mind too much if I stayed here tonight? I can plug some lights into the generator."

"Yes, I'd mind."

"Seriously, Grant—"

"Seriously, Stephanie. I don't want you here alone."

All she could think about was the ticking of the clock and the thousand dollars she needed to come up with to pay the lawyer before the end of the month. Not to mention the more time she spent with Grant, the harder it became to remember she was leaving soon and would probably never see him again. She crossed her arms, prepared to dig in. "I'll be fine."

"What if I won't? Did I ever tell you I'm afraid of wind?"

Stephanie smiled at the ridiculous comment. "No, I don't think you mentioned that."

"Besides, you're the only one who can get the dogs to go outside." He tilted his head, making a pout face that was rather adorable. "I *need* you."

"I really do have things to do."

"Whatever it is, bring it with you. Pack up what you need. I'll wait for you."

He was all but impossible to resist. "Fine!" Exasperated, she spun around to head to her room behind the kitchen to get her things. She tossed some clothes and a few of the files pertaining to Charlie's case into a backpack. As the wind howled and beat against the wooden walls of the cavernous building, Stephanie was secretly glad not to have to spend the night there alone, even if the admission made her feel like a wimp.

Grant jumped up when she returned and led her out to the truck. They rode back to Janey's place in silence.

"What're you thinking about over there?" he asked as he navigated around branches on the road.

"Baby Hailey. Isn't she so beautiful?"

"Of course she's beautiful. She's my niece."

She snorted with laughter. "Your ego knows no bounds."

"They seem really happy," Grant said wistfully.

"Yeah." Stephanie wondered what it would be like to be Maddie with a husband who clearly worshipped her and two gorgeous children. Had anyone ever worshipped her? Hardly. Charlie had loved her and done his best to protect her, but their relationship these days was all about undoing the injustice of the past.

Because she and her mother had moved from town to town, from apartment to apartment, Stephanie hadn't had many friends growing up. In fact, she couldn't think of a single person, other than the stepfather who'd gone to jail for her, who had ever truly loved her. Now that was a depressing thought.

Grant's hand landed on her leg, infusing her with warmth. "You okay?"

Stephanie snapped out of her morose thoughts to discover he'd pulled into Janey's driveway and cut the engine. "Sure. Let's go in."

They ran through the driving rain and collided on the front porch, dissolving into laughter.

"That was a graceful landing," Grant said when they were inside.

"I can't see over this huge hood." Stephanie shed the overly large jacket and handed it to him to hang up to dry. "How much longer is this storm going to hover over us, anyway?"

"Mac said at least another day. It's stalled over the island."

One more day, she thought wistfully. What then?

They tended to the animals and met in the living room, where Grant lit the fire. "Are you hungry? I can roast you a hot dog."

"As appealing as that sounds, I'm still full from the fireplace soup you cooked earlier. I wouldn't mind some wine, though. Do we have any?"

"Let me check." He took the flashlight and headed into the kitchen, returning a minute later with a bottle in hand. "Merlot. I'll add it to our tab." They'd been keeping a list of all the canned goods and frozen food they'd consumed during the blackout. "I heard someone say today that the island is nearly out of gasoline, there're no more eggs or milk at the grocery store and all the ATMs are out of cash. Shows how much we rely on the ferries and all the supplies they bring."

"What'll we do if we don't get power back before we

run out of food?" Stephanie asked as he opened the wine, poured her a glass and joined her on the sofa.

"I suppose we'll have to get out our fishing poles."

The thought of running out of food sent a jolt of fear through her. "You think it'll come to that?"

"No, silly," he said, laughing. "I don't think it'll come to that. Between what we have here, what we have at the marina, what we have at Mac's—all of which is being kept cold by generators—we'll be fine."

"Oh." She took a sip of wine and let it warm her on the inside. "Good."

Grant sobered as he studied her. "Could I ask you something?"

Wary, she glanced at him. "I guess."

"Was there a time in your life when you didn't have enough to eat?"

The question caught her completely off guard. Because she didn't know where else to look, she studied her wineglass.

"Steph?" His voice was so soft, so gentle, so loving.

A deep breath shuddered through her as memories she'd locked away years ago surged to the surface.

"It's okay," he said, running his hand over her thigh. "You don't have to tell me."

"She tried her best, but she was an addict." The words spilled from her lips, almost against her will. She kept her gaze fixed on her wineglass, sensing that if she let her eyes meet his, she'd lose her composure. "All she cared about was her next score. There was nothing she wouldn't do or sell or overlook to get what she needed. It wasn't her fault. She had a disease."

He slipped an arm around her.

Stephanie rested her head on his shoulder, transfixed by the dancing flames in the fireplace.

"Did she forget about you?"

"Sometimes."

"For how long?"

Stephanie shrugged. "A few days. A week once." She felt and heard the breath catch in his throat.

"How old were you?"

"Six, maybe seven. The first time."

His arm tightened around her, and his lips skimmed the top of her head. He all but vibrated with what she assumed was rage.

She appreciated that he didn't say anything. What could be said, anyway? It had happened, and she'd survived. As she watched the fire and sipped the tasty wine, she was glad she'd come home with him. For one more night, she didn't have to be alone or lonely or hungry for things others seemed to take for granted.

She'd give him one more night, and then she had to get back to reality.

Grant stared at the wine bottle, wishing he hadn't chosen such a bad time to quit drinking. Hearing that Stephanie had not only been abused by her mother but neglected, too, was more than he could take. And then what happened to the stepfather who'd come to her rescue . . .

As he held her close, it occurred to him that she was a true survivor. Sure, he'd taken his share of lumps in the last couple of years as his relationship with Abby hit the skids and his career tanked. But compared to what Stephanie had endured, he had no real problems.

"What're you thinking?" she asked in a small voice that told him his brooding silence had worried her.

"I'm thinking about how much I admire you."

"For what?"

"After all you've been through, it's a wonder you can put one foot in front of the other."

"What choice do I have? There was no way I was going to let myself end up like my mother, and besides, I have to work to pay for Charlie's lawyers."

"I could help you with that, you know."

She sat up and moved out of his embrace. "That's nice of you to offer, but I've got it covered."

"Let me rephrase—I *want* to help you."

She was shaking her head before the words were even out of his mouth. "It's my problem. I didn't tell you about it because I expected you to do something."

"I know that." Grant turned to her and reached for her hand. "But I also know people, Steph—people who might be able to help you."

The look that crossed her face was full of yearning until he watched her rein it in. "I appreciate that you want to help—"

"How much have you spent on lawyers in the last four-teen years?"

The question took her by surprise.

"How much, honey?" he asked, softening his tone.

"Close to half a million," she said almost sheepishly. "Almost every dime I've ever made except the small amount I needed to live on."

"How in the world did you come up with half a million dollars working in restaurants?"

"That's not all I did."

Grant wasn't sure he wanted to hear this. "What else?"

She looked at him defiantly. "Whatever I had to. For one thing, I discovered strippers make a *lot* of money."

He ached for what she'd endured all on her own. "Are you any closer to a new trial today than you were at the beginning?"

"We have a new lawyer, and he's optimistic."

"Please let me help you. Let me call every lawyer I know. Let me write about your story and tell people that Charlie doesn't belong in jail."

She was shaking her head as he spoke.

"Let me talk to my uncle, the superior court judge."

That stopped her cold. "Your uncle is a judge?"

"Yes. My father's brother is—"

"Frank McCarthy. Oh my God."

Grant took the wineglass from her and placed it on the table. "Let us help you, Stephanie. You've been fighting this battle alone for most of your life. You don't have to do that anymore. I have friends and connections and money. My family does, too." He leaned his forehead against hers. "Let us help you."

"Why?" she whispered.

"Because I can't bear to think of you continuing to fight this battle on your own when I could so easily help you— and I know my parents would feel the same way if they knew what you're going through."

She pulled back to meet his gaze. "I meant why do you care?"

"I don't know. I just do." He tipped her chin and kissed her. "If you let me tell your story, if you let me do what I do best, maybe it'll help."

"What if . . ."

Grant cupped her cheek and compelled her to look at him. "What if what?"

"What if I agree to let you help me and this thing between us, whatever it is, doesn't work out . . ."

"My offer of help has absolutely no strings attached. I promise."

She eyed him skeptically. "And what's in it for you?"

Grant had to remind himself that she'd never had anyone help her with anything—other than Charlie, of course—so naturally she'd be suspicious of someone offering no-strings-attached assistance. "I'm not thinking about me. I'm thinking about you—and Charlie."

"You said you'd been suffering from writer's block until I told you about Charlie and what happened. Is that what this is about?"

Grant released a long, deep breath. "I won't lie to you and say I'm not glad—and relieved—that the desire to write has come back. It's been a long dry spell. But I meant it when I told you I wouldn't write a word about you or Charlie if you don't want me to. You have my word on that."

"How would it help if you wrote about us?"

"People need to know the truth about what's happened to Charlie. I have friends in Hollywood who can ignite a media firestorm with one phone call. I could get you more coverage of this story than you could ever imagine possible. I could arrange an appointment with my uncle. In other words, I'd raise some holy hell about the injustice of an innocent man rotting in jail when his 'victim' is willing to testify that no crime was committed."

"Why would you do that for me? You barely know me."

"Because what happened to you—and to Charlie—was wrong. And because I care about you." Smiling, he added, "And I can't help but wonder what you'd do with all your time if you didn't have to think about getting your stepfather out of jail anymore."

Stephanie released a laugh. "I haven't the first clue what I'd do. I can't remember a time when fighting for Charlie wasn't at the center of my life."

"Will you let me help you?"

She studied him for a long moment before she said, "Okay," so softly he almost didn't hear her. "In all the years this has been going on, you're the first person who's offered to help us."

Grant pulled on her hand, bringing her closer to him.

She settled on his lap and linked her arms around his neck. "Thank you for caring."

"I hope it helps."

Her head dropped to his shoulder. "What do we do first?"

"I want you to tell me the whole story. Every detail. We'll go from there."

Releasing a deep sigh, she said, "It makes me tired to even think about revisiting it all."

Grant hugged her and kissed her forehead. He realized that she was sitting on his lap and for once his body wasn't behaving like that of a middle-school boy. At some point during the emotionally charged conversation, things had changed for him. Freeing her from her awful burden mattered to him. *She* mattered to him.

"Start at the beginning," he said. "We've got all the time in the world."

Chapter Sixteen

"We were living in a rundown apartment in South Providence when Charlie moved in next door."

Grant kept his arms around her and watched the play of emotions on her expressive face. "How old were you?"

"Eleven. My mother had been sober for a couple of months, and things had been pretty good for once, even if we had almost no money and the apartment was a pit. At least she was home and keeping her hands off me, so it didn't matter much where we lived. She could be so nice when she wasn't drinking or using. She was a totally different person."

He could tell by the tone of her voice that she was far away from him, locked in memories.

"Charlie's ex-wife had taken him for everything he had, so he was starting over. That's how he ended up living in the same crappy building we were in."

"What did he do for work?"

"He was a high school science teacher. He had so many cool stories about the planets and trees and dirt." A hint of a smile graced her lips. "I remember thinking how odd it was that this grown man loved to do things like play with mud and bugs and worms. He was fun to be around. I'd never known anyone like him. He talked to me like I was a person and not a stupid kid.

"Even though I was still young, I knew there was something going on between him and my mom. She was pretty, and when she was clean, she took good care of herself— did her hair and makeup. I could tell he was really into her."

"That must've made you happy since you liked him so much."

"I was a nervous wreck over it. I wanted so badly to warn him off her, but I couldn't bring myself to do it because I didn't want to lose my new friend. Do you know how many times over the last fourteen years I've wished that I hadn't been so selfish? None of this would've happened if I'd said something."

"Aw, Steph, you don't know that. You could've given him all the warnings in the world, but if he was in love with her, he would've seen what he wanted to see."

"At least he would've known what he was getting into. By the time he figured it out, they were married, and he'd bought a cute little house for all of us. We were living in this fantasy world for a couple of years, but my stomach was in knots the whole time . . . waiting. Just waiting . . ."

Grant's heart broke for the young girl she'd been and the woman she was now, having to relive it.

"They'd been married about eighteen months the first time she came home high. I can't say for sure if it was the first time she used when she was with him, but it was the first time it was obvious that she'd been doing something. I felt so bad for him. He was shocked by how nasty she was. It was like someone had flipped the switch, and *she* was back. Of course he had a million questions for me about whether it'd ever happened before . . ." Her voice trailed off, and tears filled her eyes.

Grant wanted to tell her to stop. He wanted to tell her he'd heard enough, but he needed to know what'd happened so he could try to get her the help she needed so badly.

As if she was willing away the tears, she closed her eyes and took a deep breath. "When Charlie asked me if it'd happened before, I lied. I pretended to be as surprised as he was."

"Because you were afraid he'd leave," Grant said.

Nodding, she said, "Once again, I did what was best for me."

"You were a kid, and he made you feel safe for the first time in your life. No one could fault you for wanting to protect that."

"I can fault myself. He's been in hell almost since the day he met us, and I could've prevented that."

"I hate that you blame yourself."

She shrugged. "Can't help it."

"Did she get loaded again?"

"Yep," she said with a sigh. "As always, she fell hard. It didn't take him long to realize that she was a drunk and a junkie, and I was a liar."

"I'm sure he understood why you lied to him."

"We've never talked about that. I'd like to think he gets it, but I don't know."

"How did he end up taking you from her?"

"He came home and found her beating me," she said in a matter-of-fact tone that chilled Grant to his bones. "She was screaming and pounding on me with her fists. He pulled her off me and picked me right up off the floor. I was more or less out of it by then. When I came to, we were in a motel room. He'd cleaned up my cuts and tucked me into bed." She paused, seeming to collect her thoughts. "I wanted to ask him what'd happened, but my mouth was cut and swollen. It hurt to talk."

"Jesus," Grant whispered, wanting to commit violence on the woman who'd hurt her so badly.

"Charlie was sitting by the window, staring out into the darkness. There was this orange sign in the parking lot. I can still see him outlined in an orange glow as he probably tried to figure out what the hell we were going to do next. The next time I woke up, the police where there, and they were arresting him." Her voice caught on a sob. "The bitch had reported me kidnapped and told them he'd been sexually abusing me the whole time we lived together."

Grant was afraid to say a word for fear of scaring her with his anger. He'd never heard anything so outrageous in his life.

"Because my clothes had been bloody and ruined, he'd put me to bed in just my underwear. I was black and blue and swollen and mostly naked. With hindsight and adult maturity, I can see that it looked really bad. I kept telling them he'd never laid a finger on me, but they didn't believe me. They took me to the hospital, subjected me to a rape kit." Her slim frame trembled as a shudder rippled through her. "It was the worst thing I've ever been through."

Grant hugged her tighter and pressed a kiss to her forehead. "I'm so sorry, honey. I wish there was something I could say that wouldn't sound stupid and insignificant." His eyes burned with unshed tears over what she'd endured.

Using her sleeve, she wiped the dampness from her face. "That was just the beginning of the nightmare. The day before, my friend had been trying to teach me how to ride her bike."

Grant had a flash of Big Mac teaching each of them to ride a bike when they were six or seven, running through the marina parking lot after them, laughing and yelling his encouragement. How lucky they'd been, and they hadn't even known it.

"I'd fallen on the bike and had bruises on my upper thigh and . . . And . . ."

"The bruises cemented their case," he said for her.

She nodded. "No one would listen. I felt like I was screaming at the top of my lungs, and no one could hear me. I told every police officer, lawyer, social worker and doctor that he never touched me. I offered to take a lie-detector test, to swear on a stack of Bibles. Didn't matter. Every one of them patted me on the head like I was a stupid baby who didn't know whether or not she'd been raped. No one listened."

"I'm listening. I believe you. I believe you, Stephanie."

Leaning her head on his shoulder, she looked up at him with big trusting eyes that slayed him. "That helps. Thank you."

"What about your mother? When did you see her again?"

Her expression darkened at the mention of her mother. "She showed up at the hospital and gave an Oscar-worthy performance with tears of gratitude that her baby had been found safe and maybe not so sound, but alive. She was calling Charlie every name in the book and going on about how a child predator had been taken off the streets. Of course, for once, she was stone-cold sober. I found out much later that he'd recently threatened to divorce her and file for custody of me if she didn't go to rehab. She was out for revenge, and she got it. Boy, did she get it."

Grant linked his fingers with hers, wanting to comfort her in any way he could.

"Things happened really fast after that. Charlie was charged with kidnapping, sexual assault of a minor and a bunch of other felonies. Nothing he or I said or did made a bit of difference. I felt like I was drowning for months, forced to live with my mother in the house Charlie had bought for us with all his things around. His planet models and the fish tank and the ant farm he got me for Christmas." A sob broke loose, and she began to cry.

All Grant could do was hold her and let her get it out.

After a long while, she finally settled, and he wondered if she'd fallen asleep. He sort of hoped she had. If her story was unbearable to listen to, he could only imagine how it must hurt her to relive it.

"I'm sorry," she said, resting a hand on a damp patch her tears had left on his shirt. "The ant farm gets me every time."

Moved by her attempt at humor in the midst of such darkness, Grant ran a soothing hand up and down her back. "Please don't apologize."

"What you must be thinking . . ."

"God, Stephanie. I'm in awe of all you went through and the strength it's taken for you to keep fighting for him all these years."

"I'll never stop fighting for him."

"I'll help you. We'll figure something out. I promise."

"I appreciate that you want to help, but don't get your hopes up. I've learned that nothing good comes of that."

Grant refused to believe there wasn't *something* he could do to help. He had things she didn't—money and connections. He'd use every dime and every contact he had to get her out of this nightmare if that was what it took.

"Where's your mother now?" he asked.

"She overdosed six weeks after the so-called kidnapping— without ever telling the truth about what really happened. They put me in foster care, forced me to testify against my stepfather, threw him in jail and left me to fend for myself in the system. The day I turned eighteen was the first time I saw him after I testified at his trial. It'd been four years by then. I went to see him in prison and was shocked by the change in him. He'd become this hardened, bitter man who

I barely recognized. He told me to go away, get on with my life and forget about him. I said that wasn't going to happen, and he'd better get used to seeing me because I planned to go back again the next week."

As she spoke, the devastation seemed to leave her, and determination took hold. "That's what I did. It took three months for him to say another word to me, and he again told me to go away and leave him alone. I talked to him for the full hour every week. I told him everything that'd happened since I last saw him, I talked about the case, about the lawyer I was going to hire as soon as I had the money. I pretended like I didn't care that he never said a word to me in return. I took it as a good sign that he tolerated my visits."

"He probably lived for them."

"Maybe," she said with a shrug. "He didn't have much family of his own, and his friends had deserted him after he was charged. I was all he had. I still am. Anyway, it took a year, but I was able to hire an attorney—the first of many. Some of them took my money and never returned my calls. Others said they'd look into the matter and reported back there was nothing they could do. It was a constant battle. This new guy seems different. I guess we'll see."

Grant's mind raced with scenarios and plans and ideas about things he could do to bring attention to her plight. "You said you saw *Song of Solomon*," Grant said, referring to his Academy Award–winning screenplay.

"Three times. I loved it."

Pleased by her praise, he said, "A story about a death-row inmate must've struck close to home for you."

"Far too close, but the ending . . . When the DNA exonerated Solomon. It gave me hope, you know?"

Grant nodded. "I did a lot of research on death-penalty cases, met with high-profile attorneys and became a quasi-lawyer myself. Have you heard of Daniel Torrington?"

"Of course I have. He's only the top defense attorney in the country. Who hasn't heard of him?"

"He's a friend of mine."

She sat up straight and sucked in a sharp deep breath. "Are you *kidding* me?"

"No," he said, chuckling at her reaction. "I'm not kidding. How about I give him a call tomorrow and see what he has to say about all this?"

"God, Grant. My heart is pounding." She brought their joined hands to her chest. "Do you feel it?"

He flattened his hand over her heart, and for the first time since she settled on his lap, his libido woke up and took notice. "Yeah."

"I'm afraid to hope."

"Don't be afraid," he said, moving his hand to her face. He bent his head to kiss her. "Whatever happens, you're not alone in this anymore."

"It's not just Charlie and the case. It's you, too." She reached up to comb her fingers through his hair. "You make me want things I've never wanted before."

"Don't be afraid of that either."

Her brows knitted with aggravation. "What about Abby?"

"Who?" he asked, kissing her again.

"Grant . . ."

"I'm not thinking of anyone but you, Stephanie. Only you."

Chapter Seventeen

With his lips still fused to hers, Grant stood and carried her to the bedroom. "You have to be exhausted."

Stephanie kept her arms linked around his neck and drew him down with her onto the bed. "Not completely," she said, infusing her tone with a dash of coyness. Her heart beat fast as she waited in the pitch dark to see what he would do.

"Hold that thought." He left her with a kiss and got up to light the candles on the bedside table. As he tugged off his shirt, he kept his gaze fixed on her. Leaving his jeans on, he stretched out next to her and propped his head on his hand. With his free hand, he reached for her.

Stephanie turned into him, absorbing his appealingly familiar scent and the soft brush of his chest hair against her face. He'd given her so much by listening to her story and providing the perfect amount of outrage. "I've never told anyone all of it before."

"I'm honored that you told me."

As she focused her lips on his collarbone, his hand ventured under her sweater.

"Your skin is so soft. It's like silk."

"It's the one good thing I got from my mother."

He pushed her sweater up as he explored her back.

Stephanie took the hint and pulled it off.

"I love that you don't believe in bras," he said as he dipped his head to lave at her nipple.

She arched into him, grasping a handful of his dark hair. "I don't have much need for them."

"You've got more than enough to make me happy."

She smiled at the compliment as she watched him feast upon her small breasts. "Feels good," she said, squirming against him, looking for more.

He raised his head to focus on her lips. "I want to make you forget," he said between kisses. "Just for a little while. Will you let me?"

Stephanie's heart ached in her chest as she stared at his arrestingly handsome face. *God, I've gone and done it. I love him.*

"Steph? Are you okay?"

Biting back the swell of panic that seized her, she said, "Make me forget."

His sweet kisses became hot and ravenous. His tongue was persuasive as it dueled with hers.

The realization that she loved him made everything about this more than it had been before. *This is love*, she thought, astounded to think that only a couple of hours ago, she'd been convinced that one more night with him would be enough. Now it was clear that a lifetime of nights with him wouldn't be enough.

He broke the kiss and gazed down at her, an odd combination of befuddlement and desire in his expression. Something had changed for him, too, and he clearly had no idea what to make of it, which provided her a measure of comfort.

Stephanie placed her hands on his face and urged him into another carnal kiss. She was under no illusions that their relationship would last beyond the end of summer, so she was determined to enjoy every minute they had together before they went their separate ways.

She pulled on the button to his jeans until it gave way and then pushed her hand into his boxers.

He let out a gasp when her fingers encircled his erection. She loved listening to him moan with pleasure as she stroked him.

The next thing she knew, he'd removed their jeans and was rolling on a condom. "Turn over," he said.

"Why?"

"Just do it."

His insistent tone stirred a flurry of nerves in her belly as she did what he requested.

His hands traveled from her shoulders to her hips and then back up as he used his knees to push her legs farther apart. He brought his hands to her bottom, kneading and caressing until she was half-crazy with desire.

"Grant . . ."

"What, honey?"

She lifted her backside into his embrace. "Now."

"Patience."

"I don't have any."

Laughing, he bent his head and bit her left cheek—hard.

Stephanie cried out as an orgasm took her by surprise, rocketing through her in a streak of heat and energy. When she came back down from the high, she discovered her hands were gripping the sheets, and he had positioned her on her knees to receive him. The blunt head of his cock nudged at her sensitive opening, teasing and tempting.

She pushed back, urging him to take her, but he wouldn't be rushed.

By the time he finally slid into her from behind, he had her hovering on the brink of yet another release. He squeezed her ass so hard she was certain there'd be bruises, not that she cared. She was glad he couldn't see her face, so he wouldn't know that he'd undone her defenses.

He suddenly withdrew from her. "Turn over," he said, his voice husky.

Even though she was wary of showing him too much, she did as he asked.

He slid his hands under her and held her close to him. "Hold on to me," he said, kissing her softly as he entered her again. "I've got you."

Overwhelmed by the way he looked at her as well as his sweet words, Stephanie wrapped her arms around his neck and held on tight.

"That's it," he said. "You can count on me, Steph. I won't let you down."

Did he have any idea how much those words meant to her? She bit her lip to keep from bawling her head off and buried her face in the curve of his neck. The scent of plain old soap had never been so appealing.

As she tasted his skin, he picked up the pace.

"Come for me, baby." He slipped a hand between them to coax her.

The instant his finger made contact with her clit, she erupted with a scream that was met with barking from the dogs across the hall.

Grant laughed his way through his own climax and collapsed on top of her.

"The natives are restless," Stephanie said, running a hand over his back. His hair was soft against her face, his whiskers rough against her chest. She wanted to keep him right there forever. But then she remembered that while he'd been kind and loving to her, he wasn't hers to keep.

With self-preservation in mind, she released her tight hold
on him.

Rather than roll off her as she'd expected, he kissed his
way down the front of her, reigniting the insatiable desire.

"Grant . . ."

"Shh," he said, focusing on her belly.

Helpless to resist him, Stephanie let her hands fall to
her sides and gave herself over to him, hoping she'd find
the wherewithal to let him go when the time came.

Owen couldn't remember when he'd last enjoyed a rainy
day so much. Coffee had turned into soup and then a
spirited game of Monopoly in which he'd lost his shirt to
the deceptively shrewd Laura McCarthy. He'd gotten a
kick out of watching her elation as she collected an obscene number of hotels and houses while racking up a
huge chunk of cash. Earlier in the day, they'd spent a few
hours cleaning the manager's apartment she would occupy
on the third floor, and he'd helped her move her belongings
there from her aunt and uncle's house.

"That's it," Owen said, tossing his last five dollars onto
the board. "You've bankrupted me and crushed my spirit.
I'm a shell of my former self."

She hooted with laughter. "You can't fool me. I know
you've got all that money stashed away from skipping the
married-with-children phase."

"I never should've told you that."

"No, you shouldn't have. I'll use it against you forever."

"Promise?" he asked with a flirtatious grin that made
her blush. While her cousin Janey was petite and adorable,
Laura was all cool, blonde beauty with an inner warmth
that saved her from being untouchable.

"Now you're just being silly."

"It's kind of fun to be silly, isn't it?"

She thought about that for a second. "Yes, it is."

He watched her sort and order the play money so that each bill faced the same direction. "I much prefer you silly to sad, Princess."

"I rather prefer it myself."

"Why is it so important that all the bills face the same direction?"

"I don't know. It just is."

Left to his own devices, Owen would've tossed the money and cards in the box and shoved the game back on the shelf. He was fine leaving the sorting to the next person who played the game.

"Do you require that level of order in all things or just Monopoly money?" He couldn't say why he wanted to know, but for some reason he did.

"Pretty much everything, which is why what happened . . . with my husband . . . really rocked me." She got busy arranging the Chance and Community Chest cards.

Owen turned a chair around and sat facing her, wondering if the property cards would be put into color order next. "It went against your plan."

She nodded, and sure enough, she started organizing the cards by color.

Owen took her hand to stop her. "You can't plan everything, Princess."

"So I've discovered."

"It doesn't mean anything is wrong with you."

"There must be something wrong with me if my husband was cheating before the ink was dry on our marriage license."

Owen linked their fingers and resisted the urge to bring

her hand to his lips. It was a move he'd used hundreds of times in the past, usually with outstanding results. For some reason, it seemed oddly inappropriate to trot out his usual moves with Laura. "I hate to hear you say there's something wrong with you. This one is all on him."

"See, I know that. Really, I do. He made a choice to cheat. It had nothing to do with me, but yet . . ."

"It had everything to do with you."

She rolled her lip between her teeth and nodded.

With his free hand, he tucked a strand of hair behind her ear. "He messed with your plan."

"That's the part that really pisses me off."

She was so damned cute, he couldn't resist laughing, even though he suspected it would make her mad. "The lying and the cheating didn't make you mad, but messing with your plan . . ."

"Infuriating," she said with a self-deprecating smile.

Owen reached for her meticulous piles and swirled them into chaos. "Maybe it's time to shake things up a little."

She tugged her hand free from his hold and messed the cards up some more, which pleased him.

"There, now doesn't that feel good?" he asked.

"Actually, it does."

Owen scooped the mess of cards and money into the box and put the lid on. "Someone else's problem."

She flashed him a winning grin that made his heart sing.

"Tell me the truth—will you sneak down here some night when you're here by yourself and fix it?" he asked.

"I will not, and I resent the implication. This is the new me." She got up and twirled around with her arms over her head.

Owen made an effort to focus on her face and not the

tantalizing view of spectacular breasts. "Easy, tiger, or you'll sprain something."

As she stuck her tongue out at him, a knock on the window startled them.

Two faces appeared in the window that looked out on the porch. Evan and Adam wore pleading expressions and held up six-packs of beer.

Laughing, Owen got up to let them into the small suite of rooms he kept at the hotel. "What're you two fools up to?"

"Linda is driving us nuts," Evan said. He pulled off his foul-weather coat and hung it on the door. "To her, a slow-moving tropical storm is an opportunity to pump us for every ounce of information about our love lives that she can suck from our bone marrow."

Adam cracked open a beer and handed it to Owen before opening another for himself. He offered one to Laura, but she shook her head. "Dodging Voodoo Mama gets exhausting."

Laura's delicate laugh rang through the room, warming Owen all the way through. *What was that all about?*

"Remember how mad she used to get when you guys called her that?" Laura said.

"Ev found out earlier that she still gets mad when we call her that," Adam said with a sly grin that earned him a punch in the arm from his brother.

"Why don't you tell her what she wants to know and be done with it?" Laura asked her cousins.

Adam stared at her, an expression of horror marking his face. He was a younger, shorter, equally handsome version of his brother Mac. "*Because.*"

"Oh," Laura said. "Of course. I get it now. Thanks for clarifying."

Owen laughed at her dry delivery and gestured for the new arrivals to help themselves to the chips and salsa on the table.

"Because," Evan said, stuffing a chip loaded with salsa into his mouth, "if we give her anything, even the slightest mention of a *possible* girlfriend, she's planning the wedding ten minutes later."

"Especially since Mac and Janey screwed everything up by getting married," Adam said. "Now she wants us all shackled and domesticated. No, thank you."

Owen clinked his bottle against Adam's. "With you there, my brother."

"First Mac, then you, Laura, then Janey and Joe, then Luke and now Grant." Evan shook his head. "It's a world gone mad, I tell you."

"What's up with Grant?" Owen asked, noting the hint of sadness that crossed Laura's face when her cousin mentioned her marriage. "Did he get back with Abby?"

"Nope," Evan said with a salacious glint in his eye. "From what I hear, he's hot and heavy with Stephanie over at Janey's place. Apparently, the two of them have been joined at the hip and fighting like cats and dogs for weeks while they worked at the marina. Looks like the fighting was actually foreplay—or so we suspect. Ned's taking bets on how long it'll be before they're engaged."

"Interesting," Owen said. "I thought he was all about getting Abby back."

"He was when he first got here, but now it seems someone else has his full attention."

"I love how Stephanie cuts him right down to size," Adam said with a wicked grin.

"Calls him on his bullshit," Evan added.

They clinked bottles in solidarity against their older brother. "It's about time someone brought the high-and-mighty Grant McCarthy back down to earth where the rest of us live."

"You guys," Laura said, smirking at the three of them.

"What?" Adam asked.

"Just wait until it happens to you. I want to be around to see that."

"I hope you're planning a *long-ass* wait, Cousin," Evan said. "I've got things and women to do before that happens." He jiggled his hips suggestively. "Lots and *lots* of women."

Adam nodded in agreement. "What he said. Every word."

All eyes turned to Owen. "What?" he asked. "Don't look at me." He tugged at the neck of his shirt. "You can't put a collar on me. I'd die."

Evan and Adam dissolved into laughter along with Owen, but when he recovered from the outburst, he found Laura watching him with that strangely intuitive thing she did so well—as if she knew something he didn't. As he studied her elegantly beautiful face, he decided he was better off not knowing what she was thinking. Definitely better off.

Chapter Eighteen

Grant's ringing cell phone woke him in the morning. As he extricated himself from Stephanie and fumbled for the phone in the pocket of his jeans, he noticed sunshine streaming through the blinds. Hallelujah!

He grunted out a hello while rubbing the sleep from his tired eyes. There hadn't been much sleep . . .

"Grant, honey," his mother said. "Wake up."

"Mmm, I'm awake." He stretched out on the bed and smiled when Stephanie snuggled up to him.

"The storm's over, the power has been restored and the ferries are running again. We're all going down to the ferry landing to see off the honeymooners. They're leaving on the nine o'clock boat."

"What time is it now?"

"Seven forty-five. You'll be there?"

"Uh-huh."

"Grant? Are you really awake?"

"Yes, Mother. I'll see you there." He ended the call before she could ask him again if he was awake.

"What's going on?" Stephanie mumbled into his chest.

"Storm's over, ferries are running, so Joe and Janey are making their escape."

Stephanie sat up straight. Her short red hair was spiky and disheveled, which he found adorable. "I need to get to the marina."

He reached for her to keep her from getting out of bed. "There's no rush."

"The restaurant. I have to open. Let me up."

"Not yet," he said, pinning her under him, oddly sad to know the storm was over, and with it, their escape from reality. He focused his lips and tongue on her neck. Even after a night filled with passion, he still wanted more. He craved her soft skin and the wild way she responded to his every caress.

"*Grant*," she said with a moan. "I have to go."

"Five more minutes won't matter."

"It never takes five minutes with you."

He snorted out a laugh. "I think there was a compliment in there somewhere." As he continued to work on her neck, he cupped her breast and tweaked her nipple with his fingers. When her hips rose to meet his, he knew he had her. "That's more like it."

"You're a bad influence on me."

He shifted his focus to her kiss-swollen lips and reached for a condom, intending to linger much longer than five minutes. "It's okay. I'm in good with your bosses."

She rolled her eyes at him. "Hurry," she said, curling her legs around his hips. "I've got doughnuts to make."

Afterward, Grant lured Stephanie into a blissfully hot shower. Then he gave her the keys to his father's truck and sent her to work. He tended to the animals, shaved two days' worth of scruff off his face and brewed a pot of coffee. His phone rang again just as he was getting ready to head for the ferry landing. He glanced at the caller ID and saw his agent's number.

Surprised to hear from him, especially before six in the morning Pacific time, Grant said, "What's up, Jimbo?"

"Hey, man. Glad I caught you. You guys all right out there after Hailey?"

Grant pictured Jim on his deck in Malibu watching the sunrise from his hot tub. "No worse for the wear. I got a new baby niece out of it—named Hailey."

"That's cool." Never one for small talk, Jim barely skipped a beat before he dived into business. "So listen, I got a very interesting call yesterday. Remember that project Tony Zuckerman was working on a year or so ago? We had a couple of meetings with them?"

Grant recalled the meetings as a huge waste of time. "What about it?"

"He's finally got the green light and the funding. He wants you. No tryouts, no more meetings. The job's yours if you're up for it."

Grant's heart thudded with excitement. Tony Zuckerman was the up-and-coming son of one of Hollywood's top directors. Any project of his would get top-tier attention thanks to his pedigree.

"Grant? Hello? Are you there?"

"Yeah, I'm here."

"This is what we've been waiting for, man. I figured you'd be a little more excited."

"I am excited." He thought about the night he'd spent with Stephanie, the story she'd told him, the promises he'd made. "I need some time to think about it. Things here are sort of complicated at the moment."

The comment was met with complete silence.

"Could I call you back in a day or two?" Grant asked.

"Sure, whatever you want, but this is it, Grant. If you want to stay in this business, here's your shot."

"I know. I'll get back to you."

"He wants you here in a week to get started, so don't take too long to think."

Oh, God, a *week*? He needed more time with Stephanie. As he stared out his sister's kitchen window, it occurred to him that if he had a month, six months, a year, he'd probably still want more time with her. A surge of panic brought him back to the moment. "I'll call you, Jim. As soon as I can."

"All right."

The line went dead, and Grant stood there a long time, holding the phone, thinking about the offer that would resurrect his career.

His phone rang again, and this time it was Adam. "Dude, are you coming? Mom's having a cow looking for you."

"On my way," Grant said. He left his sister's cottage and jogged the short distance to the ferry landing where the family had gathered—less Maddie and the new baby—to see off Joe and Janey. His sister glowed with happiness and excitement as she hugged and kissed her parents, Ned, Mac, Thomas, Evan and Adam.

As she approached him, Grant held out his arms and lifted her off her feet. "Have a great time, brat."

She scowled at him. "You're not supposed to call me that anymore."

"So I've heard."

Looking up at him, she seemed to take a full inventory of his features.

Grant squirmed under her scrutiny. "What?"

"You look tired."

He shrugged. "Maybe a little."

"Did you and Stephanie find a way to pass the time during the storm?"

Leave it to his sister to cut right to the chase. He tweaked her nose. "That's none of your business."

"I like you with her. I'm not sure I like you with her in my bed, but . . ."

"I thought you liked me with Abby," Grant said, surprised by his sister's comment.

"I did, don't get me wrong. I loved the idea of you married to one of my best friends."

"But?"

"For whatever reason, things fell apart between you guys, and now she's really happy with Cal. I'm hoping you'll be happy, too."

He looked around to make sure he wouldn't be overheard. "Could I ask you something kinda personal?"

Always an open book, Janey shrugged and said, "Sure."

"When you were first with Joe, was it, you know, sort of different than it was with David?"

"Night and day," she said without hesitation. "Sometimes it still makes me sick to think I could've married David and missed out on everything I've had with Joe. When it's the right person, it's *earth-shattering*."

Grant felt like he'd been struck by lightning as his sister so aptly described what he'd experienced with Stephanie.

"Grant? Are you okay?"

He forced himself to meet her gaze. "How could I have thought what I had with Abby was 'it' when it wasn't?"

"Just like me with David, you needed to go through that so you'd know when the real thing came along."

"Maybe," he said, wondering when his baby sister had gotten so wise.

"Is Stephanie the real thing?" Janey asked with a coy grin. She was, after all, Linda McCarthy's daughter.

"Nice try, brat," he said with a smile. "I'll neither confirm nor deny in the interest of self-preservation."

She laughed and threw her arms around him.

Grant held her close.

"If it is the real deal, don't screw it up, okay?"

"I'll try not to."

She went up on tiptoes to kiss him. "Love you, big brother."

He tugged on her ponytail the way he had when she was six. "Love you, too, brat. Have a good time in Aruba. Go easy on poor Joe."

"Poor Joe," she said with a snort, "loves every minute of it."

Grant groaned. "Spare me the details." He nodded at his new brother-in-law, who was gesturing for Janey to come on. "Your husband is looking for you."

She cast a glance over her shoulder and sent Joe a reassuring smile. What passed between them was nothing short of electric, and Grant was suddenly envious of his sister.

"Thanks for taking care of my zoo for me."

"My pleasure. Don't worry about anything."

The ferry's final warning horn sounded, and Janey left him with another spontaneous kiss to the cheek. He watched her run through the family scrum to Joe's waiting arms. With one last wave, the newlyweds bounded onto the ferry.

After the ferry steamed out of port, Grant's parents said good-bye to their sons and took off to do some errands in town.

"When are you guys heading out?" Grant asked Adam and Evan.

"I'm hanging for a bit," Evan said. "With the recording on the CD finally finished, I've got nothing pressing going on in Nashville. Owen needs me to help him out at the Tiki."

"Sure, he *needs* you," Adam said, grinning. "I'm going back to New York this afternoon before the morons that work for me run my business into the ground." He was the cofounder of a tech company that provided IT services to a wide range of businesses in the city.

"What about you?" Evan asked Grant.

"I'm still covering at the marina, so I guess I'm here for a while yet."

"I could use one more week," Mac chimed in as he held Thomas on his shoulders. "The little guy starts preschool right after Labor Day. I can come back to work then."

One more week. Janey and Joe would be back to collect her animals before they took off for the fall semester in Ohio, freeing him from pet-sitting duties. All the planets were aligning for him to return to his life and his work in Los Angeles in one more week. Everything he'd worked so hard for was within his grasp. Why, then, did the thought of leaving make him ache from head to toe?

"I heard Stephanie is back to makin' doughnuts," Ned said to Grant. "Can I give ya a lift to the marina?"

"That'd be great," Grant said.

"Oh, crap! Did I miss them?"

He turned to find Abby red-faced and breathing hard. She'd obviously run to the ferry landing hoping to catch Janey and Joe before they left.

"Just," Grant said, gesturing to the ferry as it cleared the breakwater on its way from South Harbor to the mainland.

"Damn. Oh, well, I'll see them when they get back."

Grant realized Ned and his brothers were subtly moving toward Ned's cab to give him a moment alone with Abby.

As she re-secured the ponytail that'd broken loose during her sprint, Grant zeroed in on her impressive engagement ring. He expected to feel something—sadness, yearning, disappointment. Curiously, he only felt happy that she'd found someone she wanted to share her life with. Sure, he'd always be a little sorry that things hadn't worked out between them, but he'd never be sorry for all the good years they'd spent together. It had once been very good—before it all went very wrong.

"What?" she asked.

Grant realized he was staring. "Nothing, sorry. I was just thinking that it's cool you're so happy with Cal."

She looked up at him with those big brown eyes that used to slay him. Not anymore. "Really? You mean that?"

"Yeah, I mean it. You deserve to be happy. I'm sorry I was so clueless and that I didn't pay more attention to what you needed. I want you to know that."

"Oh, jeez, Grant," she said, dabbing at suddenly damp eyes. "I came to see Janey off, and now you've got me blubbering."

"Sorry," he said with a smile.

"No, no, it's fine. I appreciate you saying that. It helps to know that you get why things happened the way they did."

"I get it, and I regret it."

She reached out to squeeze his arm. "Thank you. I meant it when I said I want us to still be friends. I can't imagine my life without you and all the McCarthys in it."

"We're not going anywhere."

"Will you be heading back to LA now that the wedding is over?"

Grant wished he could tell her about the offer his agent had called with earlier, but the days of hashing out career moves with her were over. "I'm not sure yet. I've got a few things to take care of here before I make any plans."

"Like Stephanie?" she asked with a teasing grin.

"Maybe."

"Don't forget what I used to tell you all the time—you can write anywhere, Grant. Anywhere at all."

Her words went straight to the heart of his current dilemma. "How's Cal's mom?"

Shaking her head, she said, "Not good. They think she's going to survive the stroke, but apparently she's in bad shape."

"Damn, that sucks."

"It really does. I guess he's going to be there awhile."

"Wow, what does that mean for the clinic?"

"I heard they asked David Lawrence to stay on for a couple of weeks to fill in for Cal, and he accepted the offer."

"Interesting," Grant said. "That's the job he always wanted. Before he got sick with lymphoma, he was in line to take over the clinic when Doc Robach retired."

"I know. Cal and I have talked about how his illness created the opening at the clinic. Without that, we never would've met." She checked her watch. "Well, I'd better get up the hill and open the Attic for the day. We've had a nice break thanks to the storm, but back to reality today."

"For me, too. Back to the marina."

She went up on tiptoes to kiss his cheek. "Take care of yourself."

"You, too." As he watched her walk away, Grant discovered he was truly over her. In fact, he couldn't wait to get to the marina so he could see Stephanie again. Making his way to Ned's cab, Grant felt lighter and freer than he had in a long time. Knowing that Abby forgave him for the way he'd treated her and wanted to remain friends made it possible to move forward guilt-free.

Ned, Evan, Adam, and Mac with Thomas on his shoulders eyed Grant with thinly veiled curiosity.

"What?" Grant asked them, exasperated by the way Gansett Islanders were always minding other people's business, especially in his family.

"What yourself," Adam said. "What'd she have to say?"

"Better yet," Evan added, "what did you say to make her all weepy?" He made a pout face and dabbed at his eyes.

Enough, Grant decided as he lunged for his youngest brother and had him in a headlock in under a second. He'd forgotten, of course, how freakishly strong his "baby" brother was, which was how he found himself rolling on the pavement under Evan.

"Oh, for Christ's sake, you guys," Mac said as Thomas giggled at his uncles' antics. "Get up before Mom hears you're brawling in the parking lot like a couple of drunken tourists."

Mac knew exactly what to say to stop the wrestling match before it spiraled further out of control. None of them had any desire to be compared to a tourist. Year-round Gansett Island residents had a love-hate relationship with tourists. They loved their money but often hated their behavior.

Grant got up and brushed gravel off the seat of his shorts. His recently injured hand pulsated with pain, and he hoped he hadn't busted open his stitches. He glanced at Ned and gestured to the cab. "Still good for a ride?"

"Thought ya'd never ask. I'm ready fer a doughnut after three days without."

"Let's go." While Grant felt like a fool for engaging in idiotic behavior in public with Evan, he'd succeeded in dodging their questions about Abby.

The arrival of the first ferry in days had brought a flood of people and cars and bikes. Ned carefully navigated the downtown area, dodging baby strollers and mopeds and pedestrians.

"What a madhouse," Grant muttered.

"Nice ta be open fer business again."

"I guess."

"Yer brothers are just razzing ya, same way ya would them."

"I know that." Grant instantly regretted his snappish tone. Ned had been a good friend to all of them and had covered his ass more than once when he was a teenager. "Sorry to be cranky with you," Grant said, staring out the window. "I've got a lot on my mind."

"Yer thinking about Stephanie."

"Among other things."

"Has she told ya 'bout her troubles?"

Surprised by the question, Grant looked over at Ned. "Has she told *you*?"

Ned shook his head. "I got the Google. I know how ta use it."

Amused by Ned's indignant tone, Grant asked, "What're you doing Googling the employees?"

"Somethin' about her was familiar. Couldn't put my finger on it. So I used the Google."

Grant wanted to laugh at the absurdity of it all, but there was nothing funny about Stephanie's situation.

"So has she told ya?"

"Yeah."

"Whataya gonna do about it?"

"I have a few ideas in mind."

"Yer uncle Frank might be able to help."

"He's at the top of my list."

"Good," Ned said, seeming satisfied that someone was planning to do something to help Stephanie. "If she needs money, ya come to me, boy. I like that gal. I'd be happy ta help her out."

"That's really nice of you, Ned, but I doubt she'll take money from any of us."

"Damned foolish pride ain't gonna get her stepdaddy outta prison."

"How do you know he shouldn't be in prison?" Grant asked.

"I read about how she's been fightin' for him ever since he's been there. Figured she wouldn't a been doing that if he was guilty."

"She says he never laid a hand on her. It was her mother who beat her up and left all the bruises they found on her."

"Ya believe her?"

"I do."

"Then ya gotta help her. Poor gal has been fighting a long battle all by herself." Ned pulled into the marina and cut the engine.

"Let me ask you something, Ned."

"Anything ya want."

"How is it you always know what's going on before the people involved even know?"

The question was met with a smirk from Ned. "Cuz I pay attention. Ya might want ta try it, my friend."

Grant rolled his eyes at Ned, but he couldn't deny he'd been told that before. "I'll see what I can do."

"Don't let that little filly get away," Ned said, eyeing Stephanie inside the restaurant. "I have a feeling she's just whatcha need, Grant McCarthy."

Since he'd been having the same feeling himself lately, he didn't bother to deny it. "Thanks for the ride."

"Any time."

Chapter Nineteen

Grant went inside to have a word with Stephanie before he got to work on the docks, but she'd suddenly disappeared. He asked Amelia, the teenage girl working the register, where she was, and Amelia gestured to Stephanie's room behind the restaurant.

He went down the short hallway that led from the kitchen to her room, but stopped short at the sound of her agitated voice.

"But you said I have until the end of September to get you the money!"

Grant knew he shouldn't be listening, but he couldn't seem to move.

"I can give you nine thousand now, and the other thousand at the end of the month. *Please* file the appeal. I promise I'm good for it."

As Grant waited breathlessly to see what she would say next, his heart beat fast, and his stomach ached over what she was dealing with. He knew he should stay out of it. She wouldn't appreciate his interference, but he simply couldn't bear to listen to the fear and panic in her voice.

He stepped to her open door. "Fire him."

She gasped and gestured for him to get out.

Grant didn't move. "*Fire* him."

"*Get out*," she whispered.

"Tell him you no longer need his services," Grant said loud enough for the scumbag lawyer to hear him. More softly, he added, "I'll get you someone better. I promise."

Stephanie's expressive eyes shot daggers at him. "Yes," she said into the phone, speaking through gritted teeth. "You heard him right. I don't have the money, so I guess you're fired."

As she ended the call and turned to him, Grant was braced for her fury. She surprised him when she didn't yell at him for butting in to her business. "You shouldn't have done that."

"Why not? You're prepared to pay him nine thousand dollars and that's not enough to retain his services to file an appeal? He was extorting you, Stephanie. He was going to take your money and run."

"You don't know that! He was going to file the appeal, and now I've got no lawyer and no appeal. What am I supposed to tell Charlie when I see him on Friday?"

"I'll have a new lawyer for you by the end of the day."

"I won't be able to afford your lawyer."

"A lot of the guys I know would handle a case like this *pro bono* because of the publicity it'll generate. Let me make a few calls and see what I can do."

She rested a hand on her stomach and grimaced.

"What? What's wrong?"

"Stomach pains. I can't believe I just fired our *new* lawyer. We had all our hopes pinned on him."

Grant closed the small distance between them and put his arms around her. "Breathe, baby. Deep breaths."

Keeping her arms hanging loosely, Stephanie took a couple of rattling breaths.

"I promise I won't let you down." He ran his hands up

and down her back as he surveyed the austere quarters that included a twin bed, a beat-up dresser and a view of the marina's gas tanks through a small window. "I bet your stepfather has nicer accommodations in prison than you've got here."

Stephanie pulled back from his embrace. "I like it. It's free, it's clean and it's close to the water."

"You would've liked my place in Malibu."

"*Anyone* would like a place in Malibu," she said, rolling her eyes at him and starting to sound more like herself.

He caressed her cheek. "Will you be okay?"

"I will be as long as you keep your promise and find me another lawyer."

Grant bent to kiss her gently. "I'll keep my promise."

She looped her arms around his neck to keep him there. Teasing him with flirtatious strokes of her tongue, she had him breathless with longing in two seconds flat.

Grant tightened his hold on her and kicked the door shut, sealing them off from the hubbub of the marina.

"What're you doing?" Her eyes were closed and her lips were slick. "I have to work."

As he smiled at her halfhearted protest, his hands were already under her tank top, seeking out her nipples. "I just need a minute," he said, backing her up to the door.

She arched her back to encourage his attention to her breasts. "I guess I have a minute."

A minute turned into five when his hand ventured under her skirt as her talented fingers freed him from his shorts.

"No condom," he somehow managed to say through the thick haze of lust that had stolen his sanity.

"I'm on the pill."

Oh, God . . . Was she saying . . . Without a condom? *It's official*, he thought as he tugged her panties off, *I've died and gone straight to heaven*. Pressing her against the closed metal door, he arranged her legs around his hips and surged into her heat. The sensations were so exquisite, so intense, that he nearly came with one stroke.

"God, that feels good." He bit his lip to refocus the attention on the pain rather than the growing crisis below.

Stephanie didn't help when she arched enthusiastically into him and clawed at his back. "I can't believe we're doing this at *work*," she whispered between hot kisses.

"There was no way I could wait until tonight." He squeezed her ass cheeks and had to bite his lip again when her tight channel clamped down on his cock.

Suddenly, he needed more. Sweat streamed down his back as he tightened his hold on her and shifted to bring her down on the twin bed, where he came face-to-face with a stuffed Pooh bear.

"Harder," she said, driving him crazy with the harshly spoken word.

"I can't. Pooh is looking." While she laughed, he turned Pooh so he was facing the wall, and gave her what she wanted. They came together in a cataclysmic moment of complete unity that left them panting and sweating.

"Mmm," she said, her lips vibrating against his neck. "If we get in trouble for this, it was all your idea."

"Absolutely," he said, capturing her lips for another heated kiss.

"Stephanie! Are you still on the phone?"

"Oh, crap." She pushed on Grant's chest to dislodge him. "Amelia needs me."

He withdrew from her, got up and extended a hand to help her. When he tried to "help" with her clothes, she slapped his hands away, so he focused on pulling up his own shorts.

"I'll go out first," she said, running her fingers through her spiky hair. "How do I look?"

Grant hooked a hand around her waist and kissed her swollen lips. "Like you've just been thoroughly ravished."

"Fabulous."

"Yes, it was."

She smiled, kissed him once more and opened the door, looking both ways in the hallway before she ducked out.

Grant closed the door and dropped onto the bed. He'd never done anything quite like what'd just happened in this tiny room. Before Stephanie, sex had always been a civilized encounter between two willing participants. Before Stephanie, he now realized, sex had been kind of boring. The thought made him feel guilty toward Abby, but he couldn't deny the truth.

Mindful of his promise to Stephanie, he pulled his cell phone out of his pocket and scrolled through his contacts until he found Dan Torrington's number. He was told Dan was in court and left a message for him. His next call was to his uncle Frank, who was also unavailable at the moment. Again, Grant left a message. In both cases, he used the word "urgent."

He stashed his phone in his pocket and left Stephanie's room. On the way past the kitchen, he caught her eye and winked at her. She smiled at him, and if he wasn't mistaken, a bit of a blush colored her cheeks, which was deeply satisfying to Grant. Whistling a chirpy tune, he stepped into the bright sunshine to find his father, brothers and Ned occupying one of the picnic tables.

The whistle died on his lips when he realized they were staring at him. "What?"

"What yourself," Big Mac said with a glint in his eye. "Where ya been?"

"On the phone, if you must know."

Evan elbowed Adam. "Is that what they're calling it in LA these days?"

For the second time that day, Grant wanted to kill his youngest brother. Rather than jump him, though, this time he chose to ignore him. On most mornings, he might've joined them for coffee and a doughnut, but today he wasn't interested in sitting on the hot seat.

His ringing phone gave him an excuse to head down the main pier. He was relieved to see Dan Torrington's name on the caller ID.

"Counselor. Thanks for calling me back."

"No problem. Don't tell me you finally got yourself arrested."

"No," Grant said, laughing, "not yet. Listen, I have this friend . . ." Grant relayed a synopsis of Stephanie's story.

"Wow, man, looks like you've stumbled upon your next screenplay."

"Maybe," Grant said, once again ignoring the buzz of interest that overtook him. He was dying to write this story. "But that's not my primary concern. She needs help, Dan. This whole situation is insane."

"It certainly sounds that way. You say she testified, but it didn't do any good?"

"She said it was like she was screaming at the top of her lungs, and no one was listening."

"You believe her?"

For the second time that day, Grant said, "I do. She loves him. I think he's the only person in her life who was ever kind to her or took an interest in her. She's eaten up with guilt over the fact that his kindness toward her resulted in fourteen years in prison."

Dan sighed. "I hate cases like this. They make me see red."

"Can you help her?"

"You bet I can. Let me check the schedule and see how soon I can get there."

Grant's mouth fell open in shock. "You're going to *come here? You yourself?*"

Dan laughed. "I do actually work, you know. And miscarriage-of-justice cases like this interest me."

"She doesn't have a lot of money, so let me know what you need to get started."

"Don't worry about that for now. We'll see what's what after I've had a chance to dig a little deeper."

"I owe you big for this."

"Yes, you do. At the very least, I want a consultant's credit on the screenplay."

"You got it," Grant said with a chuckle.

"I'll be in touch."

Grant sprinted down the main pier, past the picnic table full of nosy McCarthys and straight into the restaurant. He did a one-handed leap over the counter and made a beeline for Stephanie. When he reached her, he picked her up and swung her around.

"What the heck has gotten into you?" she asked, her eyes darting around nervously to see who might be watching them.

"I just got off the phone with Dan Torrington."

She clutched his shoulders and looked up at him with those big blue-green eyes that did him in. "And?"

"He's coming here."

"Wh-what?"

"He's coming to Rhode Island to see you and Charlie. He's taking the case, Steph."

As if she couldn't believe what he was saying, she shook her head.

By now they'd attracted a crowd of onlookers, but Grant didn't care. When he realized she was crying, he gathered her in closer to him and turned his back on the crowd. "Talk to me, honey. What're you thinking?"

"I can't believe it."

"If anyone can get you and Charlie out of this nightmare, it's Dan. A lot of times, just having his name associated with a case is all it takes to open doors."

"I can't afford him," she said, wiping at the dampness on her face.

"He said not to worry about that for now."

She looked up at him again. "He's really coming here?"

Grant nodded and hugged her again, relieved that he'd been able to do something for her. As he held her close, it occurred to him that there was nothing he wouldn't do for her.

Owen poured a cup of coffee, filled it with cream and sugar the way Laura liked it, and started up the stairs to the manager's apartment that used to belong to his grandparents. He was on the third-floor landing when he heard what sounded like retching noises.

He gave a gentle rap on the door, which swung open. "Laura?" Putting the coffee on a table, he tried to decide what he should do. Another round of violent vomiting spurred him into the bathroom, where he found her draped over the toilet. "Jesus, Laura, what can I do?"

"Go." She waved a hand at him. "Go away. Please."

For a second, Owen considered doing as she asked, but then she was heaving again, and he couldn't leave her. He wet a washcloth under cold water and crouched next to her to bathe her face.

"Owen, *please*. Go."

"Shhh. It's okay."

"So gross."

"Nah." He smoothed the hair off her forehead. "You think it's something you ate?"

She shook her head.

"Maybe a bug, then."

"Not a bug." She flushed the toilet and sagged against him like a rag doll.

Owen felt like he was missing something, but his immediate concern was her white face and limp body. "Is it over?"

"I hope so. You don't have to stay."

"I don't mind." Oddly enough, Owen discovered he rather liked having her snuggled up to him, even if she was sick. Owen in his right mind would've turned tail and ran the first time she told him to. "I brought you coffee, but I doubt that holds much appeal at the moment."

Her moan answered for her.

He slid an arm under her legs. "Hold on, Princess."

When she linked her arms around his neck, he hoisted her off the floor and carried her to bed. He tucked the covers in around her and sat on the edge of the mattress. "Can I get you anything?"

"No, thanks."

Reaching for her hand, he held it between both of his. "You wanna talk about it?"

As tears flooded her eyes, she shook her head.

"It's okay. You don't have to."

Keeping her face turned away from him, she stared out the window at the view of the vast ocean. "I'm pregnant."

Shock ricocheted through him. "Oh, Princess . . ."

"Pathetic, huh? Knocked up by my cheating husband. I'm like a bad chick flick."

"I'm sorry. How long have you known?"

"Since the day before I came here for the wedding."

Owen winced. "Ouch. Well, if it's any consolation, no one would've known you were suffering at the wedding. You were a devoted bridesmaid."

She ventured a glance up at him. "How do you know that?"

"I had my eye on you."

"Oh. You did?"

"Uh-huh. It can get sort of boring up there on the stage singing the same old songs night after night. Checking out the pretty girls keeps things interesting."

For the first time, a tinge of color appeared in her ghostly pale cheeks. "You don't have to say things like that to make me feel better."

"Hang around with me long enough and you'll discover I never say anything I don't mean."

"I'm sorry you had to see me puke."

"Everyone does it at one time or another."

"I've been doing it a lot lately."

"Maybe you should see a doctor about that."

"It's on the agenda when I get home."

"When are you going?"

"I had planned on today, but I don't think my stomach could handle the ferry ride."

He leaned in to arrange her hair on the pillow. "Could it handle a cup of tea?"

"Do we have tea?"

"I bet we do. My grandmother left behind anything she thought someone might be able to use someday. I remember making Depression jokes for which I was soundly chastised."

Her lips quirked with amusement. "Tea actually sounds good."

Telling himself it was for her and not because he needed to touch her, Owen placed a quick kiss on her forehead and got up. "Let me see what we've got." As he went into the small kitchenette, he wondered why things were so easy and familiar with her when he normally went out of his way to keep it loose and casual with women. It was probably better not to delve too deeply into that particular subject, he decided. He dug through what was left of his grandmother's pantry and found a box of tea way in the back.

"We're in luck," he called to Laura. "We've got tea, but it's nothing special. No flavor or anything."

"I'd prefer it flavor-free."

"Stand by." Owen washed a small pan and put the water on to boil. By the time he'd steeped the tea and brought it to her, she'd fallen asleep. She looked so pretty and peaceful, and he was grateful that she had gotten a reprieve from all her troubles. They'd be waiting for her when she woke up.

Sad for the predicament she found herself in and wishing he could do more to help her than boil some water, Owen put the tea on her bedside table and left her to sleep.

Chapter Twenty

After downing his usual daily allotment of three sugar doughnuts, Ned left the marina and drove into town. As he approached Gold's Pharmacy, he took a sharp left into the parking lot and got out of his cab before he could ponder the wisdom of this mission. On the way into the store, he nodded to a number of acquaintances.

When he zeroed in on Francine working the register, he ducked behind one of the shelves so she wouldn't see him. Like a teenager in the throes of first love, he spied on her for a good long time through an opening between the shelves, watching her ring up purchases while she forced a friendly tone with the customers.

Ned knew that didn't come naturally to her.

Francine was between customers when she nearly made eye contact with him.

He pulled back and realized he was standing next to the condom display. The idea came to him fully formed and crystal clear—and imagining her reaction made him giggle. For the first time in more years than he could count, he studied the various options, which had vastly expanded since the last time he'd been in the market for protection.

He settled on the brand that proclaimed to be dedicated

to "her pleasure," and made sure to choose the extra-large ones, which set off a new round of laughter. After taking a moment to get himself together, he picked up a bottle of massage oil and some candles before heading for the register.

When Francine saw him coming, she dropped the change she was handing to her customer, sending coins scattering all over the place. "I'm so sorry," she said, her hands shaking as she gathered up the money.

An awkward minute later, the customer ahead of him left, and Ned dumped his items on the conveyer belt.

She glanced down, gasped and then looked back at him, her cheeks pink with embarrassment. "What're you about?" she whispered.

"Just making some plans," he said as casual as could be.

"What kind of plans?"

"Do ya grill all yer customers like this?"

She scowled at him. "*What kind of plans?*" she asked through gritted teeth.

He leaned in close enough to invade her personal space. "The kinda plans ya make when yer hoping yer girlfriend's gonna come to her senses."

Francine took a quick look around to see if anyone was watching them. "I don't know what you think you're doing, but I told you I need some time."

"I ain't asking ya fer nothin'. Ya happen ta work at the only pharmacy on the island. I can't stay outta here forever."

"You don't need that stuff," she said with a sweep of her hand.

"Better not let Mrs. Gold hear ya say that. Ya'll get yerself fired. Now, are ya gonna ring me up or not?"

She snatched up the condoms, and her face turned bright red when she saw the brand. The massage oil was next, and the candles landed in the bag with a thud. "Thirty-two sixty-three."

Ned made a big production of reaching for his wallet and counting out the bills, which she snatched from his hand.

She returned his change with the same finesse.

"Thanks, doll," he said with a wink. "Have a great day now." Yep, he'd gone and made her good and mad, but he'd also given her plenty to think about. He could feel her eyes boring holes in his back, so he put a little wiggle in his ass.

On his way out the door, he grabbed a free copy of a special edition of the *Gansett Gazette*, which was full of coverage about the tropical storm, and then hightailed it to the ferry landing to get his cab well positioned for the arrival of the next boat. He was propped against his cab reading all about Tropical Storm Hailey when the toot of a horn caught his attention.

Sydney Donovan, driving Luke Harris's truck, pulled up next to Ned's cab. "Would you mind taking custody of himself for a minute while I go drive the truck on the boat?" she asked, gesturing to Luke.

The stormy expression on Luke's face took Ned by surprise.

Luke got out of the truck, retrieved his crutches and hobbled over to where Ned was standing.

"Be right back, hon," Sydney said cheerfully as she drove off.

"Take your time," Luke muttered under his breath.

"What's yer beef?" Ned asked his young friend.

"She's driving me crazy, hovering over me like I'm some sort of invalid."

"Well, I hate to break it to ya, sport, but ya kinda are somewhat of an invalid at the moment."

Luke's scowl was so dark and fierce and unlike him that

Ned would've laughed if he hadn't also sensed the despair lurking just beneath the surface of his friend's misery.

"Are ya going to get the MRI?"

Luke nodded.

"Good. Then ya can figure out what's wrong, get it fixed and get back to being nice to yer lady and the rest of us."

"I'm nice to her," Luke said with sullenness that was also not like him.

"I sure hope yer bein' nice to her. Ya pined after her fer enough years. I'd think ya'd be whistling Dixie every day, goin' outta yer way to make her happy rather than frowning at her."

"I'm not frowning at her."

"Whatever ya say."

"It's just . . . this totally *sucks*."

"Yep, it does. But it ain't her fault. Ya did a great thing that day at the marina. Ya saved Big Mac's life. Maybe Mac's, too." Ned shuddered just thinking about how close they'd come to losing both of them at the hands of a drunken boater. Luke's leap onto the boat from the main pier had finally caught the bastard's attention. Without that . . . Ned didn't want to think about what might've happened.

"It was worth it," Luke said. "I'd do it again if I had to."

"Stay focused on that. This too shall pass. I promise."

Luke nodded in agreement, and Ned watched him make an effort to smile at Sydney when she returned carrying an overnight bag.

"Ready to go?" she asked Luke, seeming surprised by the smile. It'd probably been a while since she'd seen one from him.

He nodded. "See you tomorrow, Ned."

"Good luck to ya."

"Thanks."

Ned watched them head off to catch the next ferry, hoping they'd get the answers they needed so badly. He returned his attention to the paper and was fully engrossed in the retelling of baby Hailey McCarthy's dramatic entrance when the clearing of a throat caught his attention.

"'Scuse me. I'm wondering if you can tell me where I might find Francine Chester?"

Startled by the question coming from a distantly familiar voice, Ned looked up and could barely hide his shock. He was older, he had lines in his face that hadn't been there before, his hair had gone from blond to gray, but it was those dazzling blue eyes that gave him away. Bobby Chester.

Ned felt like he'd been punched in the gut. Was *this* the business she needed to take care of? A reunion with her ex?

"Do you know her?" Bobby asked, clearly not recognizing Ned. Then again, it wasn't like Ned had ever registered as any kind of serious threat on Bobby's radar. Quite the other way around.

"No," Ned said over the panic that gripped him. "Never heard of her."

"All righty, then. Thanks, anyhow."

Whistling as he walked, Bobby strolled up to Main Street like he owned the place, like he hadn't once hopped a ferry out of town with nary a look back at the wife and daughters he'd left behind.

Thinking of Francine and Maddie and Tiffany, Ned snapped out of his stupor, jumped into his cab and peeled out of the parking lot. He walked into Gold's ten minutes later and stormed right up to Francine's register.

"*What're you doing?*" she whispered sharply as she looked around for Mrs. Gold's prying eyes. "You'll get me fired!"

"What the hell is Bobby Chester doing here?"

All the color left Francine's face, and then the starch left her spine as she crumpled into a heap on the floor.

The marina was dead after the boats that'd been trapped there during the storm departed. Since it was midweek, they probably wouldn't get too many new boats in until the long weekend, so the day was somewhat relaxed. During lunch, Grant mentioned that he'd like to read up on Charlie's case.

Stephanie put down her spoon and got up. Without a word, she disappeared down the hallway that led to her room.

Puzzled, Grant picked up his bowl and polished off the last of his New England clam chowder and wiped his mouth with a napkin.

Stephanie reappeared, holding her laptop. Approaching the table they shared, she handed it to him. "Read away. It's all on here."

Recognizing this for the huge gesture that it was, Grant took the computer from her. "Are you sure?"

She bit her lip and nodded. "I've tried everything. I've spent every dime I have, and I'm no closer to getting Charlie out today than I was fourteen years ago." She shrugged. "I need help."

Grant put the computer on the table and got up to hug her. "It's no sign of weakness to let someone help you, Steph."

"I know. It's just that I'm not used to having anyone around who *wants* to help."

He kissed her forehead and then her lips. "Now you do."

"Means a lot to me. More than you know." She linked and unlinked her fingers in an unusual show of nerves. "Even if this . . . whatever this is between us . . . doesn't work out, I hope you know how much I appreciate—"

Grant kissed the words off her lips. "I'm not doing this for your appreciation. And I'm not doing it because we're sleeping together."

"Quiet," she whispered, her cheeks blazing even though they had the vast building to themselves at the moment.

"No one can hear me," he assured her, amused by her embarrassment. "I'm doing this," he said, punctuating his words with kisses, "because I *care* about you, and I hate that you've been living this nightmare by yourself all these years."

She appeared to be processing his words as she looked up at him.

He kissed her once more. "And I don't want to talk about whatever this is between us not working out. Why don't we pretend like it's going to work out and see what happens, huh?"

"Really, I don't expect . . ."

She didn't expect *anything*, he realized, which only made him want to give her *everything*. Wow.

Seeming to read his mind, she said, "Don't make promises you can't keep, Grant." Her quiet dignity went straight to his heart. "You've got a great big life with all kinds of options open to you. It wouldn't be wise to limit yourself."

"That may be true, but the only option I seem interested in is standing right in front of me."

She released a deep sigh that told him he had a long way to go in convincing her that his intentions toward her were honorable and suddenly long-term. Of course, the nagging voice in the back of his head that reminded him he was due back in LA in a week's time put a damper on that thought.

"I've got to get back to work." She gestured toward the takeout counter and then pointed to the computer. "And so do you."

"Do you mind if I make a file on your computer to take notes?"

"Have at it."

Grant's blood zinged through his veins as the challenge of a new story awaited him.

"Are you getting a buzz?" she asked, smiling up at him.

Amazed by her insight, he said, "How'd you know?"

"Your eyes just got all bright and excited, the way they do when . . ." She gestured for him to fill in the blanks.

Grant barked out a laugh and drew her in close to him. "The way they do before I come?" he whispered in her ear, pushing his hips against hers.

"Yeah," she said breathlessly. "Just like."

"Shit," he growled. "You've got me all hot again."

"Doesn't take much." She slapped him on the ass and pulled away from him. "Get to work, stud. I'll take care of your other problem later." With a saucy wink, she sauntered off, leaving his tongue practically hanging out of his mouth.

Slumping into his chair, he willed his sudden, raging erection into submission. Damn, she was hot, and damn, she turned him on so fast and furious he barely stood a chance when she was anywhere near him.

What might she be like, he wondered, without the weight of the world on her slim shoulders? Determined to find out, he fired up her computer and dug in.

Stephanie wondered if Grant knew that his lips moved when he read or that he talked to himself when he was writing, two rather endearing qualities. Oh, who was she kidding? *All* his qualities were endearing.

She had to tear her gaze off him and get back to work on the food inventory she needed to complete so she could get the order in for the next week. As she added, subtracted and multiplied on her calculator, her thoughts were full of him. For so long she'd wondered what it might be like to be in love. Now she knew the emotions were all-consuming.

She wanted to spend every minute of every day with him and every night wrapped in his arms. She wanted to hear his every thought, share his every dream and do everything within her power to make him as happy as he'd made her.

And more than anything, she wanted to believe that he felt the same way about her. Wouldn't that be nice? When she realized she was once again staring at him, she let out a deep sigh and tried to focus on the spreadsheet that needed her undivided attention for at least thirty more minutes. Then she could ogle to her heart's content.

Ten minutes later, she'd lost the battle and was staring at him.

"Quite a sight, isn't he?" Linda McCarthy asked with a knowing smile on her face. "He reminds me so much of his father at that age. I remember standing right about where you are," Linda said, gesturing to the takeout counter where Stephanie had laid out her paperwork so she could surreptitiously watch Grant.

Apparently not surreptitiously enough.

Stephanie was mortified to have been caught gawking by the man's mother, no less—and her boss!

"Big Mac was working on the docks," Linda continued, "and I'd be in here serving up chowder and doughnuts, hoping he'd pop in to say hello at some point."

Even though she was embarrassed, Stephanie was curious, too. "Were you dating then?"

"Oh lord, no. We'd been married five years by then with Mac underfoot and Grant on the way."

Astounded, Stephanie said, "And you were still hoping for a glimpse of him."

Linda leaned in close to whisper. "I'm *still* hoping for a glimpse of him." She grinned. "Nearly forty years later."

"That's so sweet," Stephanie said with a sigh. "I've never known anyone who's been married that long."

"Well, it's not always sunshine and roses, but most of the time it is." Linda's smile faded a bit as if she was recalling something unpleasant. "It's been a bit rough since his injury."

"I'm sure that's been very difficult, but to know you're still in love after all these years, well . . ." Stephanie searched for the words she needed.

"What, honey?" Linda asked with the same kindness she'd shown her since they met last winter in Providence.

"It gives me hope." Stephanie hadn't had much use for the word "hope" in her life, but suddenly she was filled with it. That Grant's friend might be able to get Charlie a new trial, that Charlie might one day be released, that she and Grant . . . It was probably best that she not get ahead of herself where he was concerned.

Linda placed her hand over Stephanie's. "We all agree that he seems quite smitten with you. It might be okay to allow for a tiny bit of hope."

Startled, Stephanie forced herself to meet Linda's gaze. "You really think so?"

Linda nodded. "Personally, I think you're very good for him. You call him out and keep him on his toes."

"Abby didn't do that?" Stephanie asked, making an effort to keep her tone casual and not too interested.

"Abby's a doll—an absolute doll, and we love her. But she didn't challenge him the way you do. I think he needs that."

"What're you up to, Mother?"

With a conspiratorial smile for Stephanie, Linda turned to her son. "Not a thing, darling. I'm simply here to invite the two of you to dinner tonight."

Grant looked around his mother to Stephanie. She nodded to let him know she was willing if he was.

"Okay," Grant said cautiously. "What's the occasion?"

"No occasion, my suspicious son. Just dinner."

Grant rolled his eyes. "Dinner with an ulterior motive for dessert."

"I'm going to pretend I didn't hear that," Linda said with a breezy wave on her way to the big garage doors that opened the restaurant to the pier. "I'll see you both after work."

"Bye, Mom."

"Bye, Linda," Stephanie said. "And thank you."

Grant got up and stretched. As he came toward her with a predatory look in his eye, Stephanie planted her feet and lifted her chin, letting him know she couldn't be intimidated.

"Why are you thanking my mother?" He put his arms around her and squeezed her ass. That was all it took to make her want to crawl all over him. She settled for resting her hands on his muscular chest.

"Because she invited me to dinner. Why else would I be thanking her?"

"Maybe because she butted in and took your side against me? She likes doing that kind of stuff."

Stephanie would've giggled at his laser-sharp insight, but his lips had found the spot on her neck that drove her mad. It had taken him no time at all to figure out just how and where to touch her to ensure maximum results. She should probably be worried about how easy she was where he was concerned, but with his lips working their magic on her neck and his hands gripping her ass, she couldn't be bothered with worrying about much of anything.

"Is it later yet?" he asked gruffly.

Stephanie took his hand and led him back a few feet so she could reach up to untie the drop-down board that would render the takeout counter closed.

His eyes lit up with unrestrained lust. "Are we closing early?"

"Looks that way."

"Let me grab your computer from the table." He darted out to the dining room and was back in two seconds flat, putting the computer on the counter. "Now, you were saying?"

She smiled at his childlike glee and stepped into his outstretched arms, holding on to him and the hopeful feelings he inspired in her. Maybe . . . Just maybe . . . Wanting to show him how much he'd come to mean to her, she tugged at the button to his shorts and pushed them and his boxers down, freeing his erection.

Using both hands, she stroked him and ran her thumbs through the pearly fluid that suddenly appeared at the tip.

He tightened his grip on her ass. "Steph . . ." His eyes were closed, his lips parted and his Adam's apple bobbed in his throat.

She loved rendering him helpless with desire. "Sit up here," she said, patting the countertop.

His eyes popped open. "Seriously?"

Nudging him, she encouraged him to do as she asked. After he reluctantly raised himself onto the counter, she bent her head to take him into her mouth.

"Oh, God," he whispered, his fingers tightening into a fist in her hair as he sucked in a sharp deep breath. "*God*."

Stephanie opened her throat to accommodate him and lashed at his shaft with her pierced tongue, knowing he loved the combination. The second time, she squeezed his balls, too.

He held out for a long time before he finally bucked his hips, moaned and flooded her mouth. "*Holy shit,*" he said through gasping breaths.

She stood up straight and was pulled into a deep, possessive kiss. "You're amazing, and you blow my mind."

"That's not all I blow."

Grant laughed and cupped her face, looking at her with a curiously intense expression on his handsome face.

"What?" she asked, unnerved all of a sudden.

"Just looking."

She took the opportunity to look her fill, too. Would she ever get enough of his superbly beautiful face, the dark hair, the gorgeous blue eyes? Probably not. As they drank each other in, Stephanie felt a subtle shift take place between them. What had begun as a casual fling during a tropical storm had turned into something much more significant. When she could no longer stand the intensity that arced between them like a live wire, she diverted her gaze and rested her head on his chest.

"You okay?" he asked, stroking a hand over her head and neck before kneading her shoulders.

She nodded, unable to speak over the riot of emotions storming around inside her. With her hands propped on his hip bones, she breathed in his scent, committing every detail to memory for the inevitable day when they'd go their separate ways.

"I'll never look at this counter the same way again," he said drolly.

Of course she laughed at that, which relieved some of her tension. She wondered if that's why he'd said it.

All at once, he hopped off the counter, pulled up his shorts and reached for her, lifting her and curling her legs around his hips. "We've got time for a nap before dinner at my parents' house."

"Do we?" she asked with a smile, crossing her hands behind his neck.

Nodding, he said, "Plenty of time to even the score."

"What score is that?"

"The orgasm score. I owe you one."

Laughing as he walked them into her room, Stephanie knew she'd never love anyone the way she loved Grant McCarthy. This was the all-consuming, last-forever deal his parents seemed to have, and the greedy little girl who lived inside her wanted the same thing with him that they had. For now, though, she'd take what she could get and file away the memories to sustain her when it was over.

Chapter Twenty-One

Forgetting all about Bobby Chester, Ned flew around the counter but wasn't quick enough to keep Francine's head from cracking against a shelf on the way down. Adrenaline coursed through him as he cradled her head in his lap, patted her cheeks and prayed for her to come to.

"Francine, honey, wake up. It's okay. Whatever's going on, we'll handle it together. Just wake up."

A crowd gathered around them. "Should I call the rescue?" Mrs. Gold asked.

"Give 'er a minute. She's had a shock." Ned wanted to shoot himself for dropping the news about Bobby on her without a warning. Any suspicion he'd had that Francine invited her ex-husband to the island was gone after seeing her reaction to the news that Bobby was here.

It seemed like a lifetime passed before her eyes finally fluttered and opened. "Wh-what happened? What're you doing here?"

Ned realized how badly he'd bungled this. "I, uh, I came to tell ya—"

"Oh, God," she said, her eyes closing again. "Bobby."

"Yep."

"What's he doing here?"

"I was kinda hopin' ya might know."

She looked up at him, her eyes full of genuine concern. "I didn't ask him to come, if that's what you're thinking."

"Pardon me," Mrs. Gold said in her nasally New York accent. "Could we maybe take this soap opera elsewhere?"

Ned scowled up at her. To Francine, he said, "Do you think you can get up?"

"Of course I can." She pushed his helping hands away and pulled herself up. When she swayed, his hands on her shoulders steadied her.

"Take it easy, doll."

"Yes, Francine, take it easy," Mrs. Gold said. "Go on home. I'll cover the rest of your shift."

"I'm so sorry, Mrs. Gold," Francine said. "I'll be in on time tomorrow."

Ned fumed as he watched her grovel to the cranky woman she worked for. If she married him, she wouldn't have to work another day in her life.

"Take tomorrow off and work out whatever you've got going on," Mrs. Gold said. "I'll see you Friday." Despite the kind gesture made in front of several concerned customers, Ned had no doubt Mrs. Gold would make Francine pay for the scene she'd caused.

"Thank you," Francine said with meekness that was so out of character he wanted to rant and rave.

Ned extended an arm to her, and she reluctantly tucked her hand into the crook of his elbow. "Take it slow, doll."

They made their way to his cab in silence. He held the passenger door for her and settled her inside. On the way around to the driver's side, he chastised himself for being a stupid fool. "Ya better take it easy on this one," he muttered to himself. "Don't be a fool and lose her now."

He slid into the car and rested his hands on the wheel. "Where do ya want to go?"

"Home, I guess. If you don't mind."

"'Course I don't mind. Is yer head okay?"

"It will be."

"Should we stop and get some ice, or do ya have some at home?"

"I did *not* invite him here," she said a second time, more emphatically this time.

Ned didn't bother to mention that he'd been talking about ice, not Bobby. "It's just kinda interesting to me that ya tell me ya got 'stuff to take care of,' and then suddenly yer ex-husband shows up on the island. Interesting, don'cha think?"

She folded her arms and set her chin mulishly.

"Ain'tcha gonna say anything?"

"What does it matter what I have to say? You won't believe it anyway."

"Try me."

She held her silence until they arrived at her place. The passenger door flew open, and she was halfway up the stairs before he could fumble his own door open.

"Now wait just a minute, Francine Chester," he said, going after her. He'd be damned if he'd leave before he got some answers.

When they were inside the apartment, she spun around and jammed a finger into his chest. "You wait a minute, Ned Saunders. You're not my husband, and you can't tell me what to do."

"Why am I not yer husband, Francine? Answer me that one, will ya?"

She stared at him with green eyes filled with fire, and all he wanted was to kiss her until she forgot all about why she was mad at him, mad at life and about to see the ex-husband who'd left her alone with two babies decades ago.

"First of all," she said, "you've never *asked* me to marry you, and second of all, I can't marry you because—"

A knock on the door startled them, and Francine moved to answer it.

Ned wanted to stop her and scream at her to finish what she was going to say.

"Hi there, Francine."

When Ned heard Bobby's smooth voice and saw Francine's knees start to buckle, he rushed over to her and put his hands on her shoulders.

"What're you doing here, Bobby?" Francine asked, the quiver in her voice betraying her emotions.

"Marion said you were looking for me. She said I've got some grandkids these days, so I thought I'd come over and see what's what. Hey," he said, noticing Ned standing behind her. "You're the guy from the ferry dock. You said you didn't know her."

"Ya," Ned grumbled. "I lied."

Francine stood up straighter and shook Ned's hands off her shoulders. "You thought you'd come over to see *what's what*? Let me tell you *what's what*, you miserable excuse for a human being. The daughters you left when they were babies are now in their *thirties*. They have lives and families of their own. They've had everything they needed because *I* saw to it with no help from the father who left them and never looked back. So whatever sweet family reunion you see happening here *isn't going to happen*. You got me?"

"They're old enough to speak for themselves," Bobby said sullenly.

"They will *never* be old enough to deal with you after you've disregarded them their entire lives."

"Then why'd you want me to call you?"

"Because, you son of a bitch. As far as I know, we're still married, and I have someone else I want to marry—

someone decent and kind and two hundred million times the man you'll ever be. I can't marry him as long as I'm still *shackled* to you."

Ned felt like he'd been hit by a stun gun. She wanted to marry him? She was still married to Bobby? Well, if that didn't beat all. He wasn't sure whether he wanted to dance a jig or shake her until her teeth rattled for not sharing her dilemma with him.

"Mom?" Tiffany asked from the landing outside the door. "Is everything all right?"

Oh, God. Ned wanted to rush outside and protect Tiffany from the body blow she was about to withstand. Apparently, Francine had the same urge. She pushed past Bobby and went to her daughter.

"Honey, let's go down to your place." With her arm around Tiffany's shoulders, she tried to direct her daughter toward the stairs. "There's something I need to talk to you about."

Casting a glance over her shoulder, Tiffany said, "Who's that man, Mom?"

Tiffany wouldn't be redirected, and Ned suspected she already knew the answer to her own question.

Bobby stepped forward with his hand extended. "Tiffany?"

With a hesitant glance at her mother, Tiffany nodded.

"It's me. Your daddy."

Holding her daughter close to her, Francine erupted. "You have *no right* to refer to yourself that way! No right at all!"

Tiffany stared at Bobby, her face devoid of color, shock reverberating through her. "Wh-what, what're you doing here?"

"I wanted to see you and your sister, my grandchildren and your mother."

"You can't just . . . You can't—" When the words wouldn't come, Tiffany went back to staring at him.

"Don't worry, honey, I already told him the same thing. I want a divorce, Bobby, and I want it now. The very least you can do is handle the details. I don't want anything from you, and God knows I haven't got a thing for you to try to steal from me."

"I want to see Maddie."

"Not now," Tiffany said for her sister. "She just had a baby, and this is not the time."

"I'll be at the Beachcomber for a few days. Let her know I'm here, and I want to see her. Once I see her, I'll give you your divorce, Francine. Not one minute before. You all have a nice day now." On his way past Tiffany, he squeezed her arm. "It's good to see you. You grew up to be a beautiful woman."

After he went down the stairs, the three of them stood there a long time, like shocked survivors following a major disaster. Tears spilled down Tiffany's cheeks, and sobs racked her petite frame.

Francine put her arms around her daughter and held on tight. "I'm so sorry you were blindsided, baby. I had no idea he was coming here."

Tiffany was crying so hard she couldn't speak.

Ned went to them and led them inside to the sofa. Once they were settled, he made a beeline to the cabinet over Francine's refrigerator where she kept her secret stash of whiskey. He poured them each a shot and took it to them.

"Here," he said. "Take a drink." He stood over them until they'd both downed the whiskey. He crouched in front of Tiffany. "Now, honey, I know ya've had a big shock, but he can't take anything from ya unless ya let him. And if ya want to see him and get to know him, that's yer call, too."

"Wait a minute—" Francine said.

"No, Francine. He's the girl's father. If she wants to see him, ya can't get in the middle of that."

"I don't know what I want," Tiffany said. "I've spent my whole life wondering about him, and then one day out of the blue, here he is."

"And it's only natural that ya'd be curious," Ned said with a pointed look for Francine. "Yer mama will understand if ya feel the need to see him."

"Oh, I will, will I?" Francine asked, her brow arched.

Ned met her steely stare. "Yes, ya will."

"Mom?" Tiffany looked at her mother expectantly.

After a long pause, Francine said, "Of course I'll understand." She rested her hand on top of Tiffany's. "Whatever you want is what I want."

"I need to think about it," Tiffany said. "What'll we do about Maddie?"

"Let me worry about that," Francine said.

The two women embraced, and the knot in Ned's belly finally loosened. He stood and stepped back to give them some space.

"I have to pick up Ashleigh from Jim." Brushing the tears off her face, Tiffany stood and shocked the hell out of Ned by hugging him. "Thanks," she said.

Ned brushed a kiss over her forehead. "Any time, honey."

After she left, Ned kept his hands on his hips as he studied Francine. "Why didn't ya just tell me, doll?"

"Because," she said, playing with her glass, "it's humiliating. All these years he's been gone, and I'm still married to him? How was I supposed to tell you that?"

"The way ya just did. Ya think there's anything ya can tell me that'll change the way I feel aboutcha?" He sat next to her, put his hands on her face and compelled her to look at him. When he had her attention, he said, "I love ya, Francine. I always have. From the first day I ever saw ya. I never stopped wanting ya, even when ya were married to him."

She blinked back tears and sniffled. "You'd have to be crazy to want to be dragged into all this madness."

"Then call me crazy," he said, kissing her. "Yer craziness is my craziness. Did ya hear what I said, Francine? *I love ya*. If it's what ya want, I'll marry ya the second yer free from him. Ya got me?"

"Ned." She rested her forehead against his. "You're just saying that because I told Bobby I want to marry you."

"Are ya *tryin'* to make me mad?"

Shaking her head, she smiled at him. "I love you, too."

"I know ya do, doll." He pressed his lips to hers, hoping she'd welcome his advance.

Her arms came around his neck, and before he knew it, he was stretched out on top of her on the sofa. "Sorry. Didn't mean to—"

Resting a finger over his lips, she flashed the seductive smile he remembered from a lifetime ago when she'd had him firmly wrapped around her little finger. "You wanna make out?"

His mouth fell open in surprise, and then he was laughing as hard as he ever had in his life. "Yes, Francine. I wanna make out with ya."

Chapter Twenty-Two

His ringing cell phone woke Grant from the best nap he'd had in ages.

"Hi, Grant, it's Uncle Frank. I got your urgent message. Is everything all right with your dad? Laura?"

"Hi there. Yes, sorry, everyone's fine." Grant slipped from Stephanie's embrace and stood to pull on his shorts. Since she was still asleep, he stepped out of her tiny room and closed the door behind him. "I didn't mean to scare you."

"Oh, good," Frank said, sounding relieved. "How was the wedding? And the storm? I haven't heard a word from Gansett."

"We're all fine. Janey's wedding was great, and you'll never believe it, but Mac's wife had their baby right in the middle of the storm. Hailey McCarthy."

"Wow, I'm sorry I missed all the excitement."

"We missed you, too."

"How does Laura seem? I've been worried about her lately. She hasn't been acting like a happy newlywed."

"I've only seen her at the wedding and in passing since then, but she seems fine to me."

"That's a relief. She loves being there so much. She loves any excuse to visit Gansett."

"It's good for all of us to get back here once in a while. So the reason I called . . . Do you remember a case in Providence involving a guy named Charles Grandchamp about fourteen years ago? Kidnapping and sexual assault of a minor?"

"Vaguely. The victim was his stepdaughter?"

"That's the one."

"What about it?"

"I've become involved with his stepdaughter, Stephanie Logan."

"Is that right? How old is she now?"

"She's twenty-eight and working for my parents at the marina restaurant."

"Doesn't that beat all?"

"Uncle Frank, she swears to God that Grandchamp never touched her with anything other than love and affection. Her mother used to beat the hell out of her, and the night she was supposedly kidnapped, Grandchamp walked in on her mother beating her and got her out of there."

"Wait a minute. As I recall, she testified—"

"And the prosecutor twisted everything she said to make Grandchamp look bad. The guy never touched her, and he's been in prison for fourteen years."

"I'm looking up who the presiding judge was in that case." He paused, and Grant could hear the clicking of computer keys. "Oh, Christ, it was Dugan."

"What about him?"

"We've had issues with a couple of his cases. He died about five years ago after a long battle with Alzheimer's."

The implication was left unspoken, but Grant heard it loud and clear. "I've hired Dan Torrington to look into it."

Frank let out a low whistle. "Heavy hitter."

"This whole thing is so wrong, Uncle Frank. Tell me there's something we can do."

"I'd like to hear the story from her point of view."

"She goes to the mainland every Friday for visiting day at the prison. I could go with her and bring her to see you afterward."

"That'd be great. I'll make dinner reservations on Federal Hill."

He expected nothing less than a five-star restaurant from his uncle. "Thank you so much. I really appreciate this."

"You know I can't make any promises, Grant."

"I understand, and she will, too."

"What's she like?"

"Brave and tough on the outside, but inside . . . The battle has taken a toll."

"I can imagine. I'll look forward to seeing you Friday."

"Me, too."

"Give my love to your parents and tell my wayward daughter to give her pop a call one of these days."

"Will do. See you soon." Grant ended the call and returned to Stephanie's room. She was facedown, asleep in bed with just a shoulder peeking out from under the sheet. As he studied her face, soft with sleep, Grant's heart beat a little faster.

He couldn't remember a time when he'd been more conflicted. Even when he'd known Abby was growing tired of their life in LA and pondering a move home, Grant hadn't felt this gut-deep conflict. His path had always been clear—career first, everything else second. That so-called clarity had cost him his relationship with Abby, and he now realized that as much as he'd loved her, he hadn't been "in love" with her. Not like he was with Stephanie.

"Oh boy," he whispered, the realization practically knocking him off his feet. He loved her. He was *in* love with her. Everything about this was different from what he'd had before, but one important thing was the same—

the career he wanted so badly required he work in a city three thousand miles from her. She'd never leave Rhode Island as long as her stepfather was incarcerated, so it wasn't like she could go with him the way Abby had.

So here he was again in roughly the same boat he'd been in with Abby, except this time the stakes were so much higher.

He sat on the edge of the small bed and bent to press his cheek to her exposed shoulder. The feel of her skin against his somehow calmed him, which was ironic, since he was rarely "calm" around her. He was either aroused or infuriated—often both at the same time. The thought made him smile as he pressed kisses to her shoulder, the curve of her neck and finally the delicate shell of her ear.

"Mmm," she said as she came to and found him hovering over her.

Their eyes met and held.

"What's wrong?" she asked, her voice sleepy-sexy.

"Nothing at all."

She raised her arms to bring him back into bed. Her nipples pebbled against his chest, her skin was silky smooth beneath his hands. Even though he wanted her again—he always wanted her—he did nothing more than hold her tight against him. Her lips moving on his neck were soft and persuasive. The hands that skimmed lightly over his back made him shiver with desire. And the contentment that stole over him, the clicking of two halves becoming a whole, made him sigh with happiness.

Somehow, they'd make this work. The alternative was no longer an option.

Grant convinced her to walk the short distance to his parents' home at the top of the hill.

"My legs are like rubber," she said with an accusatory glare for him when they were halfway up the steep hill. "We can't keep having this much sex. It's not healthy."

He laughed at her, which earned him an elbow to the ribs. "It's *very* healthy." Squeezing one of her ass cheeks for emphasis, he added, "And besides, you can't cut me off now. I'm addicted."

Wondering if he had any idea how adorable he could be, she grabbed his hand off her butt and held it tightly as they walked.

"I got a text from Luke. He has to have surgery on his ankle to repair a torn ligament. He and Syd are going to stay on the mainland since because they scheduled the surgery for this week."

"He must be relieved to know why it's not healing properly anyway."

"I'm sure. So my uncle Frank called while you were sleeping."

Stephanie stopped short and turned to face him. "And?" She could barely breathe as she awaited his reply.

"He wants to meet you and hear your story. I told him I'd go with you Friday and bring you to see him."

"Oh."

Grant tipped his head, seemingly trying to get a read on what she was thinking. "It's okay if I go with you, isn't it?"

She looked past him to his parents' house on the hill and started to walk again. "Um, sure. I guess."

Grabbing her arm, he stopped her. "What? Talk to me."

"Look at that up there." She gestured to the sprawling white home with the big deck and the million-dollar view of the Salt Pond.

"What about it?"

"That's where you come from. You're bringing me

home to your family tonight in that big, beautiful home where all your memories are kept safe from harm. When I take you to meet my family, you'll be patted down, sent through metal detectors and forced to endure the noise and the smells and the utter chaos of visiting day at a maximum-security prison."

"Do you think I care about that?"

"I care." She looked up at the house on the hill. "I don't have that. I've never had anything close to that."

"Someday you will. You'll have a home and a family of your own, and you'll create new memories—happy memories."

She wanted so badly to believe that was possible, but at the end of the day, she was a realist. Life didn't work that way for her. She didn't get happy endings and happily-ever-afters. They were reserved for other people.

Grant put his arm around her and drew her in close to him.

Surrounded by his familiar scent, she acquiesced to the comfort he provided and slipped an arm around his waist. "Thanks for calling your uncle for me."

He answered with a kiss to the top of her head and escorted her the rest of the way up the hill with his arm still around her.

Big Mac and Linda greeted them both with hugs. Stephanie had been to dinner there before, but never as their son's guest. Her palms were suddenly damp, and butterflies stormed around in her belly. The McCarthys had never been anything but nice and welcoming to her, but would they really condone their son's relationship with her once they knew the sordid story of her life? Linda had said earlier that she approved, but would she still approve when she found out Stephanie's stepfather was in prison?

"What's wrong?" Grant asked, his lips close to her ear.

"Sudden bout of nerves."

"Nothing to be nervous about. It's just dinner."

"I know." How could he understand when she didn't get it herself? She had no reason to feel inferior to these people, but she did anyway.

Over cocktails and appetizers, Linda was full of gossip, as always. They talked about the storm, the baby and Luke's pending surgery. "The town hired a new lighthouse keeper—a single gal from Maine."

"She's going to live out there all by herself?" Grant asked.

"That's what I hear. And Laura is going to stay on to manage the Sand & Surf."

Grant seemed astounded by that news. "What does Justin think of that?"

"Well," Linda said, glancing at Big Mac, "apparently that's already over."

"*What?* They just got married in May!"

"From what Laura says," Big Mac interjected, "her 'husband' decided to keep dating after they were married."

"Oh, no," Grant said. "Poor Laura."

"No kidding," Linda said. "She's been through a terrible ordeal, so we think it's wonderful that she'll be moving out here for the time being. She's always loved it here, and the Sand & Surf needs someone to love it and nurse it back to life. It'll be good for her to have a big project to throw herself into."

"I heard she's talked to Sydney Donovan about redecorating the public rooms," Big Mac added.

Linda clapped her hands in approval. "Oh, that's perfect! I love it."

"Wouldn't it be better for your hotel if the Surf stays closed?" Stephanie asked.

"Not at all," Linda said. "There're never enough rooms to accommodate everyone who wants to be here during the season. Losing the Surf the last couple of years has been a blow to the island's economy."

"I see," Stephanie said.

"In fact," Linda said with a scheming look in her eyes, "you should talk to Laura about her plans for the restaurant. Unlike McCarthy's, they used to be open year-round. She'll probably be in the market for someone to manage it. If you wanted to stick around Gansett, that is . . ."

Stephanie glanced at Grant.

"Sounds like a great opportunity," he said. "You should look into it."

"I, uh, it's nice of you to think of me, but I need to get back to Providence when the season is over."

"Tell them why, Steph," Grant said with an encouraging smile. "If you want to."

Linda looked at Stephanie, her eyes filled with concern. "What is it, honey?"

Right in front of his parents, Grant reached for her hand and linked their fingers. "It's okay."

She stared at their joined hands for a long moment before she returned her attention to his parents and told them an abridged version of her story. By the time she was done, Linda was holding her other hand, and Big Mac was shaking his head with disbelief across the dinner table.

"What can we do?" Linda glanced at her husband, who nodded in agreement. "Tell us how we can help."

"I've hired Dan Torrington, and I talked to Uncle Frank earlier," Grant said. "We're having dinner with him Friday night. Since we won't make it back to the island until sometime on Saturday, if you can cover the restaurant for Stephanie, that would help."

"Of course," Linda said with a smile. "I'd be happy to. I still remember how to make a doughnut."

"If there's anything else we can do for you, honey," Big Mac said to Stephanie, "anything at all, don't hesitate to ask."

The lump of emotion that settled in her throat made it impossible for her to speak. When Grant slipped his arm around her, she dropped her head to his shoulder.

"I've never known people like you," she was finally able to say. "The way you open your home and your hearts to perfect strangers—"

"You're certainly not a stranger," Linda said. "You're our friend now, and Grant's . . ." When he refused to fill in the blank for her, Linda said, "Well, at the very least, you're Grant's friend, too."

"Yes," Grant said, sounding amused by his mother's attempt to get him to define their relationship. He brushed a kiss over the top of Stephanie's head. "At the very least, you're my friend."

"Thank you," Stephanie said. "It means the world to me that you want to help."

"We mean it," Big Mac said. "If there's anything we can do, I hope you'll ask."

"I appreciate that."

"I think we've got it covered for now," Grant said. "Just keep your fingers crossed that it works."

"Fingers and toes," Linda said as she served up hot apple pie for dessert. "Did you hear the big news in town today?"

Stephanie was relieved that they'd moved past her troubles and back to island gossip.

"What news?" Grant asked as he shoveled pie into his face.

Stephanie filed away the fact that he seemed to love it. Wait until he got a taste of hers.

"Apparently, Cal Maitland's mother is bad off after the stroke. He tendered his resignation to the clinic board today. As one of the directors, Dad got the word after lunch. The board met this afternoon and offered the job to David Lawrence, and he accepted."

Grant seemed to have lost interest in his half-eaten pie. He put down his fork and wiped his mouth with a napkin. "So what does that mean for Abby?"

The moment the words were out of his mouth, Stephanie's stomach began to ache. Of course she would be his first thought.

"I can't imagine what she'll do," Linda said. "Her store is doing so well."

"Huh," Grant said, seeming lost in thought.

Stephanie wondered if he was considering that Cal's absence would create an opportunity for him to pick up where he'd left off with Abby. At that thought, her heart began to ache, too.

"More pie?" Linda asked her son.

"No, thanks. I'm full."

"Stephanie?"

"No, thank you. It was all very good." She couldn't eat another bite because she feared she might be sick.

A full moon hung over the Salt Pond as they walked back to the marina. Since Stephanie had her arms crossed, he couldn't reach for her hand the way he wanted to.

When he tried to put an arm around her, she stepped out of his embrace.

"All right," he finally said, "what's wrong?"

"What? Nothing's wrong."

With a hand to her shoulder, he stopped her and forced her to meet his gaze. The closed off, shuttered look in her eyes sent a jolt of fear through him. "I'm sorry I cornered you into telling my parents about Charlie—"

"It's not that. I'm glad they know."

"Ah, well, at least I've gotten you to admit it's *something*. Come on, Steph. Just tell me."

She continued on down the hill. "I don't want to talk about it."

Grant threw his hands up in frustration and trotted after her. "*I* want to talk about it."

"So that means we have to?"

"Yes, that's exactly what it means."

"You're a little too used to getting your own way all the time."

"Yeah, right. That's the story of my life. I suppose the years of nonstop rejection from just about everyone in the film business is a sign that I get my way all the time. Or of course the fact that I supposedly write for a living and haven't written a goddamned word in more than a year is another sign. That's exactly what I want."

"Don't forget the girlfriend you managed to lose but still want."

"Ah, so that's what this is about."

"She's free and clear now. Cal's not coming back. There's the opening you've been waiting for. Go get her."

Grant was so stunned by her sharp words that he had no idea how to respond. "Is *that* what you think I want?"

"It's what you wanted just a few short days ago," she reminded him.

She was moving so fast down the hill, he had to jog to catch up to her. When he did, he took her by the shoulder again. He hated that after all the time they'd spent together, the closeness they'd shared, she still flinched as the unexpected hand landed on her shoulder. "Stop, will you?" Softening his tone, Grant said, "Please, just stop."

As a family walked by them, ice cream cones in hand, the adults cast a curious glance their way before continuing on.

"You're making a scene," Stephanie said, shrugging off his hand.

"You want me to make a scene?"

"No," she said through gritted teeth. "What I want is for you to admit the truth—that your first thought upon hearing Cal isn't coming back to the island was how it would affect Abby."

"Of course that was my first thought! She's his fiancée—and my friend. One of my oldest friends. I want her to be happy!"

"Good! Then go make her happy, and leave me alone."

"Oh, my God, you're driving me crazy." He took her hand and dragged her off to a dark corner behind Moby Dick's restaurant. Mindful of the abuse she'd once withstood at the hands of her mother, he kept his grip light enough that she could've escaped if she really wanted to.

She resisted him the entire way. "*Let me go*, you Neanderthal."

"Not until you listen to me."

"I've heard everything I need to hear."

"No, you haven't." When he was certain they were out of the sight of prying eyes, he wrapped his arms around her.

Taking a handful of her hair, he tugged gently, forcing her to meet his gaze. "Are you listening?"

She looked away. "No."

Damn, she was cute when she was being mulish. Tipping his head, he brought his mouth down hard on hers. When she tried to register her protest, he sent his tongue in search of hers, stroking and caressing until he felt her fingers in his hair and the answering brush of her tongue against his. Now *that* was more like it.

He must've kissed her for ten minutes before he softened his lips and raised his head to find her eyes. "Are you listening now?"

The brat shook her head and dragged him down for more kisses.

When he had no choice but to come up for air, he said, "Who have I spent most of the last three days in bed with? You or her?"

"I was convenient."

"That's not true."

"So I *wasn't* convenient?"

He wanted to shake her until her teeth rattled, but instead, he kissed her again. "That's not what this is about, and you know it."

Their kisses were nearly violent as he set out to show her exactly why he was with her and not with anyone else.

"I don't want Abby," he said against her lips. "For some strange reason that is far, *far* beyond me, I seem to want you."

"Gee, I'm flattered." The reply was exactly what he expected from her and a sign that her usual spark was returning.

"Just like I'm flattered that you seem to want me."

She pushed against his chest. "I don't want you."

Her words were in sharp contrast to the way she had molded her body to his to kiss him senseless. "Is that so?" He moved quickly to send his hand diving over her ass to the hem of her skirt and was sliding his fingers through her slick heat in two seconds flat. "The evidence seems to suggest otherwise."

She gasped and tilted her hips to encourage his questing fingers.

"Liar, liar, pants on fire." The rhyme took him right back to sparring with three brothers and a sister.

"Shut up and don't stop."

Laughing, Grant recaptured her mouth in another torrid kiss as he zeroed in on her clit, determined to make an even bigger liar out of her. "Are you *sure* you don't want me?"

"Very sure," she said, panting and clinging to him as he stroked her to a shuddering climax.

He held her up when her legs would've collapsed under her. "I'm glad we were able to settle that to your satisfaction."

"Shut *up*," she said as her teeth clamped down on his ear, which sent a surge of lust to his already hard-as-a-rock erection.

"I don't want her." His lips blazed a trail on her neck, making her tremble. "I want you. Only you."

He took the tightening of her arms around his neck as a sign that she'd heard him and believed him. At least he hoped so.

Chapter Twenty-Three

Laura zipped her duffel bag the next morning and took a long look around the cozy suite that would be her home for the foreseeable future. The "shabby chic" antique furniture bore no resemblance to the stylish, contemporary pieces she'd chosen for her home with Justin, but she already felt more at home here than she ever had there.

As if to ensure her return, she tucked her favorite pair of black sandals into the closet. "I'll be back," she said as she shut and locked the door to her suite. She'd called her aunt and uncle earlier to let them know she'd be leaving for a few days. They wished her a safe trip and invited her to dinner when she got back.

Dropping her bag in the lobby, she tiptoed toward Owen's closed door. Between her illness and his gig with Evan at the Tiki Bar last night, she hadn't seen him since the previous morning. She was about to slide the note she'd written for him under the door when it opened.

"Thought I heard you skulking about, Princess."

His dirty-blond hair was disheveled, his eyes were red with fatigue and his smile was breathtaking. Laura wondered if he had any idea how attractive he was. He seemed to go out of his way to look like he'd just fallen out of bed. Imagining him in bed made her face heat with embarrassment.

"I wasn't skulking."

He ran his fingers through his hair as if that might bring order to it and fixed his gaze on her duffel. "Going somewhere?"

"To the mainland for a couple of days to take care of some things." Confirming her pregnancy, returning the unused wedding gifts, emptying the apartment she'd lovingly furnished, filing for divorce, breaking the news of her failed marriage to her beloved father and bringing what she could fit in her car back to the island. The usual stuff a woman had to take care of a few months after she married the so-called love of her life.

Forcing herself to focus on the here and now rather than the nightmare ahead, she tightened her grip on the folded sheet of paper. "I, ah, I was going to leave you a note."

Holding out his hand, he said, "Let me see."

Suddenly mortified by the words she'd settled on, she tucked it under her arm. "Doesn't matter now."

Before she could anticipate his next move, he had the note in his hand and was moving past her into the lobby to read it.

"That was sneaky."

Laughing, he said, "I'm the oldest of seven. I had to be quick to survive."

As he read the note she'd slaved over—trying for the proper level of appreciation without descending into the maudlin—Laura looked for something to do with her hands. She ended up folding and unfolding them.

"That's very nice," he said, stashing the note in the back pocket of his faded jeans, which were still unbuttoned.

"And very sweet. I'm glad I met you, too, Princess, and it was my pleasure to provide a shoulder for you to lean on."

She could see the button to his jeans poking at the gray T-shirt he wore over them, not that she was looking or anything.

"But you don't have to thank me. You're doing us a huge favor by taking on this place. My grandparents are happy, and that makes me happy."

For some reason, it pleased her to have played a part in making him happy. She'd have to chew on that realization when she was alone. "About yesterday . . . I just wanted to say, you know, thanks for the tea." Damn, was it hot in here or what? "And everything else. It was nice of you." She couldn't bear to think about him watching her worship the porcelain god. The thought of it made her ill all over again.

"How're you feeling today?"

"More of the same," she said with a wry grin. "Happens around the same time every day."

He winced. "Such a drag."

Shrugging, she said, "I hear it only lasts about three months."

"Oh, God, that's awful!"

The face he made had her giggling. He often reminded her of an overgrown kid.

Scooping up her duffel bag, he settled the strap on his shoulder. "You shouldn't be carrying this heavy thing in your condition." He held the door and gestured her out ahead of him.

"I'm pregnant, not feeble, and it's not that heavy. I left most of my stuff here."

"Good," he said with the irrepressible grin that was so *him*. "That means you'll be back before I have time to miss you."

As she took the stairs to the sidewalk for the short walk to the ferry, Laura was caught completely off guard by his casually uttered comment. What did that mean? He was going to *miss* her?

"You heard me right, Princess. I'll miss having you around to keep me company."

Stunned by his confession, Laura tried desperately to think of something witty she could say. "You've got Evan, Mac and Grant to entertain you."

"They're so *ugly* compared to you," he said with a pout that made her laugh again.

"I hate to break it to you, pal, but my cousins are *not* ugly. Trust me on that. Janey and I used to make fun of the daily parade of girls who'd show up at the White House looking for one or the other—or in some cases, all four of them. It was obscene."

"That may be true, but in my eyes, they're *far* uglier than you."

"Thank you. I think."

They laughed and joked all the way to the ferry landing, where he seemed to reluctantly hand over the duffel. "Take care of yourself over there on the mainland," he said, attempting a serious expression that failed miserably since he didn't have a serious bone in his body. He tucked a lock of hair behind her ear and cuffed her chin playfully. "Don't let the bad stuff get you down."

She appreciated his insight and his concern. "I'll try not to. See you in a week or so."

He surprised her when he bent to press a tender kiss to her cheek. "I'll be here."

"Good," she said, leaving him with a smile as she boarded the ferry. It was nice to know she had a friend waiting for her on the island she was planning to call home for the next little while.

Francine tossed and turned all night. Ned knew this because he'd been right there beside her. He wanted to dance a jig and shout the news from the rooftops. They'd finally done it—the horizontal bop, the *deed*—or whatever they called it these days, and it had been every bit as phenomenal as he'd remembered from the last time they were together.

Even though Ned's heart was singing a new song on this glorious day, he knew his beloved was troubled by the news she had to bring to her eldest daughter this morning.

Ned held her hand all the way to Maddie's home on Sweet Meadow Farm Road. "Everything's gonna be all right, doll," he said for the hundredth time since they woke up together and shared a pot of coffee and eggs that she'd barely touched.

"It's so unfair to drop this on her a few days after she had the baby."

"That may be true, but it's no fault of yers that he showed up here when he did. Ya had no control over that, and Maddie will know that." He squeezed her hand. "I'll be right there with ya, okay?"

She nodded and held his hand between both of hers. "I appreciate you coming with me."

"Of course I'm coming with ya. We're a team now, and don'cha forget it."

"I won't," she said, offering him a fleeting smile.

Ned wanted this encounter between Maddie and her father over with so Bobby could go back under the rock he'd crawled out from under and leave them all in peace. Ned had kept up a brave façade and pretended to eat

Francine's share of their breakfast, but he'd been a nervous wreck the whole time.

He had this vision of Mac flatly refusing to allow his wife to see her wayward father—not that Ned would blame the boy for not wanting his wife upset right after giving birth. But then where would they be? Bobby could hang up the divorce forever if he wanted to, and there wasn't much they could do about it without a protracted battle. He wanted to be married to Francine, and he wanted to help her and her girls through this crisis. That was all Ned cared about at the moment.

They arrived at Mac and Maddie's home and navigated the stairs to the deck, hand in hand.

"Take a deep breath, doll," Ned said when they were on the deck. "Remember, none of this is yer fault."

She looked up at him with her heart in her eyes. "I could've chosen a better father for them."

The significance of her words wasn't lost on him. "I'll be a damned good stepfather to them. I promise ya that."

"I know you will. Come on. Let's get this over with."

They visited with the new parents, fussed over the baby and played with Thomas for more than an hour. Fortunately, Mac and Maddie didn't seem to notice the tension that Ned and Francine had brought with them.

"David was just here to check on Hailey, and he says she's doing great."

"That's a huge relief," Francine said.

"It's nice to see you two kids together again," Maddie said as she burped Hailey.

Ned exchanged glances with Francine.

"Actually," Francine said, "we're hoping to be married before too much longer."

Ned wasn't sure his heart was strong enough for the

excitement that surged through him as she said those words.

"Oh my God!" Maddie cried. "Mac, come here! Quick!"

He rushed in from the kitchen, a towel tossed over his shoulder and his eyes wide with panic. "What's wrong?"

"Absolutely nothing! Mom and Ned are getting married!"

"Hey, that's great, you guys. Congratulations!"

"There's just one thing . . ." Francine said.

"What, Mom?"

"Well, it seems that I'm, um . . . God, how do I say this?"

Ned reached for her hand. "Spit it out, doll. Get it over with."

Francine met her daughter's gaze. "Your father and I are still married."

"Wait . . . How can that be? It's been more than thirty years since he left."

"Neither of us ever filed for divorce."

Seeming stunned, Maddie stared at her mother.

"Tell 'em the rest, doll."

"What, Mom?" Maddie's gaze darted nervously to Mac, who came to sit next to her on the sofa. "What is it?"

"I called his sister, Marion, asking if she could help me get in touch with him so we could take care of the divorce. Yesterday, he um . . . He . . ."

"He's here," Ned said. "He's on the island, and he wants to see you."

"Absolutely not!" Mac's face flushed with color. "She just had a baby! The last thing she needs is a confrontation with that son of a bitch."

"I really don't want to see him," Maddie said, reaching for Mac's hand.

"You don't have to, honey," Mac said. "Of course you don't."

Francine swiped at a tear that rolled down her cheek. "I'm so sorry to have to ask you this . . . I hope you know I never would, not in a million years, but he, um . . ."

Maddie's eyes widened with disbelief. "Oh my God. Is he demanding to see me before he'll give you the divorce?"

"Yes," Francine said, humiliation coming from her in waves that infuriated Ned.

Maddie handed the baby to her husband and stood slowly and carefully. "Then let's go."

"Maddie, wait a minute." Mac stood with the baby propped on his shoulder. With her diaper changed and her belly full, Hailey slept blissfully.

Thomas watched them from the floor, where he was playing with his cars.

"You don't have to do this, babe," Mac said.

"Yes, I do. If it'll free us from the past, then I'll give him a minute of my life and then get on with it." She flashed them a winning smile that anyone who knew her well would recognize as forced. "Besides, I want to dance at my mother's wedding."

Francine stood to face her daughter. "I'm so sorry, honey." Tears made her eyes bright and shiny.

Ned's heart broke for them as they embraced. "I'll take you there and bring you right back," he said.

"That'd be great, Ned. Thank you."

"I should be there with you," Mac said, concern etched into his face.

Maddie went to him and gave him a kiss. "Stay here with my babies, and I'll be right back, okay?"

"If you're sure."

She nodded and kissed him again before turning to her mother and Ned. "Let's go."

They rode the short distance to the Beachcomber in silence.

Ned had never experienced such tension. He couldn't imagine how Maddie and Francine must be feeling.

Inside the hotel, they were about to ask for Bobby at the front desk when Ned spotted him having breakfast on the deck. He pointed him out, and Maddie made a beeline across the crowded lobby to where her father sat enjoying his eggs sunny-side up.

Ned and Francine were right behind her.

"You're Bobby Chester?" Maddie said.

Bobby looked up with a smarmy smile that Ned wanted to smack off his face. "Who wants to know?"

"Your daughter. The one you left decades ago? The one who sat in the window for weeks after you left watching every ferry, hoping you might come back? Remember me?"

Maddie made no effort to keep her voice down, so she soon had the attention of everyone on the deck. Everything stopped, and silence descended upon them.

"You sure are a pretty thing," Bobby said.

"That's it? Nearly thirty years and that's all you've got to say to me?"

"I understand you have kids."

"Yes, I do. Not that you'll ever meet them." Her voice broke ever so slightly, but Ned heard it. Apparently, Francine did, too, because she stepped forward to place a hand on her daughter's shoulder.

"Now that you've seen Maddie," Francine said, "I assume I'll hear from your attorney within the week?"

Bobby made them wait a good long time before he nodded ever so slightly.

"Let's go, honey." Francine took Maddie by the arm. "There's nothing for us here."

Maddie managed to hold it together until she got home. At the first sight of the big, beautiful house she shared with Mac and their children, tears burned her eyes.

"You don't have to come in," she said to her mom and Ned, struggling to maintain her composure for their sakes. "I'm okay. I promise."

Her mother turned in her seat and took Maddie's hand. "Thank you so much. I'm so sorry you had to do that."

"Whatever it takes to be rid of him once and for all."

"Let's hope we're rid of him now."

Even as her mother said the words, a niggle of doubt settled in Maddie's belly. "Try not to worry. I'll see you tomorrow, okay?"

"I'll be here to help in the morning," Francine said.

Maddie patted Ned on the shoulder. "Thanks for the ride, Ned."

"Any time, honey."

She watched them drive off before she trudged up the stairs.

Mac met her at the sliding door.

She stepped into his arms and broke down.

"Aww, baby." He ran a hand over her hair. "I knew you shouldn't have seen him. Was it awful?"

Shaking her head, she held on tight to him.

"Then what happened?"

Maddie drew back from him and wiped the dampness from her face. "Ned pointed him out to me. He was sitting on the deck of the Beachcomber having breakfast. I walked over to his table, and he looked up at me. Except he never got past my chest. Only when I told him who I was did he look at my face."

"Son of a bitch," Mac muttered as a furious expression settled on his face.

"He's nothing to me. I'm nothing to him. So why does it matter so much that he looked at me the same way every other lecherous jerk in the world has looked at me for most of my life?"

"Because once upon a time, a long, long time ago, he was your daddy, and the little girl you used to be was hoping he'd recognize you."

How did he know? How did he always know? "Yes." His understanding somehow made it hurt a little less. Maddie sighed and relaxed into his embrace. "What've you done with our children?"

"Hailey is napping in her bassinet, and I asked Thomas to play in his room for a little while."

"And he just did that?"

"I might've bribed him with ice cream for lunch if he did."

Maddie snorted out a laugh and reached up to frame her husband's face. "Thank you."

"For what, babe?"

"For being the best daddy my children ever could've hoped to have."

He kissed her and then hugged her tight against him. "My pleasure, love."

Chapter Twenty-Four

"Why are you taking so much for one night?" Stephanie asked Grant as they prepared to leave for the mainland on Friday.

Grant closed his eyes and counted to ten before he turned to face her. "Because I'm not coming back with you. At least not right away. I have to go to LA for a couple of days."

"Oh." He watched surprise and disappointment dance across her expressive face before she shut it all down with the blank thing she did so well. "When did this happen?"

"Tuesday. I was offered a great opportunity to work with a hot new director. I need to be there for the preproduction meeting, but I'll be back right after."

"Were you going to tell me?"

"Of course I was."

"When?"

"You've had so much on your mind with Dan flying in next week, the meeting with my uncle, taking me to meet Charlie. There wasn't a good time to drop this on top of everything else."

She released a brittle-sounding laugh. "There wasn't a good time."

"Well, there wasn't."

"Funny that there was plenty of time for sex, sex and more sex. But apparently no time to talk about a major offer or the next step in your career or where we go from here."

"See? That's it right there. That's why I didn't mention it. I don't *know* where we go from here. I don't have any of the answers you need and deserve. You're going back to Providence, where you have to be so you can be near Charlie. I don't know if you've noticed, but at the moment, I'm homeless and jobless and rootless. I have no idea where I belong. Is it here where I was raised? Is it in LA where my business is? Is it in Providence where you are? I don't know. I wish I did. Until I figure that out, I didn't think it was fair to start a big conversation with you about what's next for us."

"You're right," she said. "You're absolutely right. Let's get going so we don't miss the boat."

Bewildered by her easy—and unusual—capitulation, Grant followed her out of the house. He'd arranged for Lisa from the vet clinic to take care of Janey's pets until she and Joe got back on Sunday. Earlier, he'd stripped and changed the bed, washed the sheets and towels and replaced the food and wine they'd used during the storm.

The phrase "the honeymoon's over" ran through his mind as he got into Stephanie's beat-up old car for the short ride to the ferry landing. Since they were taking the car, they checked in an hour early and sat in silence while they waited to drive the car onto the three-thirty boat.

"Can we talk about this, please?" he asked as the silence began to grate on his nerves.

"What's there to talk about? We had a good time, and you helped me—and Charlie—tremendously by asking Dan to get involved and by setting up the meeting with your uncle. You did exactly what you said you would do. You certainly don't owe me anything else."

Grant couldn't believe that he was suddenly on the verge of blowing yet another relationship—and this one so much more significant than the last one. After a week with Stephanie, he already had more than he'd had with Abby after ten years. He couldn't screw it up. Again.

Turning in his seat so he could see her, he said, "This isn't about who owes what to whom. It's about me and you and something between us that seems to work. Maybe it shouldn't work, but it does. You can't deny that." He wanted to tell her he loved her, that he was *in* love with her, but didn't think she'd believe him if he told her now.

"It does work," she said softly, "here on this lovely little island in the middle of a storm that trapped us together for days on end. It worked very well here. I'm not as convinced it'll work over there." She gestured to the mainland off in the distance.

He reached out to caress her cheek. "I'd like to find out. Wouldn't you?"

"Everything is so uncertain right now. After Columbus Day, I'm also jobless and homeless and rootless. I've got a lot to figure out between now and then. Let's play it by ear and see what happens. Can we do that?"

"Sure," he said, relieved that she hadn't said no.

He could work with maybe.

Ten hours later, Grant used a key card in the hotel room door and held it so Stephanie could go in ahead of him.

"Tell me again what we're doing here," she said, dropping onto the sofa by a window that overlooked downtown Providence.

"Ahh, the usual stuff people do in hotel rooms. You know, some sleeping, maybe some bathing, perhaps some breakfast à la room service. If you're really nice to me,

I might even toss in some nookie for good measure." He sat next to her and stretched out his long legs.

Despite being totally drained after the grueling evening, she was still aware of him. Wanting him, it seemed, had become a constant state of being.

He reached for her hand and brought it to his lips. "I know what you need."

"What's that?"

"Coming right up." He stood and strode toward the bathroom. "Stay there and don't look."

Since she was too tired to do anything else, she relaxed into the sofa and took in the elegant room in a hotel she'd wondered about her entire life. The Biltmore was a Providence landmark that she'd admired only from afar despite having lived in the same city all her life.

Leave it to Grant.

To say Charlie had been chilly toward him was putting it mildly. Her stepfather had been immediately suspicious of the Hollywood screenwriter who'd taken an interest in his case—and his stepdaughter. After he'd basically booted Grant from the visiting room, he'd lit into Stephanie, demanding to know what was really going on.

So she'd told him about meeting Grant on Gansett, about the bickering and the bonding and the storm and everything that'd happened in the last week. She'd left out the more personal details, but he'd gotten the picture. Somehow she'd managed to convince him that Grant genuinely wanted to help them and that they'd be crazy not to accept help from a lawyer of Daniel Torrington's caliber or whatever assistance Grant's uncle Frank might be willing to offer.

When he'd grudgingly agreed, Stephanie had left the prison feeling beat up, only to have to rally for dinner with Grant's charmingly delightful uncle. He'd reminded her of

Big Mac in so many ways, mostly in how he'd embraced his nephew's troubled friend, but he was far more urbane than his island-dwelling brother.

By anyone's standards, the evening had been a smashing success. They now had the top defense lawyer in the country handling Charlie's appeal, and a well-respected superior court judge willing to speak to a colleague about a possible miscarriage of justice. What she'd wanted for what seemed like forever was more within reach than it ever had been before. Why then did it feel like a thousand-pound boulder had landed on her chest?

The boulder had been sitting there since Grant told her he was going to LA. She had the worst feeling that if he went there, he wouldn't come back. His intentions were good. She had no doubt about that. But she was wise enough to know she couldn't possibly compete with the lure of Hollywood. The thought of never seeing him again filled her with overwhelming sadness.

He emerged from the bathroom wearing only the khakis he'd donned for dinner, and a smile directed at her. As always, the sight of his muscular chest made her go dumb in the head.

"Madame," he said with a bow. "Right this way."

Stephanie hesitated, wishing there was some way to protect her heart from the blow it was about to withstand. Since she couldn't resist him—especially this playful, sexy side of him—she got up and went to him.

"It's my duty to inform you that you have to be naked for this activity," he said with a serious expression.

She rolled her eyes. "Most activities with you seem to require nudity."

He flashed her a grin that melted any remaining resistance as he lifted her shirt over her head. "And that is bad how, exactly?"

"I never said it was bad." No, it was far too good, and that was the problem.

The second she wiggled out of her skirt and panties, Grant scooped her up, carried her into the bathroom and deposited her into a steaming bubble bath. He'd lit the candles around the tub, which gave the room a soft, dreamy glow.

Stephanie released a deep sigh as she sank into the fragrant water.

He knelt next to the tub. "How is it?"

"Amazing. Thank you." She risked a glance at him and found him watching her intently. "You didn't have to go to all this trouble, you know."

"What trouble?"

"The Biltmore and bubble baths and whatever else you have up your sleeve."

"What's wrong with the Biltmore?"

"Not a thing. It's just kind of . . . extravagant."

He ran a finger through the bubbles. "So?"

Exasperated, she flipped her hand and sent a spray of bubbles into his face.

Sputtering, he wiped the soap from his cheek. "You want to play that way?"

Before she knew what hit her, he was in the tub with her—pants and all—and the water was flowing over the sides.

"Grant! You'll start a flood!"

"I'll clean it up in a minute," he said, capturing her mouth for a deep, soulful kiss.

It'd been hours since he'd last kissed her, and Stephanie had missed the feel of his lips, the insistent stroke of his tongue, the unique flavor she'd recognize anywhere as his.

After having experienced such unbridled passion, how would she live without him for even a day?

"What's wrong?" he asked, shifting his attention from her mouth to her neck.

"Nothing. You'd better mop up the water before you get us kicked out of here."

"You're no fun tonight," he said with a long-suffering sigh as he raised himself out of the tub and got busy wiping up the puddles on the floor.

When he got close enough for her to reach, she ran her fingers through his hair.

He looked up at her and smiled.

"I'm sorry if it seems I don't appreciate what you're trying to do tonight, because I do."

"Then what's wrong? And don't say 'nothing,' because I know you better than that by now."

"This feels like our last night together."

His eyes widened with surprise. "I told you I'll be back."

"I know you did."

"You don't believe me?"

"I think you want to believe that, but you'll get busy with work, and one thing will lead to another, and you'll end up staying there." She forced herself to meet his gaze. "Isn't that what happened last time?"

"Yes, but everything is different now. When I said I'll be back, I meant it."

"You need to do whatever it takes to get your career back on track. I don't want you worried about me when you need to be focused on work."

"I will worry about you. Of course I will."

"That's very sweet of you, but it's very possible that this"—she moved a hand between them to indicate their relationship—"was intended to be a fling and nothing more."

His brows knitted with what appeared to be genuine concern. "Is that what it was to you?"

Stephanie wanted to lie. She wanted to tell him what he needed to hear so he'd be free to pursue his goals without the weight of her expectations holding him back. But as she studied the handsome face she loved so much, she couldn't do it. She couldn't lie to him. "No. It was more than that. A lot more."

"For me, too, honey, and when I tell you I'll be back, I *will* be back. I need you to believe me."

This time, she did lie. "Okay. I believe you."

He extended a hand to help her out of the tub and toweled her off with reverence. When he was finished, he wrapped the towel around her and tucked in the edges before he fought his way out of the soaked khakis. "Wearing pants into the tub might not have been the best idea I ever had."

Stephanie laughed at his battle with the heavy, wet pants. "Do ya think?"

Once he was free, he reached for her hand. "Let's go to bed."

She placed her hand in his, anticipating this one last night with him. Tomorrow was soon enough to figure out how she'd ever live without him.

Stephanie never did sleep that night. She was either making love with Grant or watching him sleep. As the first hint of dawn snuck through the blinds, her heart was heavy with dread. Of course she'd survive the way she always did, but this day would be a tough one. No way around that. She'd drop him at the airport and then head south to catch the ferry back to the island. She couldn't imagine spending an hour there without him, let alone days on end.

Drawing in a deep breath, she marshaled the fortitude it would take to hide her torment from him. He needed to seize this exciting new opportunity and take it all the way to a second Oscar. The last thing in the world she wanted to do, especially after all he'd done for her, was get in the way of that.

His hand moved slowly from her shoulder to her hip, blazing a trail of sensation, which was all it took to make her want him—again. He pressed against her from behind, his hands cupping her breasts and his lips firm against her neck.

Stephanie pressed her bottom into his erection, encouraging him as his fingers tweaked her nipples.

"Not like this," he said, urging her onto her back. "I want to see you." He settled between her legs and gazed down at her for a long, breathless moment before he kissed her softly and sweetly, as if he was trying to tell her everything he needed her to know with that one kiss.

She stroked his back and raised her hips, urging him to take what they both wanted.

He slid into her slowly and released a deep sigh when he was fully seated. For the longest time, he stayed perfectly still, throbbing deep inside her, connected to her in every possible way.

The tension built and grew and then exploded in a blast of heat and sensation that ripped through her like a tidal wave. As he picked up the pace, seeking his own release, Stephanie couldn't contain the tears that streamed down her face, giving away the torment she'd tried so hard to hide from him.

Slipping his hands under her, he grasped her ass as he

pounded into her, and sent her into a second less powerful but no less potent climax before he joined her with a cry of completion that echoed through the big room.

For a long time afterward, he rested on top of her. When he raised his head to meet her tearful gaze, he pressed one last, soft kiss to her lips. "I'll be back for you. I promise."

Stephanie nodded and drew him into a tight hug so he wouldn't see her pain.

On the short ride from the city to the airport, Grant experienced a rising sense of panic. He'd never felt this torn in his entire life. All he had to do to get his struggling career back on track was show up for a meeting in LA. Stephanie said she understood. She supported his career and knew this was important to him. But he suspected she didn't believe him when he said he'd be back.

"I'll be here for the meeting with Dan."

"Don't worry about it. I can handle it by myself. He's not the first lawyer I've dealt with."

"Still. I want to be there."

She shrugged. "If you can."

What am I supposed to do? The question nagged at him as they rode south in silence on Interstate 95. And then she was taking the airport exit and pulling up to the departures terminal. His bag landed with a thud on the curb, as if she was suddenly anxious to be rid of him.

Maybe she was. Maybe he'd read this all wrong. Last night, she'd referred to their relationship as a fling. While he'd gotten her to admit it had been more than that, maybe it hadn't been enough for her to change her plans to suit him, to adapt her life to make room for what they might have together.

It wouldn't be the first time he'd read something wrong. He was still grappling with his dilemma when she gave him a quick hug and a lingering kiss.

"Good luck out there. I hope it all works out for you."

"Thanks. Steph—"

"Don't. Please." She held up a hand. "Don't say something you think I need to hear. Just go. Do what you need to do. I'll see you when I see you." Going up on tiptoes, she kissed his cheek. "Travel safely."

Before he could summon the words he wanted to say to her or the reassurances he wanted to leave her with, she was back in her car and giving him a jaunty little wave as she pulled away from the curb.

Abby's voice echoed through his head, reminding him that he could write anywhere in the whole world. And the only place in the world he wanted to be was with Stephanie.

Suddenly, it wasn't all right that she was leaving without knowing how he felt. Why hadn't he told her when he'd had the chance? "Because you're still an idiot," he muttered. "*Steph! Wait!*" He chased after her car, but either she didn't hear him or she chose not to stop. He hoped it was the former.

Racing back to where he'd left his bag on the curb, he shouldered it and flagged down a cab.

"I need to get to Point Judith," he said when he was settled in the back seat.

The driver turned to him. "For real?"

Grant withdrew his wallet and tossed two one-hundred-dollar bills through the window that separated the front seat from the back. "Drive. Please. And quickly." Adrenaline had Grant's heart beating fast, his lungs straining for air and his hands damp with sweat. Realizing how close he'd come to once again doing the exact wrong thing had finally sobered him up.

"At least this time you figured it out before it was too late," he said, earning a wary glance in the mirror from his driver. At least he hoped it wasn't too late.

He had about an hour to formulate a plan. Withdrawing his cell phone from his pocket, he got to work.

Chapter Twenty-Five

With a loud blast of its horn, the two-thirty ferry to Gansett Island pulled out of Point Judith. Stephanie had expected it to be more crowded on the Saturday afternoon of Labor Day weekend, but she was relieved not to have to share her picnic table with anyone who might wonder why her eyes were red and swollen.

She pressed a cold paper-towel compress to her eyes, needing to get herself together before she was forced to confront Grant's family when she got back to the marina.

They were covering the docks in shifts, so it could be anyone from Mac to Evan to Big Mac waiting to greet her. Even Ned and Owen had taken turns so Grant could go with her to the mainland. They were good to each other that way, a family—and friends—anyone without such things would envy.

The thought of never seeing any of them again once she returned to Providence only drew more tears from eyes that should've been fresh out of them by now.

Determined to stop crying and get her head together, she withdrew her iPod and a notebook from her bag and began making a list of fourteen years of motions and copies of legal documents she needed to send to Dan Torrington as he prepared to file an emergency motion for a new trial.

"Is this seat taken?"

Absorbed in her music and her work, she shook her head. As a regular on the ferry, she was used to people invading her personal space even when it was obvious that she wasn't interested in company.

"What're you doing?"

Astounded by the rude question, she finally dragged her attention off the notebook and found Grant sitting across from her.

Stephanie's mouth fell open as she tugged the buds from her ears. "What're you doing here?"

"Funny thing happened when you dumped me at the curb and drove off leaving a cloud of dust behind you. And P.S., you drive like a maniac."

Frowning at his description of their parting and her driving, she said, "What funny thing happened?"

He leaned into the table, took the pen from her hand and linked their fingers. "I discovered I don't want to be without you. Not even for the three days I'd planned to be in LA."

Stephanie couldn't believe what she was hearing. "But . . . But what about the job? You need the job! You can't just blow off the meeting."

"Before I get into that, Uncle Frank called."

A shaft of tension traveled through her. "And?"

"Judge Seymour will hear new evidence in Charlie's case on October 31. He wants to hear your side of the story—the same story you told me and Uncle Frank."

She was so shocked by news she'd waited half a lifetime to hear, she felt like she'd been electrocuted. "How did that happen?" Her voice was barely more than a whisper.

"Uncle Frank told Judge Seymour that he'd recently

had the opportunity to speak with you and hear your story. Because he has a family connection to you, Uncle Frank can't hear the case himself."

"What 'family' connection does your uncle have to me?"

"We'll get to that in a minute. Anyway, he asked his colleague, Seymour, to look into it. Apparently, there've been several of Dugan's old cases that fall into the same questionable category as Charlie's. They're anxious to right any of the old wrongs that might've occurred when Dugan's illness was in the early stages."

Stephanie needed a minute to process it all. "I can't . . . I mean . . ." She took a deep breath and forced herself to meet his gaze. "Thank you. I'll never be able to properly thank you for this."

"You don't have to. All I did was make a couple of calls."

"You did a lot more than that, and you know it. But you didn't have to chase after me to tell me this. You could've called. You need to be at that meeting in LA! It's such a great opportunity."

"Yes, it is." A smile stretched across his face. "But here's the thing—I don't *want* to write that movie. I want to write *your* movie, the story that gave me the first buzz I've had in years. In the next few days, you'll get a call from my agent with an offer for the rights to your story. He'll make the same offer to Charlie. It'll be for a lot of money—the kind of money that'll set you both up for life. I've discovered I have a taste for producing my own stories rather than waiting for someone to take a chance on me. I'm taking a chance on you and your story, and I'm feeling the buzz *big-time*, baby."

He looked so high on life that if she didn't know him so well, she'd think he'd been smoking something illegal. And even though her heart beat a wild staccato, she eyed him warily. "And you have that kind of money?"

Raising an eyebrow into a positively rakish expression, he said, "Do you have any idea what houses in Malibu are going for these days?"

Stephanie shook her head. "I know what you're doing."

Amusement danced in his gorgeous eyes, which nearly caused her to lose her train of thought. "And what's that?"

"You're trying to make sure I'll be okay without you."

His smile faded. "Wow, I really buried the lead here, didn't I?"

"What the heck does that mean?"

He reached for her other hand and held both of them tightly. "I love you. I'm *in* love with you. I want to marry you and live with you and write our movie and maybe have a couple of kids together—with lots of drugs in a hospital. I want everything with you, Stephanie." He brought her hands to his lips. "The only question, my love, is do you want everything with me?"

She stared at him for the longest time as his words worked their way through the fog in her brain to settle in her heart. "This wasn't supposed to happen," she said, flabbergasted by the turn of events.

His brows knitted with confusion. "What wasn't supposed to happen?"

Damn if her eyes weren't full of tears—again! "You, me, the happy ending. That only happens to other people. Not to me."

Grant released her hands, got up and came around to her side of the table. When he had her arranged on his lap the way he wanted her, he kissed the tears off her face. "You know what the best part about being a writer is?"

She shook her head.

"You get to finesse the ending any way you want, and I say this story ends with a happily ever after. Are you with me on that?"

"Yes," she said, hugging him fiercely. "Yes, I'm with you."

"Good." He held her just as tightly. "And was there something else you wanted to tell me?"

Smiling through her tears, she met his gaze. "I love you, too, and yes, of course I want everything with you. And then some."

"I couldn't have written it any better myself."

Thank you for reading *Falling for Love*!
I hope you enjoyed it.

Watch for the next book in the Gansett Island series,

HOPING FOR LOVE

Available as a Zebra mass market in June 2019.

Keeping reading for a special look!

This moment had been a long time coming. Since fourth grade, if Grace was being truthful. That was how long she'd been madly, passionately, insanely in lust—at the very least—with Trey Parsons. Of course, she couldn't have chosen to give her heart to a mere mortal. No, she'd set her sights on a god among men, a four-sport athlete she'd adored from afar all through middle and high school. While he'd been the star of field and court, she'd been known as "The Whale," and not because of her swimming skills.

Now, ten years and a hundred and thirty pounds later, she was getting busy with her own personal god—that was, if she didn't wet the bed first. Her bladder was going to explode any second now, which, from what she'd heard about "the act," was not the part of her that was supposed to explode.

They were in the V-berth of his father's fancy boat, tied up at McCarthy's Gansett Island Marina for the night—the night she *would* part with her virginity if it was the last thing she ever did. And while she wished she could focus on the divine feeling of his lips and tongue on her nipple, a more pressing need had her full attention.

She pushed on his shoulder. "Trey."

He raised his head. "What?"

"I need to get up."

Taking her hand, he flashed a sexy grin and tried to press her palm against his pulsating erection. "I'm already up, babe."

Grace pulled her hand back. "Not you. *Me*. I have to pee."

Frustrated, he flopped on the bed. "Hurry up already."

She reached for his discarded T-shirt and started to put it on.

"What're you getting dressed for? Just go." He took the shirt from her. "You don't need this."

The Grace Ryan who'd never been naked in front of another living soul clung to the shirt. But the Grace who was more than ready for a whole new life let him take it from her.

He caressed her face. "Go on. It's okay."

The tender—and unexpected—gesture gave her the courage she needed to slide off the bunk and duck into the tiny head without obsessing too much about what her backside might look like to him. Wondering if he'd hear her peeing through the wall almost made it impossible for her to go.

Oh, I'm so not cut out for this, Old Grace thought. *Yes, you are*, New Grace insisted. *You have as much right to a hot night with a hot guy as any other girl. You've certainly earned it.*

That much was true. With her arms crossed over her abundant breasts—the one part of her that hadn't benefitted from the weight loss—she took care of business and stood just as the phone Trey had left on the counter chimed with a text message.

Honestly, she didn't intend to look at it, but he was Trey Parsons after all, the stud king of Mystic, Connecticut, and she didn't trust him as far as she could spit him. So she looked.

From "Quigs," also known as Tom Quigley, Trey's best friend since grade school:

> Did u nail the whale yet? Remember $500 in it for ya if u bring back proof of the cherry bomb.

Grace was frozen with shock and horror. It had all been a big joke! Weeks of dates and flowers and "romance" had all been a big, *fat* joke! And to think she'd almost given him her virginity so he could use it like a trophy to impress his asshole friends! Red-hot rage the likes of which she'd never before experienced surged through her.

"What the hell are you doing in there?" Trey called, no doubt impatient to seal the deal so he could collect his prize money.

Grace wished she could storm out there and tell him off, but the fact that she was naked made it hard for her to think about anything other than the fact that she was naked—and humiliated. Again.

Staring in the small mirror, she forced back the pain, focused on the rage and opened the door.

"I thought you just had to pee." Had she ever noticed that he pouted like a petulant child when he didn't get his way? "You were in there so long I lost my boner."

Grace threw the phone at him, narrowly missing his head. Too bad. "You left it in the bathroom." She pulled on her clothes with frantic, jerky movements, desperate to cover herself and get out of there.

"What're you doing?"

"What does it look like I'm doing?"

His blond hair was mussed from her fingers, and his

blue eyes shot daggers at her. What had she ever seen in him anyway? "*Why?*"

"I'm going for a walk."

"*What the hell?* I thought we were having sex here!"

"*Were* is the key word. I need more time to think about it." What she needed was to figure out a way home that wouldn't involve calling the parents who hadn't wanted her to go on this overnight in the first place.

"You gotta be freaking kidding me. We've been dating for weeks! How much more *time* do you need?"

"I don't know." She grabbed her phone and headed for the cabin door. "I'll be back."

"Don't rush on my account."

Glancing over her shoulder, she noticed him staring at his phone. Good. Let him figure out that she was on to his sick little plan. As she climbed off the boat onto the pier at McCarthy's, her hands and legs trembled from shock and anger. On her way up the dock, the pain set in. After everything she'd been through—years of obesity, the huge decision to have Lap-Band surgery and all her hard work to lose the weight—and keep it off for more than a year— she was still "the fat girl" to people like Trey, who'd never known her as anything else.

Thank goodness she'd discovered what a total asshole Trey was before things had gone any further. When she thought about being naked in bed with him and how close they'd come . . . "Ugh!" She sank her fingers into her hair, wishing she could scrub the images from her brain.

While they'd been frolicking aboard the boat, the sun had set over Gansett's Great Salt Pond. A crowd was gathered at the Tiki Bar, where two guitarists played old favorites, not that Grace paid much attention as she walked past the bar. She had far more pressing issues—such as getting as far away from Trey Parsons as possible.

"Excuse me," she said to an older man who leaned against a cab reading the newspaper.

He glanced up at her, a friendly smile on his weathered face. "How can I help ya?"

"I was wondering—what time does the last ferry leave?"

"Ya just missed it. Left at eight."

Grace sagged under the weight of the realization that she was stuck on the island until morning. "Can you recommend a place where I might be able to get a room for the evening?"

He let out a guffaw. "On Labor Day weekend? Hate to tell ya, doll, but everything's been booked for months. There's not a room to be had on the entire island. Biggest weekend of the year, 'cept fer Gansett Race Week."

Grace conjured up an image of the camper-sized sofa in the boat's salon. It was small, but it would do for one night. "Thanks for your help," she said.

"Any time."

Since she had no choice, she turned and made her way slowly and reluctantly back to the boat, taking her time to avoid Trey for that much longer. On the way, she spent a moment appreciating the two supremely handsome men who were performing at the Tiki Bar. One of them had shaggy blond hair and a smile that wouldn't quit. He seemed in his element playing the guitar and singing for the appreciative crowd.

The other had dark hair—Patrick Dempsey hair, she decided—a muscular build and a face that belonged in movies. He too seemed right at home on stage and sang with his partner as if they'd been performing together for years.

Leaning against the gift shop building, Grace hummed along to "Brown Eyed Girl" and "Turn the Page" before she reluctantly continued down the pier to deal with Trey. As she approached the spot where the boat was supposed to be, she did a double take.

It was gone.

"Oh my God," she whispered. "That *bastard*!"

She stared at the empty spot at the dock for a long moment before the truth sank in. He'd left her there alone, taking her purse and clothes with him. She was stuck on Gansett Island with no boyfriend, no place to stay and no money. In the span of an instant, she went from hurt to angry to scared and then to sad. What was supposed to have been one of the greatest nights of her life had turned into yet another disaster.

This, Evan McCarthy thought, *is as good as it gets*. Strumming his guitar in perfect harmony with his best friend on a warm late-summer evening at the docks where he'd spent an idyllic childhood. Playing the home crowd at McCarthy's Gansett Island Marina beat any stage in any venue, and he'd played his share of stages and venues.

He and Owen Lawry exchanged glances as they played the last notes of "Bad Moon Rising" and launched into their anthem, "Take It Easy." Life was good. His album would be out by Christmas, he'd had an awesome time with his brothers, sister and extended family during his sister's wedding the previous weekend and the tropical storm that followed. He'd gotten a new niece out of the storm, born to his brother Mac and sister-in-law Maddie.

After a scary accident earlier in the summer, his father seemed to be on the mend from a head injury and broken arm. "Big Mac" McCarthy wasn't quite his old self yet, but he was better than he'd been. Evan was somewhat concerned about the unusual bickering he'd witnessed between his parents since he'd been home, but he chalked that up to the strain of his father's recovery, their daughter's wedding, a houseful of extra people and the unexpected arrival of a granddaughter during a tropical storm.

A table of pretty young women had been sending flirtatious signals to him and Owen all evening. They'd have their pick of the ladies at closing time. Since he was still staying with his folks up the hill at the "White House," the name the islanders had bestowed upon the McCarthy family home, he hoped the ladies had their own rooms at whatever hotel they were calling home for the weekend.

A nice fling over the long weekend would be just what the doctor ordered after a summer of nonstop work. He'd been feeling cooped up lately, caged and unsettled. A little mindless sex would straighten him right out—the sooner the better, as far as he was concerned. When was the last time he'd blown off some steam? That he couldn't remember was worrisome.

He joined Owen for the chorus to "Take It Easy," high off the adrenaline of performing before an appreciative audience. Here he had none of the issues with the crippling stage fright that had plagued him throughout his career. That was another reason why he loved playing on Gansett so much.

Owen grinned at him, no doubt enjoying this evening as much as Evan. The gig was actually Owen's. Evan's folks had convinced O to stay on until Columbus Day, and he'd cajoled Evan into joining him tonight. It hadn't required much arm twisting, since Evan hadn't been doing anything but hanging around the house trying to dodge his mother's increasingly probing inquiries into his nonexistent love life.

The one thing Evan McCarthy avoided like the clap was commitment, which was the last thing his mother wanted to hear, especially with his siblings falling like dominoes lately. First Mac fell for Maddie, then Janey married Mac's best friend Joe, and then Grant fell for Stephanie. To add insult to injury, even their friend Luke Harris went down hard this summer after reconnecting with his first love, Sydney Donovan. Evan had no idea what was in the water lately, but whatever it was, he wasn't thirsty.

Thank God at least Owen shared Evan's commitment to bachelorhood. So did Evan's brother Adam, who'd gone back to New York once the ferries started running again after the storm. The three of them had to stick together in the midst of all this marriage mayhem.

Owen nudged him, nodded toward a woman sitting at a table by herself, and raised a questioning eyebrow.

As Evan watched her, she swiped at tears and stared off in the distance. Unlike the other women in the crowd, she wasn't paying them an ounce of attention. Evan told himself that was okay even as his ego registered the hit.

Evan shrugged as they started into "Love the One You're With." As he sang along, he kept half an eye on the unhappy woman in the corner. Thanks to the overhead lights on the pier, he could see that she had shiny, dark, shoulder-length hair, the kind of hair that would feel like silk when you ran your fingers through it. What he could see of her face struck him as exceptionally pretty—or it would've been if it hadn't been red and blotchy from crying.

When they finished the song, Owen announced they'd be taking a short break. Usually this was the point in the program when they lined up after-hours entertainment. At their table of admirers, the perky blonde he'd been making eyes with gave Evan a come-hither smile, full of invitation. All he had to do was walk over and close the deal they'd been negotiating for hours now.

"What's with the weepy chick in the corner?" Owen asked as they set their guitars into stands.

"No clue."

"Doesn't look like she's here with anyone."

Evan looked over at her again, noting that she continued to stare off into space as if she had no clue she was in the midst of a bar full of people having fun.

"We're not under any obligation here, are we?" Owen asked warily, eyeing the table full of friendly women.

"You're not, that's for sure."

"Dude, just because your folks own the place—"

"WWBMD?"

Confused, Owen stared at him. "Huh?"

"What would Big Mac do?" Evan asked, knowing the answer to his question before he asked it.

Wincing, Owen said, "Bring a gun to a knife fight, why don'cha?" He accepted a couple of beers from a waitress and handed one to Evan.

"I could ignore it and go about my life, but his voice would be in my head, ruining whatever fun I might be trying to have," Evan said. "He'd be saying, 'How could you leave that gal crying all alone, son? Especially when she's a guest at our place? That's not the kind of man I raised you to be.'"

Owen busted up laughing. "Jesus, you sound just like him."

"Years of intensive training, my friend." Evan took another look at the young woman, confirming she was still there and still miserable. With a resigned sigh, he said, "Wish me luck."

Owen touched his bottle to Evan's. "Go get her, tiger. I'll entertain the other ladies for both of us."

"Gee, you're a pal." Like a condemned man heading to

the gallows, Evan started toward the corner table. As he passed the perky blonde, he sent his regrets with a shrug and a rueful grin. Would've been fun. He approached the corner table and plopped down, startling the crying woman. "Now tell me this—what in the world could've ruined such a great night for such a pretty lady?"

Connect with Us

Visit us online at
KensingtonBooks.com
to read more from your favorite authors, see books
by series, view reading group guides, and more.

for sneak peeks, chances to win books and prize packs,
and to share your thoughts with other readers.

facebook.com/kensingtonpublishing
twitter.com/kensingtonbooks

Tell us what you think!

To share your thoughts, submit a review,
or sign up for our eNewsletters, please visit:
KensingtonBooks.com/TellUs.

Romantic Suspense from
Lisa Jackson

Absolute Fear	0-8217-7936-2	$7.99US/$9.99CAN
Afraid to Die	1-4201-1850-1	$7.99US/$9.99CAN
Almost Dead	0-8217-7579-0	$7.99US/$10.99CAN
Born to Die	1-4201-0278-8	$7.99US/$9.99CAN
Chosen to Die	1-4201-0277-X	$7.99US/$10.99CAN
Cold Blooded	1-4201-2581-8	$7.99US/$8.99CAN
Deep Freeze	0-8217-7296-1	$7.99US/$10.99CAN
Devious	1-4201-0275-3	$7.99US/$9.99CAN
Fatal Burn	0-8217-7577-4	$7.99US/$10.99CAN
Final Scream	0-8217-7712-2	$7.99US/$10.99CAN
Hot Blooded	1-4201-0678-3	$7.99US/$9.49CAN
If She Only Knew	1-4201-3241-5	$7.99US/$9.99CAN
Left to Die	1-4201-0276-1	$7.99US/$10.99CAN
Lost Souls	0-8217-7938-9	$7.99US/$10.99CAN
Malice	0-8217-7940-0	$7.99US/$10.99CAN
The Morning After	1-4201-3370-5	$7.99US/$9.99CAN
The Night Before	1-4201-3371-3	$7.99US/$9.99CAN
Ready to Die	1-4201-1851-X	$7.99US/$9.99CAN
Running Scared	1-4201-0182-X	$7.99US/$10.99CAN
See How She Dies	1-4201-2584-2	$7.99US/$8.99CAN
Shiver	0-8217-7578-2	$7.99US/$10.99CAN
Tell Me	1-4201-1854-4	$7.99US/$9.99CAN
Twice Kissed	0-8217-7944-3	$7.99US/$9.99CAN
Unspoken	1-4201-0093-9	$7.99US/$9.99CAN
Whispers	1-4201-5158-4	$7.99US/$9.99CAN
Wicked Game	1-4201-0338-5	$7.99US/$9.99CAN
Wicked Lies	1-4201-0339-3	$7.99US/$9.99CAN
Without Mercy	1-4201-0274-5	$7.99US/$10.99CAN
You Don't Want to Know	1-4201-1853-6	$7.99US/$9.99CAN

Available Wherever Books Are Sold!
Visit our website at **www.kensingtonbooks.com**